GROVE

GROVE

A Field Novel

Esther Kinsky

Translated from the German by
Caroline Schmidt

**TRANSIT
BOOKS**

Published by Transit Books
2301 Telegraph Avenue, Oakland, California 94612
www.transitbooks.org

© Suhrkamp Verlag Berlin 2018
All rights reserved by and controlled through Suhrkamp Verlag Berlin.
Translation copyright © Caroline Schmidt, 2020
Originally published in English translation by Fitzcarraldo Editions in
the UK in 2020

ISBN: 978-1-945492-38-9 (paperback)
LIBRARY OF CONGRESS CONTROL NUMBER: 2020937349

DESIGN & TYPESETTING
Justin Carder

DISTRIBUTED BY
Consortium Book Sales & Distribution
(800) 283-3572 | cbsd.com

Printed in the United States of America

9 8 7 6 5 4 3 2 1

This project is supported in part by an award from the
National Endowment for the Arts.

"Does it make sense to point to a clump of trees and ask 'Do you understand what this clump of trees says?' In normal circumstances, no; but couldn't one express a sense by an arrangement of trees? Couldn't it be a code?"

—Ludwig Wittgenstein, *Philosophical Grammar*
tr. Anthony Kenny

I
OLEVANO

I plans un mond muàrt.
Ma i no soj muàrt jo ch'i lu plans.
Pier Paolo Pasolini

vii / morţi

In Romanian churches believers light candles in two separate places. It might be two niches in the wall, two ledges, or two metal cabinets, where the candles flicker. On the left side of the partition are the candles for the living; on the right side, the candles for the dead. If someone dies for whom in life a candle was lit in the left partition, then the burning candle is transferred to the right partition. From vii to morţi.

I have only observed the tradition of lighting candles in Romanian churches; I have never practiced it myself. I have watched the candles flicker in their intended places. I have deciphered the letters above the partitions—simple niches in a wall, ledges, filigree containers made from forged iron or perforated sheet metal—and I have read them as names, designating the one space for hope, vii, and the other for memory, morţi. One group of candles illuminates the future, the other the past.

I once saw a man in a film take a candle that was flickering for a relative in the niche of the vii and move it into the niche of the morţi. From what-shall-be to once-was. From the fluttering of the future to the stillness of a remembered picture. In the film this observance was moving in its simplicity and acceptance, but at the same time it inspired disgust, obedient and impersonal, a mutely followed rule.

A few months after I saw this scene in a film, M. died. I became bereaved. Before bereavement, one might think of "death," but not yet *of "absence." Absence is inconceivable, as long as there is presence. For the bereaved, the world is defined by absence. The absence of light in the space of the* vii *overshadows all flickering in the space of the* morți.

Terrain

IN OLEVANO ROMANO I am staying for a time in a house on a hill. When approaching town on the winding road that leads up from the plain, the building is recognizable in the distance. To the left of the hill with the house is the old village, vaulting the steep slope. It is the color of cliffs, a different shade of gray in every light and weather. To the right of the house, somewhat farther uphill, is the cemetery—angular, whitish cement-gray, surrounded by tall, slender black trees. Cypresses. *Sempervirens*, the everlasting tree of death; a defiant answer to the unexacting pines, projected sharply into the sky.

I walk along the cemetery wall until the road forks. To the southeast it leads through olive groves, becomes a dirt road between a bamboo thicket and vineyards, and grazes a sparse birch grove. Three or four birch trees, scattered messengers, vagrants among olive trees, holm oaks and vines, stand at a slant on a kind of protuberance, which rises up beside the path. From this protuberance one looks to the hill with the house. The village lies once again on the left, the cemetery on the right. A small car moves through the village lanes, while someone hangs laundry on a line beneath the windows. The laundry says: *vii*.

In the nineteenth century, this protuberance might have served as a good lookout point for those who came here to paint. Perhaps the painters, pulling their handkerchiefs from their jacket pockets, carelessly and unwittingly scattered birch seeds brought from their northern-colored homelands. A birch blossom, picked in passing and long forgotten, spread rootlets here between blades of grass. The painters would have wiped the sweat from their brows and continued painting. The mountains, the village, perhaps the small columns of smoke rising above the plain as well. Where was the cemetery then? The oldest grave that I can find in the cemetery belongs to a German from Berlin, who died here in 1892. The second-oldest grave is for a man with a bold expression and a hat, of Olevano, born in 1843, died in 1912.

Below the vagrant birch trees, a man works in his vineyard. He cuts bamboo, trims the stalks, burns off the ragged wisps, brings the lengths of the stalks into line. He's building scaffolding out of them, complicated structures made of poles, formed around the burgeoning grapevines. He weighs down with stones the points where the interlocked stalks met. Here the *viti* thrives between the *vii* in the distance, on the left, and the *morți*, somewhat nearer, on the right.

It is winter, evening comes early. When darkness fals, the old village of Olevano lies in the yellow warmth of streetlights. Along the road to Bellegra, and throughout the new settlements on the northern side, stretches a labyrinth of dazzling white lamps. Above on the hillside the cemetery hovers in the glow of countless perpetually burning small lights, which glimmer before the gravestones, lined up on the ledges in front of the sepulchers. When the night is very dark, the cemetery, illuminated by *luces perpetuae*, hangs like an island in the night. The island of the *morți* above the valley of the *vii*.

Journey

I ARRIVED IN OLEVANO in January, two months and a day after M.'s funeral. The journey was long and led through dingy winter landscapes, which clung indecisively to gray vestiges of snow. In the Bohemian Forest, freshly fallen, wet snow dripped from the trees, clouding the view through the Stifteresque underbrush to the young Vltava River, which had not even a thin border of jagged ice.

As the landscape past the cliffs stretched into the Friulian plains, I breathed a sigh of relief. I had forgotten what it is like to encounter the light that lies beyond the Alps and understood, suddenly, the distant euphoria that my father experienced every time we descended the Alps. *Non ho amato mai molto la montagna / e detesto le Alpi*, said Montale, but mountains are good for this shifting of light upon arrival and departure. At the height of the turnoff to Venice, dusk fell. The darker it became, the larger, flatter, broader the plain appeared to me. The temperature dropped below zero. There were dotted lights, even small fires in the open here and there, or so it seemed to me. I stopped in Ferrara, just as M. and I had planned to do on this trip. Ferrara in winter. The garden of the Finzi-Continis in snow or freezing fog. The haze of the *pianure*. Italy, a country to which we had never traveled together.

The next morning, I found the car with a bashed-in window. The backseat and everything stored there—the notebooks, books and photographs, the cases filled with pens for writing and drawing—were littered with shards of glass. The thief had taken only the two suitcases with clothing. One of them was filled with things that M. had worn in the last months. I had imagined how his cardigan would drape over a chair in the unfamiliar place, how I would work in his sweaters and sleep in his shirts.

I filed a police report. I had to go to the Questura, an old *palazzo* with a heavy portal. A small policeman sitting behind a desk in a chair with a high, carved back recorded my complaint. His police cap, adorned with a magnificent gold cord, rested on a pile of papers beside him, like a forgotten prop from a sailor-themed Carnival celebration.

On the recommendation of the lower-ranking police officer who had handed me a copy of the report, I spent hours searching for the stolen suitcases among bushes and shrubs, near the parking lot at the foot of the city wall. I found only a bicycle carefully covered with dried autumn leaves. When it became dark I gave up my search and made a few necessary purchases. That evening I noticed the address on the Questura papers' letterhead: Corso Ercole I d'Este, the road leading to the garden of the Finzi-Continis.

The next morning I left, heading toward Rome and Olevano. It was bitterly cold, the grass atop the city wall was covered in hoarfrost, and large clouds formed before the mouths of the vendors assembling their stands on Piazza Travaglio. A few freezing African men loitered around the cafes. Market days promised more life and opportunity than other days of the week—some trading, help wanted, cigarettes, coffee.

The light beyond Bologna, the view from the highway, evoked memories of my childhood and were a strange comfort—even the gas station convenience stores, still selling those extravagant chocolate sculptures—as if the whole world could be so innocuous and incidental, as disconnected from all pain as the bright landscape that glided past me, a moving panorama-stage which tried to fool me, in my deep fatigue that no amount of sleep would relieve, into thinking it was the only thing moving, and that I remained stationary. For a time, I believed it.

But after exiting the highway in Valmontone, I was in unknown territory, remote from the space of memory. As traffic crawled through the small town, I realized that this Italy was a world away from the country of my childhood experiences. Past a small hill range sprawled a plain, mountains surging at its other end. The summits in the second and third rows were capped in snow. Perhaps it was the Abruzzi already, still linked with outdated fantasies of wolves and highwaymen in my head. Disquieting terrain, like all mountains.

On my first morning in Olevano the sun shone and a mild wind rustled the withered leaves of the palm trees crowding my view of the plain at the foot of the hill. A bell struck every quarter hour. A different, tinny one followed a minute later, as if it had required this intermission to verify the time. That afternoon the sky clouded over, the wind became cutting, and a shrill noise began abruptly in the village. It appeared so far away, the village—a peculiar illusion seen from the house on the hill, as it took mere minutes to reach the square, where a festival was taking place. At this festival Befana presented children gifts to the tune of Italo pop. Befana, the epiphanic witch; the previous evening in small supermarkets grandmothers had haggled for discounts on cheap toys in her name. They had wrenched the gifts from the sale baskets that blocked the aisles at every turn. Silver-clad Barbie dolls, neon-colored soldiers, lightsabers for extraterrestrial use. An announcer called out, a timid choir of children's voices repeated her, and again and again I heard the word Be-fa-na!, stressed on the first syllable, as the dialect demands.

On the night after the day of Befana, moped drivers dinned through the lanes, and I learned that here every sound is multiplied, broken by numerous surfaces and evidently forever sent back to this inhospitable house on the hill. I lay awake, contemplating how for the next three months to force my life into a new order that would let me survive the unexpected unknown.

Village

IN THE MORNINGS I would walk to the village via a different lane every day. Whenever I thought I knew every route, a staircase would reveal itself somewhere, or a steep corridor, an archway framing a vista. The winter was cold and wet; along the narrow corridors and stairs, moisture crackled in the old stone. Many houses stood vacant and around lunchtime the village was very quiet, almost lifeless. Not even the wind found its way into these lanes, only the sun, which usually stayed away in winter. I saw elderly villagers with scanty purchases, bracing their feet against the steepness. The people here must have healthy hearts, trained on these slopes, day after day, with and without burdens and beneath the weight of winter's dampness. Some climbed very slowly and steadily, while others paused, drew breath—whatever breath there was to draw here, in the absence of light or any scent of life. On these winter afternoons, not once did I smell food. On brighter Sundays in the early afternoon, clattering plates and muted voices would sound from the open windows on Piazza San Rocco, but on gloomy winter weekdays the windows remained closed. There were no cats roaming about. Dogs which might have remained silent had they had a bone yapped at the occasional passersby.

Then one day the sun shone again. The elderly came out of their houses, sat down in the sun on Piazzale Aldo Moro and squinted in the brightness. They were still alive. They thawed like lizards. Small, tired reptiles in quilted coats trimmed with artificial fur. The shoes of the men were worn down on one side. Lipstick crumbled from the corners of the women's mouths. After an hour in the sun they laughed and talked, their gesticulations accompanied by the rustle of polyester sleeves. During my childhood, they were young. Perhaps they were young in Rome, rogues in yellow shoes with mopeds, and young women who wanted to look like Monica Vitti, who wore large sunglasses and stood in factories by day, occasionally partaking in demonstrations, arm-in-arm.

Above the valley whitish plumes of smoke unfurled, more buoyant than fog. After the olive trees were pruned, the branches were burned—daily smoke sacrifices in the face of a parasite infestation that threatened the harvest. Perhaps the stokers stood in the groves by their fires, shading their eyes with their hands, looking to see which columns of smoke rose in what way. All was blanketed in a mild burning smell.

Cemetery

IN THE EARLY MORNINGS I would walk the same route every day. Up the hillside, between olive trees, curving around the cemetery to the small birch grove. The two kiosks with cheerful-colored greenhouse flowers and garish plastic bouquets weren't open yet. The municipality workers, busied since my arrival with thinning out the cypresses that had grown into one another, arrived in a utility van and unpacked their tools. The roadsides were littered with debris from the felling: sprigs, cones and pinnate, scaly leaves. Beside the cemetery entrance larger tree clippings piled up, thrown together sloppily and interspersed with stray tatters of plastic bouquets: pink lily heads that refused to wilt, yellow bows. Seen from here, the house on the hill lay between the village in the background on the right, and the cemetery in the foreground on the left. A different order. The village, quiet in the blue-gray morning light. Behind the cemetery wall the men called loudly back and forth to one another.

From the birch grove I looked onto the village and the cemetery; in the mornings not a sound from there reached this spot. I could see only white smoke past the wall and a row of ascending cypresses. Tree remains were being burned. The arborists were not yet felling. They first brought their small sacrifice.

They must have stood there watching the fire. When the smoke thinned, the first saw revved.

In the afternoon I visited the graves. Both flower kiosks were open. On the left fresh flowers were for sale: yellow chrysanthemums, pale-pink lilies, white and red carnations. The kiosk on the right offered artificial flower bouquets with and without ribbons, hearts, little angels and balloons of various sizes. The woman selling flowers at the kiosk on the right was occupied with her phone for the most part, but occasionally cast me a sullen, mistrusting glance.

I searched for a term for the grave walls that made up a large part of the cemetery. Stone cabinets with small plaques, mostly bearing the name and a photo of the deceased, rendered on ceramic. Rocchi, Greco, Proietti, Baldi, Mampieri. The names on the graves were the same as those above store entrances and shop windows in the village. The walls are called columbaria, I learned, dovecotes for souls. Later someone told me the grave compartments are referred to in everyday language as *fornetti*. Ovens, into which the caskets or urns are slid.

The cemetery was always busiest in the early afternoon. Young men above all fulfilled their duties as sons and grandsons then; they would race in, jump out of their cars, slam the doors and slide rattling ladders up to their *fornetti*, in order to trade wilted flowers for fresh ones, wipe off the photographs, check the small burning lights. Old men scuffled by the grave walls, exchanged greetings, carried wilting bouquets to the trash and filled the vases with fresh water for the flowers they had brought with them.

In front of each *fornetto* was a small lamp, evoking an old petroleum lamp, or a candle, or an oil lamp like in *The Thousand*

and One Nights. The lamps were hooked up to electric cables which ran along the lower edge of each tier of the grave walls, and burned at all times. *Lux perpetua*, someone explained to me. Everlasting light. In daylight their faint glow was barely perceptible.

On rainy days I would stand by the window, not wanting to go out. I fought fatigue brought on by the heavy, wet air. Sometimes the rain was mixed with snow. From the rear windows of my house, which faced north, on the low ground to my left I saw the new housing estates of Olevano, the road to Bellegra, the paved market place, the new school and the sports field, all lying between the cobbled-together, angular new construction and the hillside too steep to develop, with its narrow sheep pastures and a holm oak forest.

Above on the right was the cemetery, a darkly framed stone lodge with a view out onto the ripped-open valley. From their lodge, the dead could watch how ambulances were cleaned at the foot of the hillside, while paramedics made phone calls and smoked; how Chinese merchants set up their booths on Mondays, in order to sell cheap household goods, artificial flowers and textiles; how soccer games took place at the sports field on Sundays. Whistles and calls would echo from the hillside during soccer games, and the dull-green ground glistened in the rain, while old women on the steep path up to the cemetery slowly carried their umbrellas through the olive groves.

Dying

NOT LONG AFTER ARRIVING in Olevano, I had a dream:

I encounter M. He is standing in a doorway. Behind him is a room filled with white light. M. is like he used to be: calm, composed, plump again almost.

There's nothing terrible about being dead, he says. *Don't worry.*

Half-awake, I remembered the dreams I had of my father after he died. My father always stood in the light. Waved. Laughed. I stood in the shadows. At first farther away, then ever closer. In one dream he took me sledding and stayed behind in the white hills, laughing, while alone on the sled I glided down into a snowless valley.

In the afternoon that same day, farther down in the village I saw a dead person being brought out of a house. The body was laid out on a gurney and covered from head to toe. Two paramedics wheeled it through the building entrance into the street, where an ambulance waited. The front door to the multistory house was open behind them. No one followed the paramedics and in every apartment the street-facing blinds were pulled down. No one stood on a balcony and raised a hand to wave farewell. The ambulance blocked traffic on the steep road to the village and the tunnel into the hinterland. A small traffic jam had formed, drivers honked their horns. The gurney appeared strangely tall to me, as if distorted; an adult would stand barely a head above the gurney's edge and while contemplating the dead body, feel like a child. I imagined standing at the gurney at eyelevel with the dead man, whose eyelids had already been pressed shut, as that is the first task of paramedics and doctors once death is established. The eyelid of the dead becomes a false door, like those found in Egyptian and early Etruscan tombs. The blanket on the dead man gleamed matte. It appeared to be of a heavy, black, synthetic material, like a darkroom curtain.

Clouds

IN THE MORNING at times the clouds hung so low that the landscape all around was invisible. I heard buses droning uphill, voices, the village bells, too, which struck every fifteen minutes. Noises from a different world, and nothing visible but clouds. Over my head the village sounds met the sputtering caws of chainsaws in the cemetery. Come fog, the tree fellers still worked. Their calls could be better heard through the clouds than clear air and, as if in reply, these short, fitful reports from the land of the *morţi* followed the inquiring sounds from that of the *vii*.

Throughout the day the clouds lifted, broke open, scattered as slack veils and sunk into the valleys. They hung awhile in the holm oaks on the steep hillside, a spindly, disused small coppice, where in the thin tracks between the trunks, objects were put to pasture. Worn-out and rejected objects hung, hindered by the trunks while rolling downhill, diagonally between trees and shrubs: furniture, appliances, mattresses. Delicate vines unfurled like dreams across the covers.

In the afternoon the plain at the foot of the Olevano hill lay dark and severe below high rainclouds, which drifted across the sky over the mountain peaks in brown and blue tones, suffused with yellowish veins of light. The volcanic mountains before Rome loomed lucid and crisp against the distant glow that opened up behind them. Sometimes a remote stripe of sun would blaze a trail to the southwest and briefly illuminate the hovering Pontine Marshes, which in a different light were hardly perceptible. Smoke rose from the olive groves below Olevano and even farther, toward Palestrina. The farmers tirelessly burned the clipped olive branches and fallen leaves. Occasionally a more slender, more dazzling beam of light burst from one of the yellowish veins in the clouded sky and fell like a finger, pointing diagonally onto a column of smoke, as if it were a sacrifice, chosen by a higher hand.

Heart

ON CLEAR DAYS in the first weeks of January, the village lay as if quarried from red stone in the light of the sun, which rose between the mountains behind the cemetery. From my veranda I watched it awake into a toy world, moved by invisible hands: windows opened, a garbage truck crept backward through the lanes, and small figures in blazing vests carried over the trash cans, emptying them into the barrel. Past the palm tree I looked down directly onto the greengrocer that opened its doors around this time. The Arab men arranged the displays, bright oranges slipping into my view of the gray lane. On a large cart lay a mountain of artichokes. In the courtyard behind the closed gate next to the greengrocer, broken plywood crates towered beside mountains of spoiled oranges, tomatoes, heads of green cabbage or lettuce, visible only from here above, a concealed pendant to the neat arrangements in front of the shop. The men, the stands with fruit and vegetables, the garbage truck—it all seemed to be part of a distant theater. Or an unusual theater, whose performances are viewed only from a distance. There was no audience up close.

Behind the village, hills ascended blue and gray, the highest ridge crowned with a row of parasol pines which from here below looked like an ossified platoon, scattered colossal soldiers of an army, perhaps, a rearguard bereft of all hope and any prospect of returning home, cut off from intelligence and provisions, standing exposed at this height to all harsh and bitter weather, lost in contemplation of the valleys. From up there they would have seen boulders, barren grasslands, Olevano in the distance, maybe the village on the right, the dark cemetery lodge on the left, between them the house on the hill—a different order.

As the sun rose higher, the red wore off and the village turned gray. I set out for the gray village, for the greengrocer where Arab men in black anoraks and gloves made calls over Arabic music playing on the radio, or spoke to one another in quarreling tones. They let the weight of their fingertips rest lightly on the scales when weighing the produce and always added a gift to the purchased goods.

I bought oranges and artichokes. The bag was light, but walking home my heart was always so heavy, I thought I wouldn't be able to carry it back to the house. Again and again I stood still and stared, abashed by my weakness, up to the sky and the trees. In several conifers I discovered whitish clews in the forks of high-lying branches and twigs: bright gossamer, veiled spools, tapered downward slightly, chrysalides of remnant clouds, inside of which were perhaps rare butterflies maturing; they would hatch in summer and, spreading their wings in who knows what colors, alight, imperceptibly trembling, on the *fornetti* next to the perpetual lamps, their glow now dissolved by the glaring sun.

The heavy heart became my condition in Olevano. When I climbed up to the house, coming from the village. When I walked uphill, from the house to the cemetery.

I pictured a gray heart, light-gray with a cheap sheen, like lead.

The leaden heart grew entwined with all I had seen that took root in me. With the sight of the olive groves in fog, the sheep on the hillside, the holm oak hill, the horses that from time to time grazed silently behind the cemetery, with the view past the plain and its small, shimmering fields on cold mornings frosted bluish. With the daily smoke columns from burning olive branches, with the shadows of the clouds, with the winter-pallid thickets and violet blackberry vines along the waysides.

Pizzuti

As DAYS PASSED, the signatures above the shop entrances and display windows began to form an accompanying text to the colors of cliffs and stone, tiles and roofs, to the grain and texture of things, which shifted with the light and weather. They suited the sounds of the words, with their slurred sibilants and broken-off syllables. There were three cobblers in the village. Two often stared idly over the chest-high partition-wall of their window display featuring shoe creams, brushes, shoetrees, and some old cobblers' tools. The third worked behind a high shop counter, from a barstool. Customers and acquaintances never failed to appear before him. At times it became lively—the sound carried into the lane. High on the rear wall, practically at the ceiling, hung an old poster on which I thought I recognized, in addition to a warplane with the colors of Italy, the outline of Mussolini.

Every day I encountered the same faces, winter coats, and hats. I became acquainted with several rules of etiquette, such as not to touch the goods before purchasing them, how to politely order from the vegetable woman, and to always follow the recommendations of the cheesemonger, whose ever-smiling, chubby daughter sat on a stool at the register, making a great effort to add small sums. Only at the Arab vegetable shop, which had no name, was one allowed to touch the fruits and vegetables, to pick them up and put them back down again. This liberty must have led to the mass of spoilage behind lock and latch, which was visible only from my veranda.

Coming back from the village I passed by a bar, where even on the coldest days people sat out front on a bench. If the winter sun was shining this bench was especially well-placed, lying for several hours in the light, and so it was a popular meeting point. The people on the bench smoked and talked, some with drinks from the bar, the interior of which was barely visible behind fogged windowpanes. Perched between the smoking men was often a nervous girl, who had a baby carriage with her. If the baby cried she would jiggle the carriage forcefully, while pass-ersby stopped and bent over the crying baby, and the smoking men on the bench laid their hands soothingly onto the blanket and mumbled pleasantly, cigarettes fuming between their fin-gers. If the baby did not settle down, the girl would stand up and rock the carriage back and forth in front of the bench, all the while talking in a hoarse voice and laughing loudly. She had short hair and dressed like a boy, in a beat-up leather jacket and heavy army boots. She begged the men on the bench for cigarettes. They were generous and complied, and she lit them hastily. Her hands were nearly blue from the cold and chapped, with gnawed nails.

Located across from the bench was a butcher. Meat was de-livered in the mornings—almost every day I saw a delivery van parked there, with half-carcasses hanging inside. The delivery man shouldered a pig carcass and moved gingerly, stooped as if carrying a delicate, needy creature. The rear pig's trotter dangled limp, yellow and rindy on the man's back. After the pig, he carried a bundle of chickens into the shop hanging head-first, and occasionally additional cuts of meat, as well. Once he was done with the delivery, in his stained smock he joined the smokers on the bench and lit a cigarette, though always at a certain distance. He bantered with the hoarse girl and seemed to be altogether witty—in his presence there was laughter. All the while the rear door of his delivery van remained open, and anyone could peek at the butchered goods inside. Back at the butcher's, the delivered parts disappeared into the rear of the shop where, through a small window, positioned behind the meat counter, you could watch the sausage maker at work. The sausages from this butcher were famous and highly sought after, and day after day a vast amount of meat was pumped out of the grinder into long skeins of casing, which at fixed intervals an assistant fastened a few times with twine before twisting. Later these fastened bulges would be sealed with metal rings at the base of the sausage. The long sausage chains were then hung and looped several times around rods, just beneath the ceiling.

On the windows positioned barely above ground next to the butcher's shop was written, in elegant letters: *Onoranze funebri Pizzuti*. A few steps led down to a door, which I never saw open. Nor did I ever observe light in these windows; it must have been dark down below, even by day. I imagined that these half-subterranean rooms were also damp and freezing now in winter. But the Pizzuti undertaking business was represented not only in these vaults; it was omnipresent in the village, and the finely lettered windows might have merely advertised the place where the coffins were stored, conveniently located directly across from San Rocco, the church nearest to the cemetery, whose bells were always first to strike the hours and quarter-hours. There was a Pizzuti wreath and flower shop farther below in the village, where women were invariably occupied with putting together large, colorful floral arrangements, and farther was a large storefront office with catalogues in the display window featuring coffins and grave decorations. There the bereaved were advised on next steps. A glossy gray-black hearse, which had the same inscription as the windows next to the butcher's, often edged broadly through the narrow village lanes, usually empty, and it always caused a bit of commotion when rounding the particularly sharp and tight curve in front of the Arab greengrocer. Occasionally I saw the hearse, filled with flowers and wreaths, parked next to the church when a burial lay ahead. Funeral services were all held in San Rocco—or at least I never observed the Pizzuti hearse at any other church. The driver, in livery and a large hat, stood like a watchman beside the vehicle as singing came from the building. On such occasions the square was usually full of men. Women went into the church; I once saw the crowd part for two women in black, forming an honor guard, and as soon as they had disappeared behind the church's doors the men reconvened into the same group they had formed beforehand, smoking and talking gravely. The Pizzuti driver, who also smoked, always had company, but in contrast to those around him there was something about his posture that was almost soldierly, due perhaps to his heavy peaked cap with a golden P.

I avoided looking at the coffin, which after the service was brought out to the hearse and slid into a sea of flowers. Sometimes after arriving back at my apartment I would look out the window down to the street, where an unfailingly small funeral procession trickled to the cemetery. The guests had surely already expressed their sympathy at the square, and for many this journey would have been too arduous. I was never witness to a ceremony, never saw a coffin being lowered into a grave or slid into a *fornetto*. I only came across the accumulated bouquets and flowers, which wilted away and ultimately ended up on one of the trash heaps, evidently later dispersed among small fire pits and burned. Animals also tampered with the trash, and, on stormy days in particular, dogs appeared, having found their way in between the bars of the gate, and descended on the artificial flowers, shredding them and trailing torn petals out into the street.

Blackbird Days

THE DAYS GREW LONGER, but barely warmer or brighter. At the cemetery I listened for birds and heard none, nothing but the jeer of a jaybird in flight, the raspy sounds of magpies lingering outside the cemetery, or the hooded crows. The crows liked to gather in loose groups at the edge of the olive groves, near the road, where scraps that still yielded sustenance could always be found. The cemetery was, nevertheless, not quiet; there was always a clanking of ladders, a rush of water filling up watering cans, engine noises from the various equipment with which workers felled, sawed, and chopped, sucked up leaves in corners. Cemeteries are usually home to birds—I would have expected to find coal tits here, linnets and nuthatches, even black woodpeckers and tree creepers. In lieu of their calls, the air was filled with the drone of a radio mast, which, bounded by clumps of bamboo, rose up directly next to the cemetery. Scattered cypress saplings buckled over, as if in pain, right-angled away from the droning mast. The unbroken buzzing ran beneath the occasional small talk of grave visitors like a murmur. Elsewhere, I saw birds: in the bushes along the path to the birch grove were small flocks of long-tailed tits and, on brighter days, warblers; farther up the mountain I heard goldfinches. Above the olive groves that surrounded the house I heard the green woodpecker but never saw it. The shattering and shrill, yet often also heartrending, wistful, and anxious sequence of tones that the green woodpecker uttered became, in this winter quarter year, the sound that grew entwined with the village, the house, the groves, the hillsides, drawing everything to it—the light, the colors, and the ever-shifting layers and grades of blue and gray in the landscape. On mornings without rain, it was the first bird I would hear; with its call it seemed to be forever letting itself plummet from a high point, because despite the call's loudness and density, it faded as if dying away, as if the bird were capitulating, falling silent in the face of something larger again and again, without my ever having seen it, even at times when its call sounded so near and hung so out in the open, distant from all treetops, that the invisibility seemed incomprehensible, unfathomable, as if either this call or the invisibility were a trick, an uncanny joke played on me every day anew by someone unseen. Even the childhood lesson, to look for the green woodpecker in the grass, was no help and the bird remained a sound, which came closer to my heart each time I heard it, without ever taking visible shape.

In late January, wet snow fell. For two days the clouds hung so low that I never saw the village. I labored on my daily walks through the heavy damp air and swaths of wet wood-smoke. I met the caretaker at the gate, a nervous woman constantly busied with the fastidious cleaning, putting-in-order and arranging of the estate. She lived with her sister in a narrow house next to the entrance gate. In the mornings, at the break of day I would hear the two women exchanging words loudly. The sister stood on her tiny balcony, while the caretaker, on her equally tiny terrace, chopped wood for her oven, or hung laundry to dry. I saw her every day, yet knew nothing about her family, her history, her life—nothing aside from these reciprocal shouts at dawn, which occasionally sounded like quarrels, and the television's flickering in her room past nightfall. I preferred to keep a distance from her nervous desire for order. But on this day, shrouded in white, wet clouds, when she appeared all at once communicative and calmer, she pointed upwards—surely to the sky, which couldn't be seen—and said: *Giorni della merla!*

The blackbird days are the last of January, in Italy supposedly the coldest of the year. So cold that one day a blackbird and its young, freezing, searched for shelter in a chimney. On the first day of February the sun shone and the blackbird, once white and radiant, emerged dyed forever black from the soot, but the bird was content, grateful for the sooty chimney's warmth. This story of plight and metamorphosis with its subsequent moral— sealing the winter fairy tale like a leaden stopper—is told in several variations, but it always involves these days of the year, and they are always referred to as the days of the blackbird.

On the first of February the sun shone this year, too. The caretaker, rushing past, promised the end of winter, while the cheesemonger, accompanied by his daughter's grinning nods, explained that proper winter only begins in February. With his hand in front of his apron he demonstrated the height of the snow some winters—and never until February! he said. So much for blackbirds! He made a dismissive gesture with his hand and I paid his daughter, who on that day wore an old-fashioned mob cap, like a chambermaid from an early film.

In the afternoon I found a dead bird on my narrow apartment balcony, from which I could see only the cemetery and not the village. In the morning, viewed from this angle the cemetery hung like a colorless, angular bulk in the shadows; it could have just as well been a factory, a bunker, or a prison, untouched by the morning light. Now the sun shone brightly, and the cypresses stood as sharply excised figures against the blue sky. For the first time since my arrival, the balcony tiles were warm from the sun. The small bird lay there as if nestled against the wall to bask in the light, and it was still soft and warm, but no longer living. I found no injury. It was a coal tit, its small head bore an all-black hood, which began at its beak and left blank a white spot on the back of its head. Around its neck, too, was a black line. The hood glistened in the sun, and the cream-white down on its belly trembled in the gentle breeze. Its back was dark gray, its wings somewhat darker with two rows of extremely delicate whiteish flecks, between which the feathers appeared blacker than on the rest of its wings. How tiny, how surreally small creatures look, once drained of life. The bird lay so light in my hand, as if it were hollow: it weighed practically nothing, a pitiful thing, which now so soon after its death one could hardly imagine capable of life.

I waited until dusk and once the television in the caretaker's room began to flicker I buried the bird between the olive trees below the terrace.

Market

MONDAY WAS MARKET DAY in Olevano. Serving as the market square was the concrete area next to the school, situated at the foot of the hillsides, which were developed only after the tunnel was excavated. At some point it must have been located at Piazzale Aldo Moro, long before the square was given this name. Every town in Italy has an Aldo Moro square, and each one seems to have been torn from some pleasant former purpose, eclipsed by the shadows the new name cast. The tunnel, which had transformed Olevano into a through-town and led through the rock, couldn't have been more than a few decades old. Had my father ever found a reason to take us to Olevano, we might have discovered another village at the end of the winding—perhaps never-paved—road, which looked only to the west and toward Rome. Small paths would have led along the ridge and through the village to the hinterland, past the house where I was staying, which now sat directly above the tunnel entrance on the hill. There, curious hikers from foreign parts could walk to the Villa Serpentara in the holm oak hills and to Bellegra. The tunnel undoubtedly shifted and distorted the Olevanesi's maps. How strange it must have been to suddenly be able to go through the mountain instead of having to ascend and descend it. The tunnel was a damp pipe, which always smelled of diesel fumes from the buses. It was not long, but very narrow, and described a slight curve. Quickly it became the pride of the village—after its construction it was a frequent subject of postcards. Yellowed black-and-white photographs on the matte, sturdy cardboard of earlier days, their borders once-white, show the entrance of the illuminated tunnel at night: the opening of the mountain, crusted round with craggy cliffs, lights reflecting on wet asphalt, no vehicles or pedestrians in sight. Pictures of forbidding nights. After the tunnel construction was complete, Olevano performed another act of land reclamation: the drained flatland between thousands of river arms flowing near the sea. Houses were built on the back hillsides, which surely had once been forested, and at the bottom of the small valley, where a number of rivulets converged from the mountains, everything was asphalted, the stream courses buried beneath the school, beneath the sports field and the market square, which was occasionally used for other public events. The rivulets crept to a stretch of water, united at the edge of the leveled land, and at the foot of a rocky slope, overgrown with bushes, they flowed farther downhill between blackberry vines and willow thickets. On the terrace-like expanse above the slope were houses, their balconies and loggias hanging directly above the precipice. In many places along the road to Bellegra, similar reckless developments had cropped up, which, seen from the rear windows of my apartment, appeared unsystematic and disordered—clusters of houses, apartment blocks, skeletons of buildings partly gnawed away by time and weather in a raw state of incompletion. Dimly glowing street lamps signaled the unfinished streets which might never had names, and even in the completed houses I rarely saw an illuminated window. The terrain lay raw in the light of day and dismal by night, perhaps even inconsolable over its utter ineptitude, suited neither as landscape nor shelter.

From my veranda every morning I saw people coming from the westward small plain, where the vegetable gardens lay beneath hoarfrost. By bike or small delivery wagon, occasionally even by donkey, the vegetable gardeners brought their produce to the village. Artichokes, puntarelle, black cabbages, and endives. After the nightly white frost, a residue from the smoke plumes of olive fires would descend on it throughout the day. The vegetable farmers made rounds to the small shops and occasionally brought something to the Arab store, but they never made it to the market place, which was reserved for delivery vans and pick-up trucks, from which all the goods and fixtures for the stands were unloaded in the blink of an eye. On Monday mornings the sound of stands being assembled carried up to my apartment; the merchants were experienced, they constructed the same stands with the same hand movements in a different place every day, offered and sold the same goods—an inexhaustible supply of polyester pillows and fleece blankets, aluminum cooking pots and teacups embellished with sentimental, pseudo-Chinese sayings in bad English. A few stands selling citrus fruit and potatoes could be found as well, and from time to time a merchant hawking hundreds of tiny cactuses. There were also other items with the appearance of utility: kitchen accessories made from colorful synthetics, fake-leather jackets and faux-fur coats, hand towels, sponges and cleaning towels. The clientele at the marketplace was so scarce that I could hardly fathom how the merchants brought themselves to make the trip anew every Monday. Between the market and the road was a long, connected row of low buildings, medical facilities with X-ray labs, ECG clinics, a dentist's office, an urgent care clinic that treated minor accidents like lacerations, slight scalds, and falls from step-ladders and, as it appeared to me, these facilities also provided the market with most of its customers. The spouses of ECG candidates whiled away the wait-time there, and the injured, freshly trussed, looked for cheap band-aids to cover their lacerations after the gauze came off, searching with stiffly and conspicuously bandaged hands.

Meanwhile in the anterior, old, south and westward-facing part of the village, African men hung about Piazzale Aldo Moro on market Mondays, seeking buyers for three-packs of socks or men's underwear. When the weather was nice they would drift slowly with their goods past the elderly, who sunned themselves there, and afterwards try their luck with the young women who brought their children to the playground. Around noon necessity compelled them to be bolder, and they entered the small shops in the lower part of the village and addressed customers purchasing parmesan, oranges, or notebooks, risking the anger of shop owners and employees. I never saw anyone make a successful transaction. I once watched a group of African men meet in a neglected corner at the edge of the playground around lunchtime in order to stuff the socks and underwear back into a black plastic bag. One of them shouldered the bag, while the others searched the ground for cigarettes, rummaged through the trashcans for something to eat and triumphantly pulled out a box of rejected pizza crusts. Then they walked to the bus that would bring them back to Cave, Palestrina, or the suburbs of Rome; they probably hadn't made any money, and tomorrow would try their luck elsewhere with the socks. They never begged and their polite phrases, uttered in a practiced, singsong Italian, which they must have known, after all, almost never worked, gave them a thin veneer of belonging. I never bought anything from them, even though every Monday I intended to; I had no use now in my life for men's socks, and feared that such a sympathy purchase would tug at my leaden heart even harder than artichokes and oranges. But the African vendors and I occasionally exchanged sideways glances, and I imagined that we mutually recognized, sized each other up as actors on a stage of foreignness—surely unnoticed by the locals—each concerned with his own fragmented role, whose significance for the entire play, directed from an unknown place, might never come to light.

Hands

EACH MORNING I awoke in an alien place. Behind a tall mountain with snow lingering in its hollows, the day broke, gray and blue, sometimes turquoise and yellow. Fog often still covered the plain, at times in individual drawn-out banks, which looked like frozen bodies of water. Each morning it was as if I had to learn everything anew. How to unscrew the moka pot, fill it with ground coffee and turn on the burner, cut bread and set the table, even for the smallest meal. Memories of actions drummed against the top of my skull, as if a sea were swashing inside there, and they rose from its depths, distorted. Dressing. Washing. Applying bandages. The imposition of my hands.

I stood at the window, waiting for the water in the moka pot to boil. I looked out onto the village and the plain, which extends to the chain of dormant volcanic mountains; beyond that I pictured the seaside, even though I knew it was farther away. The expansiveness of the plain was an optical illusion—I had seen for myself that a small hill ridge lay before Valmontone—but this flat terrain, where tucked between woods and groves were small villages and farmsteads, workshops and supermarkets, and an oil mill, closed due to the olive tree disease, was a connected basin for me, a former lake whose water had once slipped away somewhere unknown, and in whose bed, while raking through the ashes from the olive fires and the crumbly soil beneath, you would readily find the remains of fish and other water creatures.

When after sweeping the landscape my gaze fell to my hands on the window ledge, I thought I saw M.'s hands beneath them, in the space between my fingers—white and delicate and long, his dying hands, which were so different from his living hands, and they lay beneath mine as if on a double-exposed photograph. Then the coffee maker hissed, and the coffee boiled over, and my living hands had to break away from M.'s white hands in order to turn off the stove and remove the pot, but I inevitably burned myself, and this pain made me aware that I hadn't relearned anything yet.

Arduously and despite what my hands had unlearned, I fumbled my way to my camera and to photographing. I lifted the camera and looked through the viewfinder. At last I clumsily tore open a box of film and began loading the camera. Over the years it had so often seemed as if the movements performed by my hands had become part of me. While working with my negatives I sensed retrospectively that each instance of changing film—the pressure of the crank, the spool, and the camera's external coating on my fingertips, the smoothness of the black film leader, the process of inserting the leader into the spindle— had left an impression on me, and that these gestures had been added to my repertoire of hand movements. Executing them had moored a memory in this part of my body, which became operative and led the process, even if in my thoughts I was somewhere else entirely. Each sheet, with its four slots for negatives, was a testament to this habit's gradual colonization of my hands. That had satisfied me. Now, sitting with my back to the sun and the view to the valley, with uncertain hands I needed half an hour just to load a roll of film. I had to recall what the numbers meant on the rings for exposure time and aperture, how to operate the light meter.

Each exposure was an effort. I stared into the viewfinder and forgot what it was I wanted to see there. I photographed details of the plain with and without the olive fires, the village in the morning light, and three columbaria in the rear, new part of the cemetery. Once I took my camera along up to the birch grove and photographed the village and the house on the hill. I photographed the vineyard, where the old man had now prepared all his grapevines for spring. Afterwards I went to the cemetery. I had one exposure left. The cemetery lay empty and silent—it was early afternoon, not the usual visiting time. Only between the columbarium walls on the street-facing side did I hear two women's voices. They spoke so monotonously that I thought they must be praying, but as I turned the corner of a grave wall I saw the two women kneeling on the stone ground, busy cleaning the gravestones of two neighboring *fornetti*, conversing all the while in this droning, prayer-like tone. Cleaning products lay beside them and fresh artificial flowers, vase and all, as if of a piece. I could barely understand their conversation; their dialect clipped words at their roots. When they caught sight of me they fell silent, as if by arrangement. "Can I help?" asked the one, then the other in echo, once she saw me. I was startled and stepped back. What was there to say? There was nothing to help with. They eyed the camera hanging from my neck with suspicion, it seemed to me. I might have appeared as an intruder to them, a meddler who had no one there to mourn. They might not have been mourners; perhaps they were busying themselves, merely out of a sense of obligation, with the *fornetti* of long-dead aunts or uncles, childless distant relatives whose legacy they had perhaps partially inherited and whom they felt to owe certain duties, like the cleaning of grave-stones and replacing of years-old artificial flowers, gone brittle and pale from the wind and weather. My wandering through the cemetery among the graves of people whose terminated lives I had no connection to might have appeared strange to the bereaved, offensive even. I took off, saving my last exposure for a different occasion.

In the evening I stood at the window and looked out into the darkness. Twilight was almost always beautiful, the sun of-ten appeared as it set, and the cemetery hovered in an orange light in which the cypresses were no longer so black that they looked cut-out, but rather blue and deep and seemed to almost lean slightly toward the village and the house on the hill. The village in turn now lay cool-gray until the street lamps were illuminated and light was flicked-on behind the windows. On the plain it was never entirely dark. One could make out points of light from larger towns in the distance, street lamps which lined smaller roads that were invisible by day, and the headlights of cars that came in a long, uninterrupted line from the west in the evenings, allowing me to trace the path that I had taken. As it turned to night the volcanic mountains stood out all the clearer against the sky, which appeared as if illuminated from a great distance. That must have been Rome reflecting.

I stood at the window for hours as if inside a bell jar which had covered me and displaced me to my childhood, when in the afternoons and evenings I often felt incapable of doing anything but look out the window. Save that now beneath my hands on the window ledge I could feel M.'s hands. I didn't see them like I had that morning, only felt them and wondered if this was what had taught me to forget my own hands.

Palestrina

SOMEWHERE ALONG THE WAY, a bit past Valmontone, a sign for Palestrina caught my eye. When I stood on my veranda in Olevano and gazed westward I would search for the town, which was linked in my mind to the composer. Lassus, Palestrina, Ockeghem, Tallis. Music that belonged to the milky, shadowless light of my life in England, a light that didn't exist here. Many years ago, I sang in a Palestrina mass and felt myself go missing from the world in the music. Without a lament, I became invisible and could no longer see.

I set off, picturing the intersection with this sign. I had spent weeks on the hillside with a view across the plain, and was now surprised by the landscape of abandon that I encountered below at the foot of the hill. It must have escaped my notice on the way there, surely because my gaze was directed only at this mountain town in the distance, where shelter was supposedly waiting for me.

Once I had the steep, winding road behind me and drove on level land, the splayed feeling faded from the landscape. The copses, bushes, avenue trees and willows along small brooks, which from above were smoothly arched lines drawn in the landscape, slid into view here below, shrinking its vastness to a series of plots. At a distance from the road were abandoned buildings, which had perhaps once been small factories or served some agricultural purpose. Flags fluttered timidly in a mild wind in front of a shop selling discount wedding dresses. In several places they had begun leveling streets into the landscape, but I could see where they had already abandoned their work. On one such obviously deserted construction site there was still large machinery, its wheels already overgrown with scrub. The land was primed for building and the crooked signs announcing the housing development, having deteriorated into jagged fragments, protruded over the fence; a mobile home, surely there for the consultation of future home owners, was stuck above its wheels in the miry ground. Starlings circled over the fields, which perhaps were already irresolute fallow land. The plowed earth was light brown, tinged violet in the winter light. I turned onto a larger road, passed by the ragged winter remains of a tree nursery next to a tropical plant nursery, beside which was a garden restaurant with *hacienda* in its name. Strings of colorful lightbulbs were wound around the bare trees. Two colossal cactuses towered beside the blocked driveway gate, looking like papier-mâché. The waiters probably wore sombreros and on weekends there would be a party band with Mexican sounds, and the musicians—hobby guitarists and dazed rumba-rattlers hailing from villages between Valmontone and Olevano, men between forty and fifty who were too old to get out of there—were given shots of tequila on the house and left with a meager pay. Now everything was shuttered and barricaded. The musicians would spend their evenings sitting in front of the television or solving crossword puzzles until spring arrived.

The road to Palestrina led uphill, with gentle curves and

steep precipices on the one side and forested hillsides rising on the other. There was a dizzying bridge over a gorge, then the small village of Cave, which in old ochre and pink wanted to be beautiful, having either avoided the ugliness of Olevano's hinterland or successfully hidden it from passers-through. Merchants were breaking down the market; had I studied the faces more closely on Monday, I might have recognized some of them.

Palestrina was a cat city. After a violent sleet shower the streets were empty but for the white, sand-colored, and calico tabby cats on every corner, entrance, and stoop, in makeshift shelters at the edge of fallows. Some were trusting and hopeful, others lurking and anxious, yet not feral and gaunt like their cousins in Eastern Europe—more like shrewd guardians of secret places, which feared you might find them out, discover their hideaways. Now and again a moped driver cruised past on the wet streets and the clattering would echo from the hillside, a phantom moped following close behind in the air. The raspy soundtrack of the hopelessness enveloping this region.

Palestrina proved to indeed be the birthplace of Giovanni Pierluigi, as they call him here. Open to the public, his birth house was gloomy and tended by a peculiar guard, who I imagined spent the long hours and days without visitors rehearsing his smoldering gaze. In our short conversation he claimed to not know that Giovanni Pierluigi is called Palestrina in other parts of the world. Maybe he was telling the truth.

I ascended the steep road until my leaden heart made itself known. Among small rust and rose-colored houses with corrugated iron roofs and bristly rock gardens, I stood and looked out to a different plain. At the foot of the mountain was the new town of Palestrina, every bit as haphazard as the rear side of Olevano, but more inhabited. At some distance, sticking out from the ochre-colored apartment buildings and gray single-family houses like a small foreign land, was the cemetery, marked by thick black cypresses, which towered behind a whitish wall—the graveyard's local dress. A *necropolis*, which perhaps had always been there, *fuori le mura*, was located precisely at the center of my field of vision from here above, but also from the temple, which was situated somewhat farther below, where the city sloped into terraces and headed for the graveyard. A bit farther to the right, to the west, the landscape opened up into a large expanse and there, in fact, began Rome. Briefly I even thought I saw the sea in the far distance. Above this expanse and the bright horizon hung a large, dark blue cloud with brownish bulges, which frayed at the edges into yellow-green trembling feathers and ribbons. The visibility beneath this cloud was clear and sharp, until it began to rain again, dissolving everything into nebulousness, and even the cemetery became a blurry speck in which the cypress tops now swayed.

I searched for shelter in the museum that sat crowning, enthroned on the old temple. The rooms were filled with grave goods, stone sculptures, vessels and jewelry. I contemplated the *cippi* of Etruscan tombs, cone-shaped hewn stones which once marked tomb entrances, and perhaps—like the pebbles once laid again and again to separate graves in Jewish cemeteries—the boundaries of the tomb. *Your realm of the dead extends up to here.* From a small gallery above a pit, water rushing in its depths, one could view the Nile mosaic, an enormous series of panel pictures composed of tiny stones which depicted the fabulous creatures, landscapes, and monsters of Egypt—a story in images on the back of a massive river which might also have inspired fear in the Romans. The Tiber trickled more modestly into the sea. The Egypt of the mosaic harbored sad centaurs— half-man, half-donkey—chameleons, and various monkeys. Black men appear as hunters with bows and shields. A hippopotamus bathes in the river. Herons in flight seem to plummet to the earth toward an enormous, half-erect snake, already devouring a bird.

It stopped raining. Through a window I saw the sun in the west, surrounded by ragged violet, orange, yellow, and brownish clouds. The light streamed through the window, watery and soft. Only because of this light, an object in a display case caught my eye: a ring, the grave good of a woman, a mother of two children by two different fathers, according to the description. The ring itself, the thin metal band, was unremarkable, but in its setting was a miniature portrait of the deceased woman, a solemn face against a dark ground, sealed beneath a crystal, not clouded by a single flaw, whose cut and curvature made it seem as if she were looking at me, alive and urgent, from an unspeakable distance.

Maria

CLOUDS SLIPPED BETWEEN the hills, draping everything in damp white. A very thin rain fell, at times in drops so wispy and wafting that it was probably only the clouds themselves, spreading out their moisture. The white fields began moving, uncovering views—the cemetery emerged, fragments of its outer wall, the grave walls, the trees, and amid this shapelessness everything seemed much closer than usual. Then it disappeared again. Sunlight seeped into the clouds and reached the cemetery, while everything else still lay in fog, hidden. The cemetery glowed golden above an ocean of clouds, an island of promise which beckoned no one, as the village was still hidden, had possibly vanished altogether.

On my walk with the camera I had lost my cable release. The golden cemetery island in the air went unphotographed. At first, I was distressed not by my loss of the cable per se, but of the cable as witness to one day two years ago in winter— the gray, mild, mistletoe-winter, a winter without abnormalities—when we wandered through the streets, thinking about "next year" and "in two years" and the "future" in general and I bought it at a shop with used camera accessories, to replace a lost one. We both ran our fingers through the slack knot of cable releases, which lay in a basket, twisted into one another like half-hibernating, languid, fearless snakelets, and M. eventually pulled out this especially robust, light-gray coated one, which I took and used and now had lost. My distress over the cable falls under one of the potential curses of bereavement that I gradually became familiar with: weighting objects qua testimony. The attribution of participation in a moment past. A small piece of back-then, which should act as if it could moor the past tense onto the broken-off banks of the present. Idle lists of a forlornness that knows not what to do with itself.

In the afternoon it became brighter and the light beneath the evenly pale sky was nearly spring-like. In the unfamiliar landscape I learned to read the spatial shifts that come along with changes to the incidence of light. I'd never lived with such an expansive view of the country and now noticed every day how new shadows formed, new silhouettes emerged, and a lower hill lying to the south, upon it the village of Paliano, became rounder and softer, appeared to move ever closer. I went out looking for the cable, tracing my route across the cemetery. The columbaria facing the street seemed like a labyrinth to me that day, ladders strewn every which way, and for the first time I noticed that one wall with grave compartments was practically empty. In the empty, nameless cavities people had placed small lamps and flowers; in one compartment was a framed photograph, so faded that I could barely make out anything at all. I scanned the ground where I thought I had been standing yesterday in front of the women. At the opposite end of the path a girl walked between the columbaria in circles, speaking out loud. At first sight I thought she must be talking to her dead, to whatever lay locked in the ornamented *fornetto*-drawer behind the marble panel, but surely she spoke only into her phone.

I found my cable in a small pile of litter which had been either swept or blown by the wind against a grave wall: tattered petals of artificial flowers, small branches, cigarette butts, a trampled green lighter. The gray cable blended in with the light gray concrete drawers and ground, and it was only the shimmering metal ends that caught my eye. It lay in front of a grave marker bearing the name Maria Tagliacozzi. She died in 1972 in August, 60 years old, and was mourned by a brother and sisters. Above the name was a ceramic medallion, featuring a photograph of the deceased. A beautiful woman, loose curls tumble over her shoulders, her face made up as if for a performance, with a polka-dotted scarf wrapped around her neck. A face characteristic of the late forties, maybe fifties. She looked a bit like a film actress, perhaps due to the angle at which she stares into the camera, her gaze somewhat tilted and upturned, in contrast to the stiff, head-on shots adorning other graves. I tried to recall a film suited to her face and expression, but came up with nothing. On the ground in front of her grave was a small Aladdin lamp. Its fluted glass chimney was crooked, and the small bulb didn't glow, although it was connected to a cable. Perhaps it needed to be replaced. Who looked after her lamp? Her brother—elderly, short of breath? Or one of her sisters? It was unlikely: this year Maria Tagliacozzi would have been 103. Did she have nephews and nieces? I would bring her a flower next time. Maria Tagliacozzi could be my dead for the remainder of my stay in Olevano, and give cause to my daily cemetery visits.

I took the long way through the olive groves and past the old man's vineyard. Everything seemed to point to spring, even if the white smoke of burning branches and leaves rose over every valley for miles and even the plain. Fire cures and blighted offerings. Without olives the region would be utterly lost.

It was already getting dark when I passed by the vineyard. Cats arched their backs in the pale grass on the wayside. In the gardens below the vineyards, which until now had lain asleep, life stirred. People busied themselves in their makeshift, cobbled-together sheds, and dogs leapt along the fences. Early spring was taking possession of the terrain. I took a long detour to the village, which let out farther down, practically at Piazzale Aldo Moro, at the small main road. The street lamps radiated a yellow light, the shops were illuminated. There were few pedestrians. I could already hear a woman's voice yelling monotonously from below. 'Tekiah! Tekiah!' I understood from a distance, well aware that it could only be an illusion. The woman shouted repeatedly, without varying the volume or urgency of her tone. As I approached, I saw her standing in front of a large house on the corner, where the lane with the post office and the courthouse met the main road, and I understood that she was calling "Maria." Relentlessly, without pause, "Maria! Maria!" It was a large house that she stood in front of, a beautiful, old building with a wide, carved entrance and many windows, and I wondered why I had never noticed it before. The light was on in several windows of the house, but I saw no one moving through the rooms. The doorbell panel was illuminated, there must have been six apartments in the building. A ways farther uphill, the Arab vegetable and fruit stands lay in dim light. No one noticed the woman. She stepped back into the street, as if to get a better view of the interior, and continued calling without pause. The street was full of her shouts for

Maria, and no one appeared who felt spoken to. It was difficult to tell how old the shouting woman was. Perhaps she was in her early fifties. She wore a light winter coat with a belt, noticeably more fashionable than what most women here wore. The whole scene, the way she called, looked up, stepped back, even her clothing had something theatrical about it, the way she first stood, then paced up and down on a very small section of sidewalk by the door, the gesture with which she ultimately raised her hand and placed it to her ear, as if straining to hear sounds from inside the house, a sign from Maria, but above all, her monotone call—all that was a performance for an audience unfathomable to me, which sat somewhere silent in the dark, maybe even holding its breath in suspense.

Trade

EVERY OTHER WEEK a man selling citrus fruit pulled up in a small, three-wheeled cargo scooter, just like the one I remembered from my childhood. "Straight from Sicily" promised the inscription on the door, as did his feverish announcements emitted from a loudspeaker on the roof. But he couldn't have possibly come all the way from the south on this old-fashioned three-wheeled vehicles. I imagined warehouses, somewhere along the Valmontone-Frosinone road, perhaps near the *Hacienda* restaurant, where mountains of oranges lay waiting for Sicilian vendors who would load them onto their old-fashioned motorized three-wheeler and, glinting with the dodgy luster of their actual or ostensible native island, drive to small mountain towns and peddle these sour oranges that no one wanted to harvest. On the cargo bed were blood oranges—he had a special fondness for his *moro*—and "blonde" oranges, clementines, and lemons. In addition to his announcements, the driver rang a bell and honked his stammering horn. A number of Olevanesi bought his goods, at times even the caretaker, who would look around nervously while standing by the Sicilian vehicle, as if she wanted to avoid being seen. I occasionally bought a few blood oranges. The man would then look at me, disappointed and somewhat contemptuous, because

I had ordered not four kilos, but four oranges. I couldn't explain to him that it was, after all, only a grief purchase, a kind of experimental ritual. M. would wait all year for the few blood orange weeks. And besides, the three-wheeled cargo scooter, the crackling calls from its loudspeaker, and the bell that swung out the driver's side window all reminded me of my childhood, when I would marvel at the Italian cargo scooters, which I found much more beautiful than the heavy, three-wheeled delivery vans that potato merchants drove through the streets along the Rhine in autumn and winter. Bent oblique beneath their weight, a boy, the "thickwit" in the lowest service of the potato merchant, carried the potatoes in hundredweight sacks into cellars while the driver collected the money.

For hours, the orange man cruised around; until evening I would hear his horn, his bell, and the tireless announcements from his loudspeaker. He frequently quarreled with other drivers, because he moved forward slowly and longingly kept watch for customers, recklessly grazing the corners of houses and parked cars in the narrow lanes. He took lunch in the graveyard. He would stop in a pull-out niche directly in front of the main gate, where the sun, if it came out, would shine into his cart. Once I even saw him there with his mouth half-open, asleep, his cheek pressed to the window. He was the only one in the region who drove an old-fashioned three-wheeled scooter. Perhaps it was part of the image he had to embody as a Sicilian orange merchant, and the carts, coated in the bitter aroma of oranges, spent summers in a long sleep in the warehouses, then empty of all fruit and hot as embers.

Several times a traveling gas fitter came around, offering his services. He only surfaced on Sundays and would perform any job that involved *cucine a gas*; he always called out *gásse* as if twirling it around his tongue, giving it two syllables, emphasizing the first and following it with a small yet distinct swerve. *Lavoro subito e immediatamente!*, he would call into his loudspeaker, and between announcements he played a kind of marching music, certainly meant to startle potential customers and lend gravity to his question: Is your *cucina a gásse* in need of repair? Are you certain? Have you recently smelled *gásse*? He would add this last sentence to his repertoire only later, likely only when not a single housewife had hurried out into the street, ringing her hands, to save lunch. The gas fitter was also out all day. Perhaps he made a detour to Bellegra or Roiate— a small mountain village inhabited exclusively by old men— but he never stayed away for longer than an hour. Depending on the route and weather conditions, his announcements and marching music sounded either clear or muffled, and on the backside of Olevano, on the street between two partially inhabited developments, they reverberated from the hillsides; tone and echo tumbled, overlapped, robbing the words of all comprehensibility, so that only the word for gas hung in the air. Spring had arrived and the days were brighter, evening came later, mimosas were blooming and small white daffodils and Star-of-Bethlehem flowers unfolded about the olive trees, while the grass on the hillsides and plains became greener and in the slopes round holes emerged, through which I suspected snakes would soon leave hibernation, and sounding into these evenings, still brisk but ringing with blackbirds, imbued with a velvety blue dusk, were the anxious questions of the gas fitter, who had since given up hope for defective stoves, withdrawing his *subito e immediatamente*, so that only the question remained: had anyone recently smelled *gásse*?

Campo

AT IRREGULAR INTERVALS I heard the gray and blue regional buses hum up the steep curves and with creaking brakes groan downhill. They connected Olevano to the surrounding countryside. Uphill they drove on, to Bellegra and deeper into the mountains to *Rocca* Santo Stefano, and twice a day to Subiaco in the hinterland; downhill they drove toward Palestrina and Rome.

From my small balcony, where in the morning I would see the cemetery lying above like a dull gray box in the shadows, I looked between olive trees and houses directly onto the bus station below in the village, across from the tunnel entrance. I saw the small toy figures waiting around the arriving and departing buses, and the mayhem of buses, cars, and humans at noon, when school let out and many people drove home to take siestas. The bus station was a flat, angular concrete building with an overhanging roof, beneath which waiting passengers could find shelter if it rained and the waiting room behind the glass wall was still locked. Next to the waiting room was a ticket counter, which was always empty, and behind it, a bar. From the bar you looked out to the plain, to a new road swerving above the precipice to the lower districts, and a kind of junkyard for discarded everyday objects, which occupied the old observation deck and had perhaps arisen at random, unintentionally—an intermediate space for the partially discarded, whose time for final absence had nevertheless not yet arrived. The tunnel and bus stop flanked the entrance to the old village like two monstrosities, fending off outsiders; at this sight many would have preferred to turn back. In summer the leafy sycamores and lindens would soften the fright, amiably inviting travelers to keep going, journey on. But now, in winter, their bare branches warned of some danger lurking ahead.

I couldn't see the bus stop for the fog, but the stammering bellow of diesel motors was all the louder for it, and the voices of invisible waiting passengers traveled uphill more distinctly than on clear days, and occasionally I could even understand the names they called.

For some time I entertained the idea of making a trial departure, and one day I took the bus to Rome. It was early morning, twilight had just begun to show faintly. Waiting passengers wore grim expressions, their heads drawn deeply into their coat collars in the light of the street lamps. Several buses exited the tunnel at once, all advertising Rome as their destination and already filled with passengers. Most of them must have been on their way to work or school, an older couple sat speechless, clinging to a small, old-fashioned leather suitcase, and I imagined the woman was perhaps accompanying the man to the hospital. Or the other way around. Below on the plain, dawn had advanced enough that I saw the hoarfrost as a matte, pale layer, covering surfaces without glittering, since the light was still absent. A few passengers exited in Genazzano and Palestrina, scattering in the frosty morning.

The bus passed the Palestrina cemetery. In the reddish morning light it lay like a monstrous bulk among the low houses, garages, shops, and pubs in the lower part of town, which had already begun fringing into something urban, the outskirts of Rome. The bus went as far as Anagnina, the last stop on the metro line. An incremental ritual for approaching the city. I was surrounded by a gray no man's land, between feeder roads and industrial buildings. Views of an empty region that was neither country nor city, unpopulated, navigated but not settled, smoothed and leveled into a ground of possibility, yet already allotted narrow functions, which withered at every attempted description. A land of eradication, a new alienated terrain, different from Pasolini's outsider land, damaged by new construction, even more cramped, further beyond recognition, dispossessed of all names.

Regional buses came from all sides, churning out flocks of half-rural inhabitants, mostly women, perhaps employed in shops or offices, and students. Like everywhere else, there were helpless and restless African men, who gathered in small groups—impossible to say if their meetings were arranged by chance or plan. In the icy morning light, they trudged from one foot to the other, looked around, exchanged a few words. Perhaps they were waiting for a sign that they alone would recognize, a signal to move into the city.

On the forecourt of Stazione Termini I suddenly lost all desire for the city. In that moment I vaguely associated it with a disconsolate state, which I could anchor in neither a time nor an exact place; I felt only a cold trepidation, pervaded by pictures of the Tiber, of bridges and views of the naked forlornness of its banks, fully unrelated to the city they abutted. I took a bus and exited at Piazza Bologna, perhaps because the name inspired confidence in me, or because Piazza Bologna itself stirred a different, fully unfixed memory that I hoped to cling to against everything inconsolable, but when I got off I found nothing that offered any kind of welcoming shelter. I walked in a random direction and followed a main road, amazed by its colorless provinciality. There were few pedestrians—at this time of day no one was interested in the shops selling cheap clothes. A handful of young people shoved into small copy shops, and in the matchbox *alimentari*, where only random customers bought things in passing, Pakistani or Indian women sat by the doors, jammed into their tiny cashier's corners. Before long I stood at a high wall, behind which I at first expected to find a park, until I saw the flower stands, a larger and more garish version of the kiosks at Olevano cemetery. The stands appeared to arrange their territories by flower color—there was a red, a yellow, and a white territory—and all the flowers looked artificial, but proved on closer inspection to be uniform cultivated varieties, blooming bare and debellished of all unnecessary leaves: gerberas, chrysanthemums, lilies.

An *onoranze funebri* hearse rolled slowly across the courtyard toward the gate. The procession consisted of five or six cars, covered in city dust, transporting mourners who looked listlessly or sullenly out the windows. Perhaps it was an unloved elderly uncle with an unsettled legacy, for whom handkerchiefs were waved all the same.

I wandered across the enormous Campo Verano cemetery, a densely cultivated graveyard. Here the *fornetti* walls were like apartment blocks. There were entire estates, interrupted by subsections with magnificent gravestones and mausoleums, their architecture in keeping with the times, from art nouveau to Bauhaus and the brutalist concrete of the 70s. Apartments, houses, villas, palazzi for the dead, an entire city for the dead, with rich and poor quarters and a ladder-sliding, cleaning, flower-planting memorial staff, and all of it enclosed by the arterial roads, street-car lines, and train tracks of the living.

At last I ended up in the *Israelitico* section of the cemetery. It was sparser, brighter, less acutely marked by black trees and grave pomp, less severely ordered. The wall that segregated this part of the cemetery was fissured where the grave markers were embedded, the ochre-colored plaster had crumbled away, and small old bricks were laid bare. The name that I came across most often on the grave markers was Astrologo, and I had to wonder which stars over Rome might they have found themselves interpreting. On the graves lay stones and pebbles, a few blanched artificial flowers. Overturned flowerpots, cracked medallions with photographs. There, for the first time, it occurred to me: no matter where they were—in Styrian villages, in Olevano, Tarnów, or here at Campo Verano, by the Tiburtina station in Rome—these sepulcher images were a plea not to be forgotten, an anxious call of the visible, which arose with the invention of photography and wanted to be more powerful than any name. I imagined those who had always been forced to count every penny, who brought what money they had left to the photographer in order to have a picture on their grave. Or those who, already half-consumed by sickness, waylaid the first available itinerant photographer they could find—and the fear of those who had neither time nor money enough. And then there was the task of having this photograph turned into an enamel medallion: a burden placed on the bereaved. What a burden, what sorrow this picture brought about. It wanted to catch the eyes of those who came after at all costs, to shout out to them something that the written word didn't seem, no longer seemed, capable of expressing.

Cerveteri

I SAT IN THE TRAM watching the cemetery wall glide past, followed by the crumbling facades of rundown houses, then wide boulevards lined with bare trees and climbing grassy stretches, which from far away appeared familiar yet remained nameless. The fractured memories flooding my mind were placeless until I saw the pyramid, and behind it the wall of the cemetery with John Keats's grave. The pyramid of my childhood memory was different: it was smaller, an endless string of cars driving around it, and at the same time it was a sharper sign than this one. The erector of this tomb ascribed the foreign to himself for all eternity. In Palestrina, while looking at the Nile mosaic, the pyramid hadn't crossed my mind. The Nile valley had left a trail through Rome—I'd forgotten that.

I continued to Trastevere, where I had arranged a place to stay. The apartment was in a sixties block, as I knew them from films with blonde women wearing big sunglasses and scarves around their heads who would step out of doorways like this one and take a seat on the back of a Vespa. A heavy gate, marble steps. In one corner was a Christmas tree that had seen better days, without lights, only a bit of tinsel still hanging from its artificial branches. A concierge from the Danube delta in

Romania pointed me to the elevator and, when I asked, advised me where to buy groceries. The Romanian woman, who wanted to be addressed by an English-sounding name that she had given herself, sat in a small, bright lodge at the end of the dimly lit entrance hall. From there she must have always had the cast-aside Christmas tree in sight, and I imagined that every day she waited for someone to pick it up, carry it into the basement, or otherwise dispose of it. The darkness brought rain and heavy winds, which I had to brace myself against while crossing the intersection at Trastevere train station on my way to the shop. People poured out of buses, trams, the train station, all traveling downhill to the opposite side of the tracks. A nowhere-land began there, with broad arterial roads, supermarkets and apartment blocks, their windows mostly dark. In the obliquely falling rain I lost all sense of the place where I found myself.

At night the wind howled about the attic apartment. Rain drummed against the panes. On the veranda it clattered metallic, perhaps from satellite dishes, antennas, awnings. In the apartment below, a man and a woman talked deep into the night. On rare occasions their voices became louder, more feverish, and had I not occasionally heard footsteps, chairs sliding, silence, I would have thought their conversation was television.

In the morning the wind abated, the rain hushed. Through the rear windows I watched day arrive. Above hill crests the sky turned gray, then pink, and against the light of dawn I recognized the inverted outline of the mountains that from Olevano I would see drawn sharply before the setting sun. After the restless night, during which I had nearly forgotten where in the world—in life—I was, that view gave me a foothold, and even a strange kind of comfort I hadn't expected. From the veranda high above the Viale di Trastevere, I looked onto the back of the Gianicolo, which now lay in the hesitant orange-red light of winter mornings, just as the old town of Olevano would have. Gianicolo, spoken in my father's voice—the name was suddenly in my ear, adjusting my map of the surroundings. Rome. Trastevere. En route to Cerveteri. I knew once again where the Tiber was from here, where Ostia was, the Appian Way—places that yesterday had been but threadbare memories, spectres wandering about my mind. I was back at a nameable place.

After returning the keys to the Romanian concierge at the lodge, I took a train to Ladispoli. Standing in a sea breeze which blew through the train station's small forecourt, I looked up at the apartment blocks in their state of winter abandon, and was whisked away to England. Seagulls, wind, a near-turquoise sky, tiny cotton-ball clouds filled with small blue shadows—suddenly Italy was pushed aside. Perhaps it was the way the light above the salty marsh landscape between the sea and the hills shimmered, as it does above every terrain that can't decide where it belongs: a flat streak above the high, brackish groundwater table, with the sea and the volcanic hinterland tumbling incessantly around it. If you leaned into the wind at the right angle you might even hear a faint click when the dice collided.

The inland bus arrived, the sea remained at my back, and with it all distant similarities to the sky and light of England. Cypresses and pines slipped into view, along with the round summits of the undulating hinterland. All the same, on either side of the road the country remained for some time a universal land. Nurseries, warehouses, small-scale manufacturers along the highways. Via Aurelia carved a route toward Cerveteri, a gray vein that cast out small bulges of commercial areas, as all arterial roads do, where at other times traffic would surely accumulate, and passers-through would find comfort in commodities.

I never went to Cerveteri as a child. M. and I had planned to take this side-trip, a day in Rome, a half-day on the coast—that's how we had imagined it. Walking between graves. Giorgio Bassani's *The Garden of the Finzi-Continis* opens in Cerveteri, with a visit to this *necropolis*, which, as I now saw, was separated by a kind of small plateau—overgrown with low, brambly bushes—from the city of the living, with its inescapable fortress. This small plain in the winter light, too, was punctuated by tumuli. The field of burial chambers—above which the stone domes arched, covered in lichens, grasses, and wild daffodils—must have been enormous, sheer "second homes," as Bassani put it, which the living prepared or maintained and looked after for their dead, until one day they themselves moved in. The *necropolis*, this undulating ocean of overgrown domes, each accommodating a family of the dead, appeared much larger than the city of the living, which lay so silent and seemed so sparsely populated as I stepped off the bus.

Only a small part of the *necropolis* was accessible, old paved paths led between the grave mounds, with groups of trees in one or two places, tiny groves, to one side an expansive view to the sea, to the hills, past additional sepulcher mounds in the pale grass. I knew exactly how we would have walked between these graves together. How we would have entered the chambers, the stony beds, the chambers, how we would have looked at the things depicted with a near-tender accuracy found in the finely crafted two-color reliefs on the walls—as if that were enough, as if the dead would know to reach through the cool thickness of the masonry and touch the object or animal's other side, invisible to us, and hold it in their life-averted hands.

The burial chambers were oddly ceremonious, perhaps because here I could imagine M. next to me on these paths, his gait and gaze, his voice, more clearly than in any other place yet in Italy. Words from Bassani's prologue that I had long faltered over came to my mind: *l'eternità non doveva più sembrare un'illusione*—here eternity could no longer remain an illusion. I am not sure if I understood them any better now, but they had become a picture: stone, moss and grasses, there between the blue-green of wild daffodil leaves, bare stalks before any buds had arrived. Were there snakes here, between the underbrush and the cracked stone, which must be very hot in summer? In warmer months it was likely too loud, from people strolling between the graves.

On my way back to the city of the living, I wondered why my father never brought us here. Tarquina was not far—why hadn't he turned from Via Aurelia and driven up to the hills? He must have known, after all, what he would find there. Was he familiar with that sentence about eternity, which here could no longer remain an illusion, a fairy tale, a priest's empty promise?

The sun had meanwhile become sharp and dazzling. Every so often a sudden gust of cool wind blew in from the sea. I sat down at the bus stop by the empty market square and prepared for a long wait. An African man took a seat next to me, looking drawn. He leaned his head against the rear wall of the shelter and I thought he might fall asleep. Had I not been afraid of offending him, I would have stood up and given him the entire bench to sleep on. But after a few minutes he addressed me in French, with the rolling R and flat, nasal accent of a West African. He rustled in a plastic bag. I expected him to offer me men's socks, but after a crackling search he pulled out sunglasses, crooked and cheap designer knock-offs. He took them out of the bag only halfway, looked at me, and let them slip back inside, without saying a word. Instead he asked what had brought me to Cerveteri. I described the *necropolis* to him. Perhaps I used the wrong words, in any case he looked at me with an expression so blank that my explanations became embarrassing, and I was relieved when the bus came. The young man didn't get on, but raised his large hand and waved goodbye to me as the bus drove off. *Chronicle of a Summer*, I thought once inside the bus. And out the other window: Pasolini. His *Notes Toward an African Orestes*. That was the last film M. and I saw together. We had mixed up the date and arrived at the cinema to see a different Pasolini film: *Uccellacci e uccellini. The Hawks and the Sparrows*. We never did watch it together.

Via

I EXITED AT OSTIENSE STATION, grazed by a memory. Glimpses of the backs of houses along the tracks had awoken something in me somewhere, which nevertheless sunk back down once I stepped off the train. Moments later I found myself at the pyramid again. The Appian Way came to mind: a spring morning, decades ago, the white light of high fog streamed through the interstices between dark trees onto the cobblestones, which shone without being wet. It had snowed in Rome the day before, but immediately afterwards spring arrived, and that morning on the Appian Way was quiet and pleasant, remained in my memory and returned in my dreams.

The sky clouded over in the afternoon and a cold wind blew. On that weekday in February the Appian Way was practically empty, save for an occasional car with tinted windows driving to one of the luxury villas located on the grounds behind the gravestones. Perhaps the people in the villas didn't know that the quarters of the living should remain separate from those of the dead. The routes of the living, the Roman roads leading out into the world and coming from the world up to the city limits were bordered by places of the dead; it was the dead who escorted the living, and not the other way around.

And one could speak of lingering in the streets only in terms of eternity, which appeared to be incidental here, which didn't call out to prove itself not a fairy tale, not an illusion. The dead marked the old streets as places one ought not to linger, as long as one can keep going.

I liked the emptiness of the streets and the pallid terrain, bleached by winter, the figures on semi-reliefs, which despite the damaged marble looked out with such seriousness and inviolability—a precursor to grave photographs, perhaps, and their models, too, but whose gaze was turned inward by the marble's uniform white, and did not search for the eye of the viewer, did not implore for remembrance, but rather was directed at something inaccessible from outside which remained invisible. This silent avoidance of any encounter with an outside gaze perhaps displayed a much greater reconciliation with death than the pleas to be remembered from the distance of a long-forgotten moment, as on the ceramic medallions that I came across in cemeteries bordered by smooth walls and black cypresses.

Across from the last tomb, which bore a white relief, was a house behind a hedgerow. As I raised my camera, preparing to photograph the stone, three white dogs appeared from a garden tucked behind the hedgerow: large, long-haired dogs, which settled down in complete silence on the ground, camped next to one another with their legs outstretched and their heads raised, staring at me. Nothing stirred on the Appian Way. A red kite circled above the pallid open terrain past the burial ground. When I turned back, the dogs seemed to have edged out farther toward the street. Their stance was unchanged. Nothing about them stirred, not a single tail-hair twitched, their pointy muzzles hadn't puckered a hair's breadth. I couldn't even see any air being quietly drawn into their bodies. Heads raised, legs out-stretched—that's how they lay, one after or next to the other, depending on your perspective, as if they wanted to invite those who happened to pass by to compare them with the gravestone showing a bust of three figures in relief.

The street leading back to the city center appeared end-less from here. I was also hesitant to walk past the dogs. They marked a border which I neither understood nor wanted to learn about. I followed the Appian Way farther out of town. Open land now spread out on either side of the road and farther in the distance I saw a traveled road, a herd of sheep in a mead-ow, and behind a half-toppled parasol pine I could make out the contours of an old factory, its short brick chimney, its dark, slightly sloped roof. Only now did I see the many crows sitting in the bare trees at the edge of the meadow. The red kite was overhead again. Pasolini-land, I thought, without any specific scene in mind. Perhaps it was only the thin blades of yellowed grass—as grows on poor, marshy ground—which might have swept around a character's leg in a film, or it was the half-lying pines, the emptiness, the sky in its unmoved gray, the desolation of the background and the street of tombs behind me, this land of upheaval and borders, the pale wasteland of the mythic on the fringes of the razed slums east of Rome.

I had to rush to catch the last bus to Anagnina. I followed the streets that I could make out on my skimpy old map, but again and again they turned out to be cul-de-sacs. I crossed a foul-smelling canal and found myself in a tangle of lanes be-tween garages and workshops, where men sat on wobbly fold-ing stools, drinking beer, and darted mistrustful glances in my direction. Boys on mopeds cruised around the bumpy lanes, all of which let out at an enormous scrapyard. Dogs threw themselves against the fence in a frenzy until a man appeared and commanded they lie down. Perhaps he had rushed over in hope of a good deal, a trunk of rusty, unknown treasures. He didn't know where to begin with the map, but when I said Anagnina he waved in a direction and pointed out a narrow passageway, wedged between the fence and the abutting shack. As if released from a magic portal, I emerged onto a major road soon after. There were residential blocks in sight, shops, a stop for a bus to Anagnina.

On every step at the bus station, tired travelers stood waiting. Dusk fell and the arriving buses brought very few passengers. The urban and the rural parted ways again at night. A number of people had already arrived for the bus to Olevano: an Indian family carrying enormous bags from an Asian supermarket; a few Somalis; a woman with a child, who spoke rolling African French into her phone. Two men in work clothes spoke Russian. Stepping on, I recognized a woman who had taken the same bus out of Olevano the previous morning. She responded to my rash greeting with a clueless look from very tired eyes.

It turned dark quickly. The bus seemed to take a different route than it had on the trip out. It crept down a highway through rush-hour traffic and stopped here and there at bus turnouts, where people stood waiting with bags and boxes. Hardly anyone spoke Italian. The highway lay above the surroundings, and one looked down onto wholesale markets for foreign groceries, bridal parlors next to restaurants with blinking signs advertising rooms for family celebrations and weddings, shops selling bathroom ceramics, cheap tiles, cell phones and satellite dishes, hotels, guest houses, flop-houses with windows illuminated red. It blinked, twitched, and flickered all around in the light of partly defective neon signs, and shoppers carrying bags came out of the stores and went about climbing the embankment up to the road and over the guardrail in order to walk to the next bus stop. I occasionally forgot where I was. This street, with these stores and advertisements, could have been in Belgrade, in Bucharest, perhaps even London's East End. Everything was passages. The weary travelers on the bus all came from somewhere and wanted to go to another place, because they were human, as a writer once said.

After Palestrina the bus emptied little by little. The Indian family exited in Cave, the Somalis in Genazzano, the Africans with the child were sound asleep and had either missed their stop or lived past Olevano.

The bus turned off the main road to the small plain, toward Frosinone, and I recognized Olevano, illuminated yellow by streetlights, up on the mountain. Hovering in the glow of countless small lamps, I saw the cemetery on the right above the village and knew that the house where I lived, which from here below couldn't be seen, was in the middle. Everything angular, everything heavy was cast off the cemetery at nightfall, and briefly it appeared to me as an island of consolation. The white glowing cemetery and the village in yellow street-lamp light were antipodes by night as by day, two worlds with their own rules of light and shadow, but from the plain, with Rome to my back, both appeared as vessels, two glowing boxes waiting to be opened, waiting to reveal something.

Carnevale

THE SPRING AIR brought an entirely new gray on days with no
sun. It was full of light, a vibrating gray which allowed no shadows yet gave the landscape more depth; I saw the gradation of
hill ranges leading up to the mountain where, on its far slope,
Palestrina must have lain, and recognized paths emerging white
in the northward forest hillsides, which I had previously never noticed—even the plain appeared in declensions and small
ascents, each bearing a different shade of blue-gray. Olevano
cast lines of allegiance in every direction, and with a naked
eye I could trace mountains and valleys and ridges progress-
ing above San Vito up to the distant hillside with the soldierly
parasol pines. Small hamlets and villages, tucked between cliffs
and sparse green, came to light and I wondered how Olevano
appeared to the residents of these places. How did they see the
dialogue between village and cemetery, in what light did they
lie for the distant observer? How did the angularity and softness, coldness and warmth of color spread out for them, in this
place where they had perhaps never in their lives been?

I walked along other lanes with a view to neither the house
on the hill nor the cemetery. They wound around the castle
square and the larger church, where women were always busy

with flower decorations and candles, tidying and preparing the altar. The women eyed me coolly, correctly sensing that I lacked their religious zeal. The church was exceedingly ugly, a bulk from the century before last, crammed between the old houses, but the view over one of the small forecourt's walls extended to a forested valley, to a ditch with a river in the distance that I'd never noticed before. No one could tell me what it was called, only that it flowed into the Sacco, which gave the plain at the foot of the Olevano mountain its name. From these paths, stairs, and tunnel-like passageways, the view opened to a different, harsher landscape which had no plain as a reference point, but only height, steepness, camber and surface quality: cliffs, groves, bushes, bright earth in the serpentine trails and paths.

Carnevale fell on a cold Sunday. Throughout the afternoon hours it was silent as always in the village, and around the attractions and stalls assembled on Piazzale Aldo Moro there were only a few roaming teenagers who smoked, drank beer and made small deals in a corner. In the lanes farther uphill, costumed children scurried about, freezing, with yellow wigs and cattish whiskers teetering about their heads. A small girl stumbled in her long, pink glitter-dress and took a spill down a set of steps; tears ran down her face—red with blush—because she had bumped herself or because the other children had laughed at her, or because her glitter pocket-purse was now soiled. Then everyone ran away as someone turned the corner, singing an old ballad in a loud female voice, jingling a set of keys. A man or a woman? And what had sent the children running so swiftly and unanimously? A bright voice, an ungainly body and the enormous feet of a man. The figure rankled with an entrance door for a while, until the key at last turned the lock.

That afternoon I walked through the olive groves, which had lost all traces of green in this uniform light gray, becoming tarnished silver crowns atop dark gray trunks. In the village the loud *carnevale* celebration had begun; a babble of children's voices rose up from the lower square, the fallen princess's surely among it. There were bursts of loud pop music and, as at the Befana festival, a woman's voice, evidently giving celebratory instructions. Time and again, in turns, her voice, then a small cloud of children's cheers, then again the music. I saw a black car stop on the side of the road by the olive grove. A man stepped out, elegant in a coat and gloves. He held a phone up to his ear, spoke agitatedly into it. Not even as he opened the passenger door and helped an elderly woman out of the car did he interrupt his conversation. The woman wore a garish coat, orange-pink; among the gray and silver of the trees, the faintly trembling leaves and the landscape in white light, it stood out, bringing to mind something raw, like the flesh of papaya or a scar from a burn wound. The man retreated from the woman and her placatory gestures and walked deeper into the olive grove with his phone, speaking quieter, more urgently, nervously. The elderly woman set off, uphill. She walked very slowly in her shapeless coat, a gaudy speck nosing forward like a sore spot in the matte surroundings. From her coat collar hung fist-sized pompoms, which swung back and forth in time with her steps. Perhaps she had a heavy heart, or a weak heart, and that's why she wore the sore coat so gingerly up the slope and about the next bend, while the music droned from below, swallowing the man on the phone's voice. Then the music hushed as if cut off and it was silent for a few moments; the entire valley had to recover from the impact of the noise. Only the man's words remained in the air, dry and stinging. He looked up, saw that the woman was no longer standing next to the car, and ended his phone call. In big steps, out of keeping with his distinguished appearance, he set off uphill. 'Mama!' he yelled, as if startled. 'Mama!' Beyond the bend I heard him call several times more. Below in the valley the children's cheers began, the entertainer's voice resounded, and a moment later the pop's stomping pounding as well.

The cemetery was quieter than usual this Sunday. *Carnevale* was probably incompatible with visiting the dead, but the celebratory clamor reached uphill, or at least to the front sections behind the gate flanked by flower kiosks. The kiosks were closed this Carnival day. I searched for Maria Tagliacozzi's grave and found that someone had left behind a small polyester bouquet, yet not garish. A short bouquet with white, star-shaped blooms, a bit jasminish, a bit lily-like, with unspecific plastic leaves suited to neither kind of flower, lay on the ground next to the lamp, which was still broken.

The next day I went to the town hall and inquired about Maria Tagliacozzi. I was directed to an *assessore* who sat in a tiny office with a view to the corner where one evening I had heard the woman calling "Maria" so persistently. He eyed me with suspicion. The name didn't ring a bell. He made a few conjectures, asked if her niche was cared for. Just yesterday, I told him, there was a plastic bouquet there. The clerk gestured dismissively. Then they aren't from Olevano, he said boldly. We only bring fresh flowers. He then paused to think and, as if fearing he might have offended me, elaborated on the advantages of artificial flowers for relatives living farther away.

Perhaps she is from Tagliacozzo, he said as we parted, like a travel agent. Tagliacozzo is a very beautiful place.

Strade

THERE WERE CAT DAYS and dog days in Olevano. The windless waiting days were for the cats. They crept around every corner and sat—gray, sand-colored, and brownish tabby—in every nook, as if born of the same quarry stone most of the old houses were built from. They were mistrustful, observant, and skittish around strangers, yet less prickly feral than the cats in Rome and on the coast. On sunny, calm days, cats flanked the bench in front of the bar like small deities who felt responsible for the smokers and the coarse girl with her stroller, and they lingered before the San Rocco portal. They avoided the cemetery, shying away, perhaps, from the rattling ladders or the lack of birds. On rare occasions a dirty white cat with a very round head sat among the bushes below the veranda, waiting for attention. The fastidious caretaker would cry shoo the minute she saw it, and the cat learned to worm its way into the bushes and bide its time. I occasionally tossed down crumbs of food and let it lie in the sun on my veranda while I read or stood at the railing and scanned the landscape for change, counted the columns of smoke, or traced paths that had emerged in the landscape. I was still trying to muster the courage to hike farther out into the terrain. The caretaker disapproved of the dirty white cat forcing its way into areas that the caretaker tended, and several times she became indignant. If she felt no one was looking she would grab whatever happened to be in reach and throw it at the cat; this must have cost her a great effort, as she kept everything in such meticulous order. Behind the house on the hill, a tiny road named after a German painter led into the valley. He died very young and I couldn't imagine why this bumpy road, wedged into the back hill, bore his name. Perhaps it was due to its view of the Villa Serpentara, that reddish, Roman architectural folly built by a German in the early twentieth century, which lay yonder among the holm oaks on the reforested hillside, across the valley and, depending on one's perspective, directly below the craggy, fortress-like, enormous balcony of the cemetery in Bellegra.

At its upper end the small road was lined by high conifers, all bearing the same whitish cocoons that I had observed shortly after my arrival. Flocks of coal tits lingered in tree crowns. Farther below were neglected sports fields, where I occasionally saw groups of boys playing ball. A bush in front of the facilities was being swallowed by an ever-replenished mountain of trash; the many cats that resided there must have lived well from discarded leftovers and spoiled food. On silent, moonlit nights I sometimes heard their catfights, their hissing and shrieking. Looking uphill over the tangled, thick scrub one could see the sharply drawn corner of the cemetery looming, with its undulating cypresses; stiff and barely legible, it was a greeting from above to everything entangled that had accumulated on this extremely steep path. Behind the sports fields the dirt road passed by the ambulance station and met a paved street which had emerged from the tunnel a few hundred meters back. A retired teacher who offered guided walks through Olevano, whose weak heart and blue lips worried me, told me at this intersection—with cars and buses roaring around us, the sounds multiplied in the valley and tunnel—that in the depression where the market place and soccer grounds are today, were once the region's brickyards. In this valley they fired roof shingles, bricks and clay tiles, and the surrounding hillsides lost their forests, the wood burnt in the brick kilns. The air here was always heavy and pushed downward, because very little wind found its way into this hollow; mixed with smoke from several brick kilns, it must have weighed even heavier on everything and settled, viscid, onto the bare slopes.

On stormy days which filled everything with a trembling restlessness, from the ample southern valley down to the smallest fissures in the terrain, the cats remained hidden. But dogs roved about, alone or in small packs, forcing themselves through fences to attack trash cans, and chasing one another. After darkness fell, their barking drifted beneath the gusts of wind in hoarse wisps, and it sounded as if they were following the moped drivers, who, on stormy nights, as if gripped by a fever, cruised around the streets for hours, letting their motors howl and their brakes squeal. The wailing wind, the ragged woofing, and the storm-possessed moped-drivers made it impossible to sleep on these nights, and it was almost calming to hear the first buses droning in the morning, groaning uphill and downhill—commuter buses, school buses, refugee buses—black clouds shooting from their exhaust pipes. The sound of their motors nearly bursting on the steep curves bore into the morning and afternoon, but after stormy nights this return to the order of things was liberating—a crack in the day that would put an end to the howling mopeds and yapping dogs, who would also need sleep and make their beds somewhere below the wind and wait.

On hunting days too the cats took cover, ceding the terrain to the dogs, who trotted through the olive groves, panting, and attempted to locate the origin of the shots that echoed off the hillsides and village walls. They hunted on calm, beautiful days, for instance when the sun tried to break through a layer of high fog, when the landscape lay pale and gray-blue without shadows, and a serene atmosphere was almost in the offing. No one could tell me what they hunted in this early spring. I took care not to walk on those days, after on several occasions in the forest above the cemetery and in the olive groves past the vineyards I was surprised by shots, which sounded as if they had been fired from only a few steps away. But I never saw anyone shooting, nor did I ever see a dog retrieve. I only heard after each shot the dogs' ascending romp from the village; with pendulous tongues, they were eager to root around for prey.

One hunting day I was out for a walk with the teacher, reverentially referred to as *professore*, when I saw for the first time the village's southwest face from outside, its steeply ascending walls with their intimated arches, and the houses upon them, watchful and in their impoverished state so vulnerable. Laundry fluttered beneath the crooked shutters, behind which they lived forever aware of the abyss before their windows.

On a small plateau below the village was a church with a painting of the Madonna, which was part of the teacher's walking itinerary. According to legend, it was brought here by angels, he explained. The Madonna had long, slender Duccio-hands; the chubby boy on her knee wore an amulet-like red necklace and held a red rose. Angels had placed similar pictures of the Madonna in several churches between Olevano and Rome, each one painted by the same Albanian hand. Yes, indeed, he meant Albania, the white land across the sea—Italy, too, tipped to the East here and there. The painting of the Madonna hung on a freestanding wall, separated by a narrow passageway from the church wall. The back of the wall was covered in writing. In the past, explained the teacher, only women were allowed to write down their pleas here. Today no one pays that any more heed. There were shaky, barely legible sentences, written over a hundred years ago, probably by the first generation of women in the villages and hamlets that could write at all; carved, calligraphed, and jotted pleas for sons to get well, for sons to come home from war, for sons to finally be born, and others yet to be released from prison. The wails, whispers, teeth grinding, beseeching and trepidation of the women of Olevano from the twentieth century, turned to script, framed by newer pleas, written in marker: to pass an exam, for reconciliation with a loved one, for a new moped.

Outside, in front of the church, I heard the hunters' gunshots in the small westward valley overlooked by the fortress. The shots, their echo, the dogs' wild yapping from the other side of the village. The teacher pointed to a small terrace, barely discernible in the bush below the village wall. In the past, children who died before they could be baptized were buried here, separate from the cemetery. And there, next to the lowermost gateway to the village, were the remains of an old quarantine infirmary for migrant workers, who came here to hire themselves out to clearcut the forests. They came from far away. People always came from far away and, eventually, they left.

All of these mountain crests, the teacher said, pointing to

the hillsides behind San Vito Romano, where the soldierly pines stood, are paths. The mountains were more important than the rivers. The mountains carried the *strade. Le strade fanno storia,* he added with an air of finality. Men came from the valley, dogs panting obediently about their feet. The men carried bundled kill, rabbits and birds which they threw into a car, parked partly in a bush, and covered with black plastic sheets. The car was behind the chapel of Santa Anna, secret patron saint of the un-baptized children from *fuori le mura* cemetery, each of whom she, subverting all rules of damnation, would lead to paradise. The chapel was always open for stray hikers in need of shelter. That was the custom here.

The hunters drove off at noon and I asked the teacher, whose lips had turned very blue from either hunger or the sun-resistant cold, where the old cemetery was, the one that came before the concrete lodge of the *morți,* up there on the right?

The old *morți* were, as it turned out, housed beneath the ugly bulk of a church in the village. The feet of the *vii* shuffled and shambled across the travertine ground during mass and prayer and while tidying up, arranging and adorning, as behooved the sanctimonious women. The *morți* lay sealed between cliff and concrete in an enormous *fornetto* beneath the church, without flowers and without luce perpetua, but among the *vii.*

Women's Day

IN EARLY MARCH the mimosas on the southern hillsides in Olevano began to bloom. Yellow clouds in blackberry bushes, still-bare pastures, among dwarf periwinkle and pale reed stalks. I heard corn buntings and skylarks in the fallow land between olive groves and vineyards, time and again the green woodpecker, too. In the evenings the blackbirds sung. In a cabinet in the apartment I found binoculars, and from my veranda I now observed the area through them. I could see vegetable farmers in their fields on the plain and farmhands poking olive fires. I made out paths leading up the sparsely forested hills in the west, which were traveled infrequently by cars, and small hamlets on distant hillsides, which to the naked eye were mere rock formations. Below the mountain crest with the rows of pines, I discovered a herd of sheep moving like a whitish shadow, slowly across the ground.

To the south my gaze now always went to Paliano, the village that sat atop the half-round of a hill that appeared as if formed by a human hand and was forested below the development. Otherwise shadow-blue, through the binoculars the coniferous forest proved to be interspersed with small islands of reddishly bare deciduous trees. At dusk I saw individual windows illuminated in the houses. The entire landscape was transformed by the binoculars, reminding me of the first time I experienced this wondrous kind of metamorphosis as a child, when my brother was given a pair, and from the highest windows of our house we could suddenly see elements on the opposite bank of the Rhine which previously from the same spot had appeared to be bluish, indistinct bulges of riparian woodland with trees lying behind them, with no connection to the riverside landscape that we knew up close from our walks. Through his binoculars, the riverside became something strange, in the inverted order of things and through the many, somewhat blurry outlines of elements: first water, then the bank reinforcement, brambles, and only then the promenade trees, which on land naturally conquered the foreground. The bank reinforcement was stained and bumpy, the outer edge of the river mile marker like a mysterious cipher. It appeared as if the *possibility* of a landscape unfolded through the binoculars, both in the staggered arrangement of the stripes of terrain and the degree of precision, a possibility that you could fall into as if it were an abyss, if you only let the terms, the ratios of size and distance, sink into oblivion.

Seen with a naked eye, Paliano was a gentle hill in the light of spring, a faint outline of houses on its crest. Through the binoculars it became a fairy tale land that existed only on the other side of the glass, a toy village with tiny figures—on one hand intriguing, but at the same time frighteningly imponderable. As soon as I set down the binoculars and looked with a naked eye, it rejoined the landscape of the plain and lowland hills, which stretched between Olevano's Monte Celeste—I had just learned this mountain's name—and the Monti Lepini in the southwest.

Women's Day fell on a Sunday this year. In the many years since I had last been in Italy, it had transformed from a holiday of demonstrations, protests and declarations into a kind of second Mother's Day: candy shops sold yellow sweets shaped like mimosas, pastry shops advertised cakes decorated with marzipan mimosas, perfumers furnished their gift paper with plastic mimosas, and on every corner stood a vendor selling mimosa bouquets. Despite all the bouquets, the stock was not yet plundered, and ample mimosa trees bloomed, yellow and soft in the landscape, decorating it for Women's Day as I set off for Paliano that morning.

It was an arduous trip. The actual streets did not coincide with those on the map I had found next to the binoculars in the cabinet; they terminated suddenly, were blocked by the cars of residents who remained hidden, or pivoted unexpectedly in entirely different, uncharted directions. I had shaken off the caretaker's warning—that Paliano is far away—as implausible, but it now proved to be true, and I found a way in only from the broad state road between Valmontone and Frosinone.

The Paliano that I walked through had little in common with the place I had seen with binoculars. It was midday, the sun gave off a sharp light, and the streets lay empty; only here and there was a mimosa vendor, hopeful for a repentant husband or son, and in a pastry shop three Women's Day cakes were still for sale. From the apartments came the clattering of dishes, a babble of voices hung in clouds around the open windows, and every pub aside from a "Bar Sport" was closed. On the small square a few boys stood clutching their mopeds sullenly, thus expressing their dismissal of Women's Day, or at least this commercialized version of it with mimosas and sweets.

The fortress at the center of Paliano proved to be a prison and a sanatorium for convicts with tuberculosis, with barbed wire curling on one of its walls, and in front of a small door below, in the large, slick, frightening fortress wall, a police officer sat on a plastic chair sunning himself. Beside him a dog with a pointy muzzle lay on the sun-warmed ground. Maybe there would be visiting hours in the afternoon and mothers, wives, brides and daughters would pass by the police officer and enter the dismal building. The prisoners might have made small mimosa twigs from fondant or colored paper to give their visitors for Women's Day.

From a winter-cold spot not yet pierced by the sun, I saw Olevano, the house on the hill, the cemetery, and it all formed the impression of a backdrop, clumsily stuck or glued in front of greenish-gray Monti Prenestini in the background, which, covered very sparsely with trees, ascended behind San Vito Romano and donned the row of bewitched pines that I always saw from my veranda. I hadn't brought along the binoculars to find the fairy tale view of Olevano from here and could hardly imagine that, day after day, I stood fixed to this thin backdrop, letting my gaze wander about the landscape I now found myself in.

I followed signs to a restaurant that was supposedly open. The road led along a hillcrest lined on both sides by open, steeply declining terrain and stretches of single-family homes with a view, some of which were like provisionally knocked-together huts, others opulently equipped with prefabricated fittings: concrete lions, ornate lanterns, garden gates like small church portals. The restaurant was in a holm oak grove, where the road dead-ended. In warmer months it must have been a popular destination for groups of daytrippers, but now only a small section was open with a few dozen tables where families celebrated Women's Day. On the lower edge, the windows were still hung with a thick brown felt against the wind and cold; above it one looked out to snow-covered mountain peaks in a sharp, bluish-white light that I had never observed in Olevano. This light suddenly gave me the feeling I had been flung an unforeseen, frightening distance, and momentarily I was homesick for my apartment in Olevano. I sat between a large family which, gathered around a taciturn and not particularly healthy-seeming mother, vociferously ordered one dish after another, and an elderly couple who exchanged not a single word. The family's attempt to coax enthusiasm from the mother with the myriad dishes was both moving and terrible: every plate that she disdained or pushed aside after momentary tasting, her sons assailed with wolfish greed. Their young, heavily made-up wives meanwhile looked bored and played with their cell phones. Perhaps no one knew how to handle the old woman's stomachless grief, not even her husband, in his suit trousers held up by suspenders, who frequently stood up and went out, probably to smoke and have his quiet. At the table he occasionally reached clumsily for his wife's hand, disheveling the mimosa branches arranged around her plate. Once she took a piece of bread and I saw that her hand was bandaged up to the knuckles. The sight of the taciturn mother made me sad, and I moved my seat so as to no longer have the family in view. The older couple sat in front of empty plates. Behind the woman's head rose the panorama of icy mountains. She had a rigid face, very masculine, and the receded roots of her dyed-red hair made her forehead appear enormous, brutal almost. At the same time, the woman was small, delicate even, with very narrow, bony hands. She wore a dress in a color referred to as Carpaccio in Italy, after the Venetian painter with a predilection for a dull, brownish red, reminiscent of raw meat or dried blood. On one shoulder she wore a scarf, folded in a manner that would have been considered elegant decades ago. The scarf had a zigzag pattern in green tones. One waitress removed the empty plates while another brought a single dessert, which they shared wordlessly. With uniform slowness they spooned away at their respective sides, emptied their wine glasses, paid, and left.

From the restaurant's forecourt I tried to spot Olevano among the oak trunks. At first, I found it difficult to get a foothold, the landscape with snow-covered peaks and craggy pitches in the background was so foreign and the light so cold that I didn't know what direction to look in. But then I discovered the village and then the cemetery. Both were tiny, flat and distant, the village strangely yellow in the afternoon light, a valley's dull close at the beginning of a wilderness. The cemetery, inconsistent with this wilderness, appeared as an angular drawer not fully slid into place on the hillside, cement gray and cypress black, an unsightly box or a single austere *fornetto*, holding inside the countless urns.

I could make out the house on the hill only narrowly, not because it was so small, but because the spatial conditions had shifted. I finally discovered it on the mountain, where it lay, stuck in the shadow of the cemetery, as if the drawer were hanging menacingly above it. From this distance, one could scarcely distinguish the many olive trees from the craggy surfaces.

On one of my car's windshield wipers sat a small blue butterfly in the sun, the first of the year. I didn't want to drive it away and so I waited until suddenly, in a gust of cold wind, it flew off.

I hadn't planned to drive back through Paliano, but along the way, which from above had appeared so simple to me, I became lost again and again. I drove through an odd region which at every turn reminded me of a different landscape I had once before traveled through, as if this terrain between the small range of hills behind Paliano and the much higher mountains— along whose foot I thought I simply had to drive north—could not decide where it belonged, as if it wanted to be everything to everyone, yet was merely a network of small false paths through some place you'd long ago visited, and some place you could no longer find. Finally I arrived at a *Strada del Vino*, a wine road, and I knew eventually it had to lead me back to Olevano. It was a long way, and in the near-evening light I passed through a town I was sure I recognized. Serrone, a name I associated with nothing. The feeling of distant familiarity might have only been due to a group of people I passed casually strolling along the road, dressed entirely in white, like old-fashioned recreational athletes. They moved toward their goal with such a leisurely single-mindedness and assurance that their undeniable sense of belonging to this place and in this late afternoon was immediately apparent, and I briefly wished to join them.

The wine road led uphill between craggy slopes, and I watched the sun go down behind the hunched-over volcanic hill, which always appeared before Olevano streaked by the red evening sky on one side only. It was near dark when I drove down from Bellegra into the valley toward Olevano. I had never approached the town that way before. The cemetery lay on the left, carried by thousands of small, fluttering lights swimming in the evening. The village was farther below on the right in the yellow light of the street lamps, rising motionless and empty above the abandoned terrain on the floor of the depression. Where were the *morţi*, where were the *vii*?

Butterfly

THE NIGHT AFTER Women's Day I dreamed about M.

He's wearing an all-white hospital gown and sits, propped against pillows, in bed. He looks cheerful, confident, and holds his left hand out to me. A strip of bandage is wound around it, covering the hematoma on the back of his hand. Dried blood shows through the bandage.

We have to change the needle, M. says, and I am assailed by a familiar fear, of my clumsiness and the blood, which I'm not able to contain. The thought of contaminating the white hospital gown terrified me.

I pull down the neck of his gown. His skin is stretched thinly over the port inserted above his heart, and I see that no needle is sticking into it at all. On the raised spot sat a small yellow butterfly.

It should be blue! M. says, sudden trepidation in his voice.

The butterfly is yellow only today, I tell him. Because of Women's Day in Italy.

M.'s head falls exhausted onto the pillow. His eyes are fixed on the ceiling and are empty. I see his skull clearly beneath his skin. M. is no longer alive.

The butterfly rises from M.'s chest and lands on the lashes of his left eye. Its wings turn light blue.

Erminia

SOMETIMES I BROUGHT FLOWERS to Maria Tagliacozzi's *fornetto*, never purchased flowers, only what I found on the wayside. Daisies, wild hyacinths, lungwort, primroses. Probably nothing that would have made her day—she probably would have wished for mimosas on Women's Day, and something more striking than these little, low-growing flowers. I put my small bouquets behind the cable sleeve that ran along the outer edge of her *fornetto*, where they wilted quickly, and the next time I came they lay on the ground like wafted-over weeds.

I went back to the town hall, looking for the *assessore*. He had implied he would inquire after Maria Tagliacozzi. The sun shone into his tiny office, where there was no room for a second chair, and so he stood up politely. Maria! he said, pointing proudly to the framed photograph of his newborn daughter, now on his desk. It seemed uncalled for, given the baby picture, to bring up Maria Tagliacozzi, and the clerk evidently remembered only vaguely the matter that had brought me to him once already. He had nothing additional to report about her, and instead spoke generally, as if giving a talk about the region to tourists. *Fornetti* are either urns or metal coffins, he informed me. The *fornetti*, like graves, were leased for a certain period of time. When the lease was up the metal coffins and urns were extracted. The remains from the coffins would then be brought into the *ossario*. He described the lie of one ossuary—there was more than one in Olevano. The cemetery was built section by section, each with its own ossuary. The graves were a different story. There were never urns there, only coffins. And they had a longer lease period than *fornetti*.

At the cemetery I looked around for the ossuaries. At the spot he had described I found only a bin for compost. I came across small fieldstone cottages with narrow barred windows which were so dull and coated in cobwebs that I could make out nothing of their interiors. The door to one such house was ajar, however, and I saw that there were only tools inside: besoms, shovels, buckets.

While looking for the ossuaries I came across a flat grave with a marker that lay flush in the ground and bore a ceramic picture of a woman. It was not a professional portrait, but had clearly been made from a photograph shot in passing, perhaps while on a vacation or an outing; in any case it showed a woman in a short-sleeved blouse, holding her face in the sun, her eyes half-closed, one arm folded over the other. In the background I could make out blurry leaves. Her nose cast a sharp shadow on her right cheek. She had black hair, curly, cut short. I pictured her at Women's Day rallies, arm-in-arm with other women, perhaps workers. Maria Tagliacozzi didn't seem like the type for demonstrations and strikes, but her studio picture might have been misleading. De Paolis Erminia, the gravestone read. Born on 27/8/1927, in Olevano. A few months younger than my father. For a moment I was startled by the coincidental mirroring of Maria Tagliacozzi's date of death, on 28/7. I brushed aside the pine needles that had gathered around the raised letters.

DE PAOLIS ERMINIA NATA A OLEVANO ROMANO IL 27/8/1927 MORTA A LONDRA IL 25/1/1979. A surge of memories that I had set aside long ago washed to the surface. January and February 1979 were the months of the London bin-men's strike. The downtown squares and fenced-in greens were full of black garbage bags, stacked meters high. It was a mercifully cold winter, with pale-gray light, clouds of crows in the sky. All around hung the smell of trash, of decay, rot. When weeks later in February garbage trucks showed up and workers began clearing away the bags, rats scattered in every direction. I stood on a corner at Nevern Square and watched the crows in the bare trees, the droves of scattering rats, the workers anxious with revulsion in their defiled overalls, and the flying, oozing bags, which the men tried with utmost haste to throw into the garbage truck. Something unnameable to me, which nevertheless was connected to every fiber of my growing up and coming of age, came to an end with this sight, and I never forgot the scene.

At night I grappled with imagining all the possible ways to die that might have been De Paolis Erminia's end. In my imagination she was run over on Shaftesbury Avenue by a red bus, stepped out in front of a taxi on Camden Road, jumped from Hungerford Bridge, died in a fire—as so often happened in the old, oven-heated flats and bedsits—or slipped away in a cancer ward. I was reminded of the washable synthetic fabric in brown-ish-pink or yellow, which, ruched like a curtain, was slid onto the screen frames; this is how beds are separated in the wards.

Like Maria Tagliacozzi's gravestone, it mentioned no husband. No bereaved were mentioned either, but she must have had a family who paid to transport her corpse for burial here, in Olevano, in a proper grave. Perhaps the coffin arrived by airplane, at the Ciampino airport, located on the Valmontone–Rome rail line. Or it came the entire way from London to Olevano in a hearse; it was winter, after all, and cold.

I accepted that I would never know. I was afraid of going back to the town hall to research another dead person, so I asked the caretaker about the name. Yes, of course, De Paolis, the auto repair shop where my window, broken from the burglary, had been replaced. On the street in the plain. A place my gaze often brushed over while looking through the binoculars.

Who knows what brought Erminia to London. Perhaps the photograph was taken here, in Olevano. Perhaps she often stood like that in the sun, leaning against the doorframe of the workshop, somewhat hardened and full of expectations. We had a small piece of London's pale gray winter of unrest in common.

Reapers

IT WAS LATE MARCH before the olive reapers reached the groves around the house on the hill. There were three—a man who gave orders and occasionally disappeared for hours at a time and his two assistants. All day long I heard the sound of pruning shears. No saws. Just the metallic snipping. The clipped branches piled beneath the trees. On the second day they cut the branches into smaller pieces. Perhaps they used different shears because it sounded clearer. The two assistants worked together, huddling and speaking quietly, occasionally laughing out loud and glancing at their employer. Maybe they were joking at his expense. He stood at a good distance and worked alone. He wore a white coat with large pockets—presumably his work clothes, perhaps a disused pharmacist's coat. Or maybe he was a chemist. He spent his days in a lab, somewhere in one of Rome's southern offshoots, near Frosinone, where industrial plants were splayed on the flatland at the foot of the hills. He was certainly not an olive farmer, even if he knew what to do now with the trees. The assistants wore old, somewhat ragged clothes and black knit caps, which they pulled down over their ears again and again, although it wasn't cold. The overseer wore a hat, and his face looked very long and dour beneath it. His

cell phone rang often. I heard the impatient *pronto* with which
he received his calls. At times he spoke loudly, in an important
voice, and on other occasions he would turn his back to his
assistants or take a few steps to the side, speaking quietly. Two
white dogs showed up one day, which I had never seen here before. They reminded me of the guard dogs on the Appian Way
and settled down at some distance from each other in the same
manor, near the street, between two trees. Very calm, nearly motionless, they rested sphinx-like and watched the three
men trim the branches. I took them for the overseer's dogs, but
when he looked up and suddenly saw them, he jumped. He
took a few ungainly steps in their direction and, arms flailing,
shooed them away; the assistants giggled quietly and, walking
in place, imitated his gait. The dogs got up calmly and trotted uphill toward the cemetery. The overseer exchanged a few
words with his assistants and drove off in his car. An hour or
two later, he returned with three rakes. They first gathered all
the branches into neat, evenly spaced piles in the sparser parts
of the grove. Then with utmost precision they began to rake together all the remnant branches and dried leaves on the ground.
It was a beautiful morning, very bright, spring-like beneath a
pale sun. While the men raked, strange clouds began to surface
behind the volcanic hills in the west, which towered above the
mountain rims like brownish rings of smoke and turned violet
as they neared the plain, as a bluish darkness approached from
the south. When the men were nearly finished it thundered in
the distance. The first thunderstorm since M.'s death, I thought;
had I been a Hasid, I might have recollected a blessing for such
an occasion, to cap my mournfulness like a lid.

The men ended their work beneath the cold wind, now

blowing in gusts, and spread wide tarpaulins over the brush-wood heaps before driving off. It took a while for the rain to set in. The thunderstorm never came, the heavy clouds moved into the north and remained motionless for a while, dark blue beneath occasional rumblings over the mountain crests.

Meanwhile a very solemn chanting sounded from Piazza San Rocco, of one or more male voices without accompaniment; perhaps it was a ritual in anticipation of Easter. As the chanting amplified, I remembered the sound of the muezzin in rural parts of other countries. In the late afternoon it began to rain, hard at first and then passing over into a very soft, quiet murmur. In the evening the rain let up. A yellow glow lay like a crown about the clouds above the mountains in the west, and the blackbirds sung in a way I hadn't yet heard this spring.

The next day was bright and clear, entirely windless. Only the man in the white coat came and burned one pile of leaves after another. He was very careful and never let the fire out of his sight. In the end he took a shovel and covered the fire pits with dirt. The smoke rose very upright in the clear windless weather; perhaps the man took it for a good omen. Despite the upright columns of smoke, the air around the house was filled with the biting smell of fire, a smell that was absorbed by every fiber and for a long time didn't abate.

Capranica

Not until the day after the fires could I see how much thinner the trees, indeed the whole grove around the house, had become—the trees appeared clipped and coifed, the grass, brushed. Traces of winter were eliminated, everything was cleared. Sunlight spread large spots onto the ground between the trees and the still-recognizable fire pits. As evidence of what had once existed and now been cleared away, the fire smell remained, clinging to everything, and even a day, two days later, it was so acute that it masked everything else and ultimately roused a feeling of mild disgust.

I drove to Palestrina to escape the smell and from there continued up. To the west, far below at the foot of the mountains a landscape unfurled before Rome, appearing almost quaint in the spring light, traversed by small rivers, dabbed with groves, until past Tivoli it adjoined the massive pale scar that is the travertine breach. From the lookout points along the road the quarry appeared like an arranged badlands, carefully measured and barren. The stone of Rome had so thoroughly penetrated every pore down there that all who passed through must have been surprised by the softness of leaves on the scarce trees lining the road to Rome.

I stopped at a small village that reminded me of France, of a summer spent with M. in a mountain town in the Alps where we felt out of place; every day brought tremendous thunderstorms, and from the hillsides we heard scree coming loose, causing the landscape to shift, pulling down trees, and rendering navigable stretches impassable. M. was afraid, his eyes gave him away: of the scree, the precipices, of the dogs that stood snarling in front of their masters' houses, blocking the small roads, refusing to let us clueless hikers pass. Nothing of the sort was here. The likeness might have been due to a certain, brief incidence of light, to the well, located right by the entrance, to the root word of both town names, signifying "goat." A few market stalls were built up on the wide square at the village entrance, without a customer in sight. There was goat cheese and sausage, and at a different stand bread, cake and large chunks of *torrone*. Two African men walked around aimlessly, holding socks in their outstretched hands; without any potential customers, this gesture looked even more miserable here than it did on market days in Olevano.

Viewing the displays, I felt the urge to buy something to bring back home from Italy. Something that would help me get through the days with smell and taste, as I settled into my empty, bereaved apartment. I asked the cheesemonger if his cheese was from here. He nodded yes and, as proof, held up a small binder filled with laminated photographs of goats—apparently his—as if, just by looking at the goats, one could see where they lived or grazed.

I put the piece of cheese I had bought into my pocket and walked through the small village. It was cold despite the sun and the houses had a strange unfinished quality about them; plastic sheets flapped in window cavities, and provisional barriers enclosed crumbling doorsteps. But no one was outside, and only a single house on the road had children's scooters lying out front in the sun. Through the gaps between houses I saw the snow-covered mountains in the east. Where the interstices widened, it was also possible to make out all the countless crests, ridges, hill chains and small plains extending right up to the mountains in the distance, presenting themselves in all their barrenness. From this distance the olive groves over in the east by Olevano no longer swayed. The entire landscape was traversed by paths and roads which linked the villages, mountains and valleys; these lines formed a forbidding script, decipherable only from here above, to those who had mastered it.

When I got back to the square the stands were already dismantled. The cheesemonger and the cake seller were loading their goods into vans, while the African men waited at a distance, their socks already back in plastic bags, and when the right moment arrived they would probably negotiate a ride.

As I sat at the bar on the square, drinking coffee, the vendors came in. The bar was run by two Colombian women who spoke Italian with coarse accents and played different music to that in other local pubs. Two men sat mutely over their wine. One looked over at the new guests. When he saw the African men, who had remained standing outside, he waved his hands about and, to no one in particular, yelled: Ha, look who's come home! They're from here! No one paid him any mind, and the African men outside, who couldn't have possibly heard him, nevertheless turned their backs to the bar, as if embarrassed, while the man launched into a didactic monologue in a drunkard's sluggish manner. He turned to the Colombian women and with sweeping gestures explained how settlements were built on these hills above Palestrina during the Roman Empire for distinguished military returning after years of service along the Nile. Black women and men, said the man at the bar, this town was full of black women and men, those were different times.

He found no audience. Perhaps this scene repeated itself every Saturday, while the cheese and cake vendors drank coffee and the African men stood outside, not wanting to miss their ride, with neither the money nor desire to linger at the bar and be welcomed as lost sons by this lonely drinker. As we walked around Olevano, the teacher had told me something that supported the drunk man's story. He pointed to these hillsides and suggested that, to this day, one could find shards of dishes from the Nile region here, because in the mountains above Palestrina, distinguished military returning to the Roman Empire from Africa were given plots to settle in their homeland. The story stuck with me because of the pines, because of their military air in my mind, which went so well with this story.

I drove somewhat farther out of town, looking for the soldierly pines. I found them quickly, on the upper edge of a slope. I sat down on a rock a bit below the row of trees and ate a piece of the cheese, which now seemed unlikely to have any significance after my departure. Covered in spring-green, low grass and tiny flowers, the entire hillside was scattered with white boulders and ragged bushes, still bare from winter, and molded ridges, while small groups of sheep and buffalo grazed silently, undisturbed by my presence. The landscape of the last months spread out before me, and the inscribed routes made clear to me how these places were linked. I saw the small road to Valmontone and part of the major road to Frosinone, I saw Paliano and the route along the small ridge up to the restaurant in the holm oak grove, and even the highway from Paliano to Oleva- no, where I had become lost. From here above I saw that it was simply a long route that brushed against many different things, and I hadn't been lost at all. I saw Serrone, the town where I had encountered the daytrippers in white, Roiate and Bellegra, and more distant places in the hinterland. Olevano was easy to recognize, and if I squinted I could even make out the house on the hill and the cemetery, but from here above they lay stacked, like steps on a path: the village, the house, the cemetery. I didn't observe a single fire across the entire vast land.

I became dizzy looking at this unfurled country which was laid so bare yet remained so incomprehensible to me. A rug- ged terrain with a restless appearance—it presented itself dif- ferently from each side. On each side the routes drew a differ- ent script, the mountains cast different shadows, and the plains, foregrounds, midgrounds, and backgrounds shifted. A terrain that left traces in me, without a recognizable trace of myself re- maining in it. Something about the relationship between seeing and being seen—between the significance of seeing and being or becoming seen, as a comforting confirmation of your exis- tence—suddenly appeared to me as a burning question, which defied all names and acts of naming. If on that hillside someone had told me that I might die from the inability to answer or simply even phrase this question, I would have believed them.

Flying

IN THE NIGHT AFTER my excursion to Capranica, I had a dream.

M. strides over to me like he used to, stout, sprightly, in jeans and a sweater, laughing.

I stretch out my arm to him, he grasps it and collapses, becomes gaunt, small, fragile; I hold him and see that he is dying. I lay his dead body on the floor and float high above the plain at the foot of Olevano. I see the mountains in the west, the hill with Paliano, the ridge with the pines and I recognize Capranica, small on the summit beside them, even though everything lies in twilight, as if in the shadow of a massive cloud.

I know I have to say something now. I have to answer a question:

vii or *morţi?*

I'm not sure how to respond and feel an increasing tugging at my chest. Hovering there, above the plain, with the village and the cemetery and the house on the hill to my back and the clouds above, strains my heart inexpressibly. In my dream, I feel I've never been so strained.

Will it wither away, the hand that I pulled back from the *morţi?*

Ortolan

IN THE LAST DAYS of March, spring arrived. The village's damp-cold reticence was broken. I heard children in the churchyard, playing soccer into dusk, and people sat in front of their houses in the sun. Cats arched their backs on the sun-warmed steps, dogs scuffled on the roadsides or tramped about in search of a mate. The shop doors stood open. The cobbler with the old Mussolini poster on his wall listened to Italo pop, and his customers and acquaintances debated cheerfully. The landscape turned from blue to green. Flowers appeared on the waysides, pale purple dead-nettle and star-shaped white flowers unfamiliar to me. Everything that had previously seemed unapproachable now wanted to be inviting.

The sky in these last days of March was blanketed by a grayish-white high fog, which neither dissipated nor condensed into clouds, only let the blue shine in as if through a veil. The light spread over everything evenly with a soft flicker, and the shadows were gray and edgeless. This flicker had nothing of summer's blinding flare, was only a mild blur, which always made me look twice, unsure if I had been mistaken when recognizing something at first glance.

Blasts came from somewhere between Olevano and the mountains in the southwest. Several times a day the noise from the explosions ripped the ground; the birds flew off, uttering brief, anxious sounds. I scoured the area through binoculars, and once or twice thought I discovered a large bare spot on a very distant hillside, but soon after I became unsure—perhaps this bald, scar-like spot had always been there, after all, since I had seldom looked out to these rugged, purple-blue mountains behind Colleferro, where I had never been. No ascending clouds of dust revealed a detonation site. Aside from the birds and me, these explosions seemed to neither startle nor concern anyone; when I once asked the caretaker about it, she didn't know what I meant.

I tidied up and packed my notebooks and books, put the stones I had collected into boxes and wrapped the exposed film in black foil for my trip. I walked through the village lanes, trying to memorize the views and changes in perspective. I owed no one a goodbye and that was a relief. I took my daily walk around the cemetery, where I saw the new vendor at the flower kiosk on the left side who was always dressed in black and still needed time to adjust to his role. An elegant woman in a pantsuit stood at his stand, wanting advice, impatiently clinking her car key, putting her sunglasses on and taking them off. The new flower vendor cluelessly eyed his narrow selection of white and yellow chrysanthemums. He grabbed a white bouquet, held it up and said: here are the white flowers. Then he bent down to the yellow chrysanthemums, pulled out a bouquet and said: and here are the yellow ones. I glanced through the gate, but didn't enter the cemetery again. I had photographed the graves of Maria Tagliacozzi and De Paolis Erminia and once I was home would see what emerged in the pictures.

I continued walking through the olive groves, between the vineyards and past the group of vagrant birch trees.

Since the olive grove had been pruned, the green wood-pecker no longer came to the house. I missed its call in the morning, but throughout the day I could hear it farther away, between trees in the small valley along the steep road named af-ter the German painter, and behind the cemetery, where it oc-casionally sounded as if it were carrying on a conversation with two Eurasian jays in the small holm oak grove, farther uphill.

Around the birches, which now stood in the thin green of first leaves, I saw yellowhammers and blue tits. On the hillside beneath mimosas, now withered, a red-backed shrike creaked in the brush.

On my last day I heard an ortolan. Through the binoculars I saw it in a low bush at the edge of the olive grove under the terrace. For a moment all other birds fell silent. I remembered a summer night in the hills near Siena, during my last summer break spent in Italy. I was no longer a child and not yet an adult. It was early August and when darkness fell, lights appeared in the surround-ing vineyards. The lights moved, I heard voices, calls, imperatives, quiet and muffled. My father stood at the garden wall, where one looked out onto the valley, past the vineyards. I saw the glow of his cigarette and heard him picking up his wine glass and setting it back down on the wall. The countless lights, wandering about the dark landscape from all sides, formed an eerie spectacle that I couldn't make sense of. Perhaps they were looking for someone. But there was occasional laughter, their voices were untroubled. My father didn't say a word and I asked no questions. The next day we saw nets stretched everywhere in the vineyards, surely for catching songbirds. It was the first day of the hunting season.

On my last evening in Olevano the sky became overcast, the sun dulled and disappeared behind restless layers of clouds, blue with torn borders.

Bassa

IT WAS STILL DARK when I set out. A very delicate, barely perceptible rain fell. The air smelled of woodsmoke, dirt and grass. Nothing stirred in the village, it lay in the yellow lamplight like a backdrop after a performance. The first birds stirred with tranquil, shy morning noises, still half-dreaming.

I followed the narrow lane that joined the main road at a sharp angle where, on one of my first days here, I saw a dead man being wheeled out of a house. Above, at the station by the tunnel, commuters stood in small groups, waiting for the bus. Coming toward me at the next bend was a near-empty bus bound for *Rocca* Santo Stefano. Near Genazzano I had once seen the large warehouse. The blue buses were parked at a site that looked like an abandoned railroad yard, full of rusty objects, with slanted sheds, surrounded by bare elderflower bushes.

Once I had the steep downhill curve behind me and had entered the plain, my leaden heart burst, like in a fairy tale, and my relief was so great that I forgot to pay a parting look to the De Paolis workshop. My headlights occasionally grazed small groups of people who, bleary and contorted from the morning chill, waited for the bus. Wherever the road met a lane was an unmarked stop for passengers from hamlets, farmsteads, villages that I had never noticed while contemplating the plain.

As I drove onto the highway outside Valmontone, day broke. It continued to drizzle but the sky didn't hang, and a whitish light spread out. I hardly noticed what was on both sides of the highway, saw only how the landscape lay there now as compared to in January, how it had lost its sharpness and ruggedness; here and there a pale-blooming bush buckled in a field, perhaps hawthorn or lilac, everything was green. My eyes searched neither for places nor names; I wanted to leave behind Olevano, Lazio, Rome and this vague, cold southernness of the past months, and have terrain back under my feet that was connected to my interrupted life. Past the final Apennine tunnel, the territory widened. The road signs said Bologna, the mountains lay behind me, and the Alps still appeared distant; all around I saw only plains, the pale earth of the flatlands, green meadows, and vast orchards with blooming fruit trees. I strayed from the route I had planned on taking and drove northeast. I grazed *Ferrara*, saw part of the Rampari, and tried to avoid thinking of that icy day in January. I drove on without a plan and reached the Po; thought saw a thin shadow of the pale blue Euganean Hills in the distance. But toward the east the entire landscape was spread out flat and billowing, with single trees, clusters of trees and copses as islands, while distant church steeples formed the masts of invisible boats. I stopped in a small town named Polesella and wondered if I had ever been there as a child. Back then I would have gladly clung to this intermediate flatland between the Alps and the Apennines, which, on account of the overwhelmingly milky light, always appeared to hover after the mountains' sharpness. It was too formless for my father, who called it *nothing land*, but he loved the river and we would stop on bridges over the Po and look upstream and downstream, to the mountains, to the sea, and compare it to the Rhine.

Perhaps the river in Polesella merely reminded me of the Rhine, and I had never been there, after all. The river was broad, grayish blue, lined by willow trees and spanned by an ugly bridge. Near Polesella the river bends broadly, only to then lose itself in the plain to the east, while the Rhine of my childhood lunges out and then turns west, where nothing stands in its way to the ocean. I walked awhile along the bank. For three months, my feet had become used to gradients and now on level land they searched for a hold. Not far from here began the enormous delta, wandering and weightless, at times earth, at times sea, always partly sky. To the east the land stretched to the horizon, to the sea; manipulated by nothing, the border between sky and earth blurred until it was but a precarious stripe, flickering gray, blue, violet.

Over toward the sea the sky was a bright, soft April-blue, almost turquoise. Clouds emerged in the north. I dreaded the Alps and procrastinated until the wind picked up, and it became cold. As I turned to go I saw an egret in a bush on the far bank. It stood motionless like an icon, painted there on the bank between the branches and the soil. *Egret*, a word I had learned from M. On a hushed strip at the mouth of the Thames, we once came across a flock of little egrets, suspended like a loose cloud of dashed snow in spindly winter wood above reddish reeds. An estuary bird, in a pact with the itinerant.

II
CHIAVENNA

la scintilla che dice
tutto comincia quando tutto pare
incarbonirsi
Eugenio Montale, l'anguilla

Altipiano

WORDS ROLLED IN MY HAND like marbles, damaged glass marbles with dull, scratched surfaces and tiny nicks, scoured by sand, dirt, concrete, the glass of other marbles. A soft click when they collided, a sound that my entire body would strain to hear, to see if it would form a picture.

Marbles were mysteries in my childhood, there were never rules for a game, nor players; they were simply something to have, in their beauty inexplicable. I once stuck a marble between my upper and lower eyelid and looked into the light. I didn't come any closer to the marble's mystery—it was merely black in front of my eye—yet I felt blinded. A short time later I had an eye infection and secretly believed it stemmed from my experiment with the marble. I lay in my room with bandaged eyes. It was summer. I felt cold in the blackish, blind darkness and studied a small world with my hands: paths from one room to the next, along walls, railings and doors. Each fingertip felt a different color.

My father read to me, but in Italian, which I did not understand. You don't have to understand everything all the time, he said and read on. Over time, the words became soothing, I found them beautiful and made my own sense of them. Sometimes I asked about a word, and my father would respond tersely in German. *Hier. Vielleicht. Links. Berg.* I'm not sure what book he read from, but it might have been a travel guide. Once I asked about a word that I had to repeat several times: *altipiano. Hochebene,* said my father eventually—plateau—and the word was just as strange to me as *altipiano.* But I didn't pursue it, because my father's explanations were endless and clarified very little, and I preferred listening to the Italian.

The eye infection was cured before long, the blindfold removed, and I was able to see again. The world hadn't changed. But I had the word *altipiano* in one hand and the word *Hochebene* in the other, and sometimes I held them furtively up to the light and tried to see through them, always taking care, however, not to bring them too close to my eye.

Some time afterwards we watched a film in school about the River Po. Only much later did I come to know that the film is called *La Gente del Po,* by Antonioni. At the time it was just one of many black-and-white films about rivers; I also remember a film about the Rhône delta and the Rhine near Rotterdam. The films flickered upon the canvas, damaged due to the many mended sections, tearing often, and the sound was accompanied by a constant crackling noise. When we watched the film about the Po, I immediately identified with the child who lay sick in bed below deck, even though it was the mother, and not the father, who read to her. Even though her eyes are not bandaged, she lies ill in the belly of the boat and sees nothing of the river or the landscape outside. I identified so strongly with this child that for a long time, when I reflected on my days of blindness, the smell of the school gym where we watched the film would rise into my nose and the sound of the heavy, rubbery blackout curtains, drawn by older children, would shuffle in my ears.

Many years later, when I had no longer been a child for some time, my father suffered from a broken blood vessel in his eye. He had to lie calmly and was not allowed to strain his eyes. I read to him; he wished for Italian stories, despite the fact that my Italian was poor. He corrected my pronunciation and interrupted me occasionally, in order to elucidate things in a very long-winded manner. One of the books that I read was *Narratori delle pianure* and I remembered the old, beautiful secret-word from long ago, *altipiano*. While my father used another pronunciation mistake as an opportunity to interrupt, correct me and to provide a long-winded account of a carousel factory along the Po, near Mantua—apparently world-renowned—I imagined a stretch of river landscape in northern Italy, blanketed in undulating fog, hovering between heaven and earth directly beneath a low-hanging cloud cover. Sparse poplar groves anchored the landscape into the skies.

Positive

MY FATHER DIED during a heatwave in June, which had already begun in the last days of May. For two weeks on my daily walks through suburban streets, parks, and dirty sidewalks around Euston station, I cut a path through the sticky city air. Fans hummed at work, dogs prowled, panting behind their owners along the edge of the park, sleepless children whined late into the night, and in the small, boxy backyard gardens people sat, drinking too much—because of the heat, the whining children, the panting dogs, because of these mild nights, which had something unprecedented about them.

On the day that my father died, while crossing a bridge over the Thames my shoes became stuck in melted asphalt and it was quite a task to free them, since walking barefoot on the steamy, hazy tar street would have been impossible. Traffic came to a halt and the police walked down the road awkwardly, nervously; they too feared becoming stuck in asphalt and moreover, they were unsure what kind of gestures they should extend, fold or cross their arms and hands into, as there was no protocol for dealing with melting asphalt, upon which wheels can no longer spin.

The call came in the early evening. Sounding from the open windows of neighboring houses, clattering dishes and children's shouts mixed with the murmuring of news anchors and television theme songs. From the large garden of the villa at the next crossroad, which was slid between the small backyards of the surrounding townhouses, like a gusset, rose plumes of smoke which became caught in the shading branches of a cedar, and it smelled pungently of burnt fish. The airplanes landed at some distance that evening, on the other side of the Thames. I stood hesitantly in front of the ringing phone and watched the ungainly airplane bodies sink from the heat-gray sky into the blueish air above the housetops. The shrieking of the throttled engines remained far away.

Death notices are like scissors or sharp knives that sever the film of the world. What cuts cleaner, a knife or scissors? A futile question, which anyway arises only years after the event—for instance while attempting to splice severed film. Never can the ends be put back together so that things line up, they always overlap or become displaced; half of the child's face, poised to laugh, might be positioned below the other half, or adhered to a rose bush or a door post much too high for the small body, and the laugh is forever failing, a never-ending miss.

I found myself from one moment to the next sitting in the dark between two dangling celluloid strands, while the soundtrack played on, for reasons incomprehensible to me.

The next day I was in one of those ungainly airplane bodies, like the ones I had watched on the previous evening, landing in the hot gray air. It was even hot where I arrived, the air similarly gray and viscous, and the landscape lay motionless, disintegrating under its weight; on hillcrests and in the occasionally visible strips of riverbank clung fragments of memory which had torn away from a larger picture and settled there.

In the evening we sat in my father's room. Even years after he had given up cigarettes it still smelled of stale smoke. It
smelled of old smoke, of sour wine, of dust, of the desk chair's
threadbare seat, the blackness of vinyl records. It smelled of
maps, of a dark-green pen, and the tasteless onyx desk set. We
played the St. Matthew Passion and when it got dark we unpacked the slide projector.

We removed two pictures from the wall and positioned the
projector so that the beam of light landed on the bare spot. It
took a while to stack the books at the correct height on the
table in order to place the projector on top. My father had always used two volumes of the encyclopedia, but they were no
longer in his room. We switched the projector on and moved
the table with the tower of books farther away from the wall,
so that the image became smaller and sharper. It was still just
a white square. The projector hummed. We closed the curtains and my brother, already drunk at this point, dragged over
the slide trays that were standing behind the door. Halfway to
the projector the stack tumbled over and the contents of a few
of the slide trays scattered onto the ground. My brother knelt
down onto the carpet and began indiscriminately stuffing the
slides back into the slots. My father had always kept his slides in
a meticulous order, unintelligible to outsiders. This order was
now torn, irrecoverable. We didn't utter a word about the fact
that we would now never know *what* was out of order. This
sudden recognition of irrevocability, however, on account of
the circumstances—his drunkenness, his clumsiness, the projector's expectant humming—had something minor, pitifully
obvious about it. My brother shed silent, drunken tears onto
the mixed-up slides and knocked-over cases. Still wordless, we

politely tried to let each other operate the projector; in the end, the role fell to me.

We were using the old projector, which held only two slides. They had to be alternated by hand, and the picture that had just been shown had to be replaced while the new one was being projected. Surrounding the projector was a cloud of heat and in front of its lens dust particles danced like tiny creatures in the white beam of light.

The first pictures were scenes from a family trip to Italy. Judging by our age, it must have been shortly after the darkroom was removed, and was thus one of the first times my father had shot slide film. Perhaps his inexperience with the material was the reason for the overexposure, for our paleness in the pictures, for the washed-out and threadbare quality of the colors, forms, landscape, through which the bare wall and the clearly delineated rectangles where the photos had been were visible. Nevertheless, I was flooded with memories of our stay that had little to do with these pictures, of the white light, the sultriness, of walks between fields where corn stood high, of the smells in the guesthouse, of the saltless bread, of the evening walks through the village with my father when he still had purchases to make after dark in the small stores and I, at my request, was allowed to wait outside alone, among boxes of tomatoes and peaches, among conversations and laughing passersby, as if I belonged there, as if I were familiar with the street and the customs that prevailed there, as if I lived in that evening space, filled with new sounds, together with the people there, who carelessly brushed me by on the street corners, on the waysides.

It became unbearably stuffy and hot in the small room behind the drawn curtains, and after viewing half of the first tray

I ended the show. As I pushed the pile back into its corner, it occurred to me that this was a collection of my father's gaze. Through his eyes we looked at these scenes cast on the wall, and for a moment I believed that the thinness and paleness of the images might have resulted from the irrevocable absence of his gaze. Each slide projection humbly staged an instant, the blink of an eye. Perhaps that's why my father had given up the dark-room and developing photos. He was tired of being the sole witness to the picture's slow emergence in the sloshing chemical bath and wanted to stage his gaze on a grander scale. For a mo-ment, the decades-long grudge that I had harbored against him for giving it up disappeared.

The night had become black and dense. Above the low hills beyond the river heat-lightning flickered distantly, making the outlines of the hill-crests briefly visible before disappearing again into the darkness, which felt so clammy and palpable, as if you could shape it in your hands: the opposite of snow, hot, soft, and black. My brother walked up and down the garden, his footsteps silent on the lawn and only the glowing tip of his cigarette, floating back and forth, was visible.

Night

THROUGHOUT MY CHILDHOOD we often drove to Italy. We had neither family nor place there, but my father spoke Italian and there was a connection between his speaking, or his desire to speak, in a language unintelligible to me, and the trip that I accepted without question. The journey to the Italian border, or at least to the linguistic border that we would cross already in Switzerland, always felt to me like a deep breath, drawn and held and released at last when my father spoke. This release of tension and the disorder of air in my lungs and head that came with exhaling were forever connected with the names of the towns that we encountered first on the south side of the mountain pass which, as if under a spell, always lay in the sun. Airolo! said my father, in a voice already different than usual, and farther down the valley a reddish city would spread out in a bright spot of sun, while we were still stuck in snow.

Once we stayed overnight in Chiavenna. We found a guest house, managed by a woman with a severe expression. Every piece of furniture and every step creaked. We were given a family room, which smelled of mothballs. The beds stood somber and massive in the large room, as if randomly placed and left there standing. My parents had an argument and my father went out. I lay under the stiff sheets, pretending to sleep. My mother sat at the window, waiting for my father. The dull-yellow light from the streetlamps filtered through the trees along the avenue. The guest house must have been located at a crossing or at the approach of a curve on the through-road; the droning and squealing of cars and trucks braking could be heard again and again, bringing a breeze which caused the shadows of the leaves to tremble restlessly in the dull-yellow puddles of light on the floor. The lamp was switched off and my mother sat quietly in the dark in a chair, black like the beds, while I listened into the night. Not a word was uttered. I must have silently wondered where my father might have gone and if he was even coming back. Perhaps he sat in a bar, drinking and talking, self-consciously eager to cover up his not belonging. Or he strolled through the lanes, looked into the illuminated apartments of strangers, ascended a mountain path; maybe he would never return. Or he had climbed back into the car and kept driving, toward Milan, Padua, Bologna—the entire country was stretched out before him. What would become of us here in Chiavenna? My mother didn't speak Italian. How would she feed us? I lay stiff in the saggy bed and tried to recollect the overheard fragments of Italian that were set aside somewhere in my mind, but they seemed wrong for the situation. They were flatland words, not suited for that mountain village, whose barren hinterlands I had seen on the journey in; unsuited for a light defined by shadow, unlike the white light of the lowlands, which casts everything in the same shadowless smallness. Would I have to climb the stairs and steep lanes up to a tiny village schoolhouse, dressed in an apron or smock, like the ones I had seen the local children wearing? Was I afraid? What remains in my memory is only a feeling of inner excitement, brought on by the thought of my father's potential disappearance and the ensuing upheaval of our lives, stranded in an entirely foreign place called Chiavenna. A word I quietly muttered under my breath, half in expectation of a future in which, when asked where I lived, I would answer, *Chiavenna. Yes, kia-vein-na, not chee-a-venna.* Admittedly, a beautiful name.

It wasn't the first time that my father had simply walked out after an argument and stayed away for hours. My mother, standing in front of the open window of the children's room, staring out into the night, was a familiar sight. I lay in the far end of the room in bed, looking up at the black sky which seemed to recline around her head. My eyes adjusted quickly to the darkness, its blackness fading the longer I stared, gradually revealing itself as a gauzy layer atop a distant, diffuse, and inexplicable shimmer. The impermeability of night was an invention. A fairy tale, meant to inspire fear. My father always came back, usually in the early hours of the morning, peacefully drunk, speciously invoking unexpected encounters with relatives who happened to be passing through, strangers' emergencies, old acquaintances; the train station always played a role—delays, changeovers, missed departures. Later I would often imagine my father in the musty 24-hour cinema at the train station, where he would occasionally drop us children when he had something to do. The cinema was frequented predominantly by men, some unwashed, some swathed in a cloud of aftershave, clutching small suitcases on their laps, some sipping silently from beer bottles and smoking, while others would cry at the passé, kitschy films that ran between the newsreels and often tore, their tears provoking in us children a nervous giggling above all.

My father's return to the bleak guest house in Chiavenna escapes my memory. Either I was asleep, or I let the hissing dispute that undoubtedly followed his return sink into oblivion. On the following morning it rained thinly. It was now quiet in the street and drops of rain fell audibly onto the leaves of the trees. In the breakfast room, which was equipped with the same blackish furniture, we, the only guests, surrounded by quite a number of tables covered in white linens, were served coffee with milk and bread. The drizzle persisted past Milan. Then it yielded to the even, vibrating white light of the plain, in which the abandoned and partly dilapidated farms seemed to hover.

Katzelmacher

MY FATHER LEFT HIS ROOM and desk in the disarray that we had come to associate with him. Deep in the heavy desk drawers, which we were never allowed to open, he still had provisions stashed away: an anxious habit that he never was able to cast off. As a child, on my first forbidden rummage I came across tinned fish and packets of pumpernickel bread; they frightened me like an ugly secret, which weighed all the heavier because to mention it would have meant revealing my transgression.

In his provisions drawer I found an old photograph showing my sister and me with our grandmother. It was likely one of the last photos that my father had developed and printed himself in his darkroom. Before he transitioned to slides and dismantled the small darkroom, which then became a storeroom for disused things, he made pictures like this one, with matte surfaces, and when I reflected on what they felt like to me as a child, things seemed farther away in these photographs than in the glossy ones. These pictures always had flaws, smudges and blurs, but they were printed on beautiful, rigid paper, which felt more pleasant to the touch than glossy photos.

The picture of my sister, our grandmother and me was taken not long after the death of our grandfather, who, one rainy

evening in November, while walking home from buying cigarettes at the kiosk only a few meters from his house, was hit by a
truck. In the photo it is spring, and we pose on a garden bench
before a blooming bush, its blossoms all puffed cotton, and my
sister has my other grandmother's handbag draped across her
arm like an elegant elderly lady. After the death of her husband,
my grandmother first collapsed inwardly, then cut off her long
hair, which she had previously worn twisted into a bun at the
nape of her neck, and adopted a waved hairstyle, thereby becoming a different person for us. Next to photos of her cats, all
of whom had been run over on the busy road beside her house,
was now a photograph of our grandfather in dark, severe clothing. But above all, she—who had countered each of our trips
by alluding to her insurmountable homesickness, brought on
by even the shortest absence—took to traveling. This photograph was taken shortly before she embarked on her first grand
tour; she might have even paid us this visit to say goodbye before her departure and a few days later, equipped with a large
brown suitcase with a checked lining, caught a train to Genoa
and from there boarded a ship to Haifa. While looking at this
picture I thought I recalled her singing to us on that afternoon, shortly after we posed for the photo. A song from her
childhood, which we always begged for when we were young.
She called it the *Katzelmacher*-song, and had heard it from the
Italian knife grinders and cutlery makers, who sung it while
rolling their stands past the houses. The lyrics were a marred
Italian, sung from memory, strung-together syllables that made
no sense, but my grandmother enjoyed singing it with her eyes
half-closed, which gave her an enraptured air which embarrassed me. On the photo one can already detect her contorted

lower lip, a distortion that would advance in the following de-cades, eventually making it impossible for her to sing, which saddened her.

When we brought my grandmother news of our father's death, she was standing at the window, as if she had been keep-ing watch for us. I already know he's dead, she said when we walked in. I dreamed I was ice skating, I was a young girl and I sang, but then below the ice I saw his face.

Eel

IN ONE OF THE LAST PHOTOGRAPHS taken of my father, he is on a boat. It is an old-fashioned wooden boat. We see fishing tackle and standing to the right and left of my father are two men: friends, acquaintances, fishermen—I don't know them. My father holds an eel in his hand, which is still squirming; the animal is out of focus because it is moving, but we can identify its snaky form. My father stands slightly hunched over, his legs apart, his hands and arms outstretched, a smile on his face.

I never found out where this photograph was taken or who the two men were. The day is overcast and the light is gray. The water banks have small reedy coves and one side rises gently to a meadow. An orchard, perhaps—I can make out trees in the distance. For a long time I wanted to believe that the photo was taken in Italy, but at some point, I had to admit that the light was too northern.

My father would not have spoken Italian with these men. I wished he could have in situations like this. He was not a fisherman. Sometimes he paddled us children up and down a dead tributary of the Rhine, and he was a good swimmer. On trips to the seaside he would always swim so far out that we could no longer see him, alarming us on more than one occasion, because we thought he'd never come back.

Most of our rowing trips on the dead tributary's still waters took place in a light similar to that in the photograph of my father with the eel. My father would paddle us up onto the island's sandy tip, where the actual river began; this location was marked by an eel-catcher's boat, a painted black boat with long rods at its downriver-end, from which hung nets. My father never paddled up to the height of these nets; at times he said that the river was too dangerous for him, while other times he said eels were scavengers, that he wanted nothing to do with them. After these excursions on the dead tributary, on the way home we passed by an eel smokehouse, run by the boat's owner and his sons. Sometimes the storefront door was open, and a neon lamp blazed inside; in its bluish light we saw the long, snaky bodies, a glossy brown from having been smoked, hanging on a rod. Below the hanging eel bodies was a heavy stone table; on top of it, knives. The thought of consuming an eel that had first filled its fish-insides with carrion left me cold with revulsion. The eel smokers stood expectantly at the door, waiting for customers. My father urged us to hurry past.

Eventually the eel smokehouse closed and eeling was prohibited, because the Rhine water was too toxic. The eel catcher's black boat remained there and the owner kept it in good condition; its sides were always painted a glossy black, and the cabin on top was green with red window frames. By contrast, shortly after its closure the low smokehouse building was already ringed by willow bushes and stinging nettles, and in their protection it decayed. Rust-colored veins dripped from the corrugated iron roof down the walls.

Even if I had learned from my father about the underwater wanderings that eels make between the Sargasso Sea and the rivers of Europe, I nevertheless knew that his aversion to snakes also extended to eels. That's why the photograph frightened me for a moment, so many years after our rowing excursions. Again and again my father tried to get a grip on his aversion to snakes, as he referred to it, and he liked to make others witness to his efforts. On his excursion with these two strangers, who might well have been his friends, his getting-a-grip seems to have been successful, even if it was not a snake but an eel, made ghoulish by its gluttony for carrion, and I didn't want to imagine how he felt, holding in his hands this fish which was so vile to him, and yet so frightened itself, a foreboding of death in a black, foreign skin.

During the hot Italian summer, hardly a day passed without him returning from one of his very long and lonesome walks in the vineyards or sparse copses, reporting an encounter with a snake. Blue, green, and earth-brown snakes, zigzag-patterned and iridescent ones, shot across his path, swished, twitched, disappeared into burrows or, eerily quiet and matching the color of the bark, disappeared up the trunks of trees.

We spent one summer in a rundown house near Florence. Small black scorpions dwelled in the cracks of the walls, moving across the tiles at night with a barely audible, dry shuffling. In the morning we would find them in our sandals and in the coffee bowl on the kitchen window ledge. My father paid them no attention, yet asked the elderly caretaker-couple about snakes. *Ci sono serpenti?* was a question I learned early on, which I quickly also knew to be superfluous, since the answer in Italian was always the same.

The caretakers, who invariably appeared as a couple and who performed every task together, naturally affirmed it as

well. Absolutely, snakes live here. They said 'live', while drawing my father a glass of their sour wine, which was sealed air-
tight by a layer of oil that always left behind small beads on
the walls of his wine glass. In the evenings they shuffled across
the terrace and added water to the saucers below the geranium
pots. The woman watered with a small watering can while the
man hauled a large, dented lead can, filling up the woman's
small one again and again. Because of the resident snakes, outside we had to play in closed footwear and, if possible, always
carry a stick for knocking vigorously on the ground when we,
for instance, searched for a shuttlecock in the shadows of trees.
Below the terrace was a trail leading to a small pond where the
midday heat gathered above in such clumps that it felt as if you
could reach out and pick handfuls of it. On this path my father
discovered in the cavity of a wall, in the small half-shade cave
where a stone had broken away, a quiescent snake. He claimed
it was blue and lay very still, but would make eye contact. Every
day he went back to the same place and encouraged us to join
him, but no one did. The blue of the snake sounded appeasing
and almost promising, and perhaps it was these visits to the blue,
squinting, unaffected snake in the cracked wall near Florence
that brought my father to try and get over his aversion and pho-
bia, until on a gray summer day in a northern country, probably
not far from his birthplace in Rhineland, he finally held this eel
in his hands, flanked by two men, whose friendship he might
have sought only to this end.

Migration

ON A TRIP WE STOPPED at a river. The Alps lay just behind us, still casting shadows onto the vast, barren expanses, covered in scree, as if it had fled the mountains, highlighting the scattered riverbed, interrupted here and there by earthy islands amid the gravel, where scrub grew alongside thickets and small trees, forming low ridges, round against all the angular stone—miniature forests, green-gray in the dusty summer light. The landscape widened here and light-reddish church steeples, which due to their narrowness appeared especially tall, protruded from the scattered villages on the plain. The scree field was interspersed with green streams which expanded as if to form small lakes before tapering back into rivulets. The broad scree strips skewed something in the landscape; they lay like a scar at the foot of the hill, making visible what was missing: the water. This landscape of river and stone with small groves in between nevertheless had something enchanted about it, something detached from the valleys and villages. Here and there bicycles lay on the gravel, and children swam and played in the blue-green streams, jumping from the banks, submerging even though the water appeared so shallow. They couldn't care less about the approaching clouds, beneath which I froze, perhaps more because of the sudden sharpness of light and shadows than the temperature itself. Even the distant thunder that sent us running didn't startle the children at the river.

On the way south, toward the sea, a heavy thunderstorm broke out which must have caused the river to rise in its gravel bed. Once the rain had let up and the sun hit the steamy street, there was nothing left to be seen of the Alps behind us. We spent the night in a small town near the sea. The road into town was lined by grassy walls with wooden steps leading upwards. On top of the walls were small sheds and stalls, from which fishing rods projected obliquely into the sky.

Later that evening we went for a walk. Small canals ran through the town and in the light of the street lamps, the fronts of houses reflected in the still water. Men thronged in a sports bar, where pool tables stood in the middle of the room and thick swaths of smoke hung in the air; noise came from the bar in waves, a tangle of voices woven with a thin thread of radio-sounds. My father liked to stand in front of bars like this one. Perhaps he would have rather gone in than walk with us, and would have stood between strangers, drinking, smoking, gesticulating—although I could picture my father gesticulating only with difficulty. The small *alimentari* was open and old women shuffled across the sidewalks and carried milk and lemons into their houses. I always hoped for a short trip to the grocery store, for an opportunity to dip into that small world, filled with the strange aroma of bread, oranges, and herbs—at every shop the same—and humming fans and a murmur of radio voices, coming from backrooms or courtyards. It was summer vacation—perhaps that's why the vault-like fish shops were still open—and in the evenings there were naturally no fresh catches. The stone tables where fish were gutted, cut and weighed in the morning had been scrubbed clean while the tiled floor, where bloody fish entrails piled up during the morning hours of operation, now gleamed wet and free from any trace of butchering, but the fishmongers stood ready to sell prepared and preserved eel. They wore clean aprons and galoshes, their hands stuck in their apron pockets or resting, folded on their stomachs, some smoking and talking with customers. Behind them were eels on view, swimming in large glass pools; the refrigerated counters housed smoked eels and eel pieces; on the shop's walls hung large panels with pictures of eels and framed photographs of fishermen, who, either alone or in a group, proudly presented their catch. The eels were a major attraction for vacationers, who in the evenings strolled along the canals and curiously viewed the pools full of tired and anxious entangled bodies, which awoke an indescribable revulsion in me. I was relieved that my father didn't stop at any fish shops or snare any fishmongers in conversation.

Later that evening, we children lay in bed in the hotel room with the windows open. Voices and shreds of music sounded from the small piazza, and the air was heavy and somewhat sticky, despite the short thunderstorm. We couldn't sleep because of the noise and my father, who sat outside on the small balcony and smoked, talked to us from this blue-damp twilight. He was no natural history expert but on this evening, probably because we had asked him about the town's eels, he told us about their mysterious wanderings, all of them born tiny, glassy fishes in the faraway Sargasso Sea. In large schools these whiteish translucent fish-children move through the Atlantic Ocean until they reach Europe, where in swarms they select rivers to swim up. Once they have made it from saltwater to fresh, they turn brown and long and fat and snakelike from their diet, carrion for instance. They live hidden in sludge, always in groups. There at the bottoms of rivers and lakes, every year they become darker and larger. At some point, following a secret signal not recognized by any human or other living being, they assemble back into schools and begin their journey home. They first have to find the ocean. They follow the rivers, but in order to take shortcuts they are able to cover stretches over land, even uphill. Snapping his fingers and quietly clapping his hands, my father attempted to explain the sound of a large school of eels crossing a field by night, driven by an insurmountable urge to return to their birthplace. It was a strange story, and I wasn't sure if I should believe it. My father told it indifferently, aside from the noises at the end, which he made with abandon. He also paused here and there, to pour himself more wine or light a cigarette. Many eels, he finally explained, converged on their way home in the area where we were now, in order to slip back into the ocean, where they would once again change their appearance, becoming lighter and thinner, because on their journey through the saltwater they wouldn't eat until arriving back at the Sargasso Sea, where they came from. But the fishermen there knew enough about the migrations of eels to lie in wait with nets, and would catch many of them.

Half-doubting if it could all be true, I lay awake a while longer. I wondered if the eels passed through the furrowed riverbed where we had stopped. The voices outside became sparser, and eventually it was quiet. Without losing my aversion toward them, I sympathized with these sad, entangled eels in the show-pools, which saw themselves robbed of any prospect of returning home.

I was long pursued by the idea of accidentally ending up one evening in a meadow where thousands of eels, writhing in unbelievable exertion, would slap forward through the darkness toward their fabled home.

Mosaic

ROME WAS A WORD filled with expectations, which, in the place itself, soon had a different ring. Despite the promise of this short, marble-like name, how it rolled in the palm of my flat, child's hand, Rome was not a city that could be opened and read. The first time we traveled there we stayed in a guesthouse on a narrow lane, with attic rooms. Pigeons cooed, crows flew over the houses and past the rooftops I saw cupolas, towers and countless antennas. The pigeons and crows were at odds; from up close I watched a pigeon fight a crow for a bit of prey, and the pigeon's eyes frightened me, so round and smooth with determination—I had never seen bird eyes at such close proximity and this sight suddenly exposed doves as symbols of peace as a lie.

During the day the narrow streets in the city center were filled with traffic and we had to press ourselves against the raw, porous house walls to escape the honking cars as my father led us from one place to the next where there were sights worth seeing. In the quieter districts, where Vespas, mopeds, and three-wheeled delivery vehicles were on the roads, a pleasant cloud of noise hung above our heads—voices, clattering dishes, family sounds—and below it I felt in good hands, as if under a shelter, which could be abruptly withdrawn, however, if the street hit a broad intersection with traffic that followed baffling rules on all sides. We became lost several times on the clever shortcuts that my father took, hoping to lead us to something significant, and on one such route we ended up farther and farther from the city center, stumbling through streets with half-finished yet already-inhabited blocks, where laundry hung from lines stretched in front of the windows, camping chairs stood on tiny balconies without balustrades, and here and there someone sat on a railingless balcony, reading the news; everything was under construction and a narrow strip of scrapyard extended in the distance, where there were shanty-like workshops, while hobbling dogs and scruffy cats brushed about our feet until we reached a wide street in dusty light, lined by long buildings on either side, where groups of men in caps waited to enter the lopsided, dusty buses. Exhausted from the long walk and unsettled by my father's disorientation, much to the bewilderment of the workers we squeezed into the buses that took them home and stood, unwelcome, among the tired and taciturn men. The workers clung to their briefcases, perhaps full of crumpled paper with grease spots from consumed cheese and salami, worn wallets, breadcrumbs, keys. The few women on the bus stood bunched together, forming a small fortress against the men with their less-battered bags. My father stared out the bus window, visibly relieved when we reached areas that he recognized. We exited at a bridge. Far below, bordered by high stone walls, coursed the Tiber. It was interspersed with sand banks that had collected garbage and on its narrow shore people sat alone in the dusty grass, everyone seeming to watch a man in rolled-up pants who stood on a sand bank trying to fish something out of the river with a pole.

When I later thought back to our days in Rome, I saw myself and my family walking the streets as dwarves; to this day I would believe that even my father, despite being able to speak the language, was hardly tall enough to see over one of the restaurant tables lining the busier streets. Who fit in here, in this city with its thrust-aside river, its churches and antiquities, which crowded every path? Emerging in the humid twilight was at times something that remained hidden in the brightness of day: something about the somber fronts of houses resisted the befogging maelstrom of the monuments and the slick men who stood in front of bars in service of this maelstrom, and the vying calls of souvenir sellers at their countless stands. One or two floors above street level a life began that was turned away from the magnificent, which made everything on the street conceived in this maelstrom seem small and puny. This monument-averse life even hung in the lanes around the guesthouse, ready to seep into every pore not already clogged by the magnificent. In the bars men stood huddled together, some of whom we had perhaps ridden the bus with; the television was on, ceiling fans cast oval shadows and drove swaths of smoke into the corners. Children wandered about, sent to the *alimentari* in pairs or threes, swinging their half-full shopping nets on the way home. Girls thronged against the lattice parapets of tiny balconies to talk with adolescents in the street below, at least one of whom would have a Vespa, its motor left quietly humming. In the evening my father would stand at the window for a long time, looking down at this distant lane-life. At times he would go out as well, but only briefly. Maybe he lacked the courage in Rome for one of his all-night absences, or was aware of how small he had become, looking at the sights worth seeing.

On our last day we went to a church. We stood beneath an enormous mosaic and were allowed to use the opera glasses that my mother always brought with her on trips, while my father carried on a long conversation with a bald man who stood expectantly behind piles of books on a table. When they were through, the man held out his hollow hand, supported by his other hand as if it were a cup, and my father put money inside.

The mosaic spread out like a sky in gold and blue and green, full of birds in golden fields among floral ornaments. In one spot I caught sight of a pair of red birds, surrounded by white flowers, feeding its young in its nest. Whenever it was my turn to look through the opera glasses I would search for this pair of birds, and each time I found it only with difficulty, but would discover instead four-legged mythical creatures, angels, and, ultimately, at the bottom edge, a black cage placed over a blue bird. The bird clawed at the black grid with its orange feet and looked straight ahead while other animals lined up as if in a procession. It weighed heavy in this domed sky of delight, and I couldn't fathom how the pair of birds related to this caged bird. Through the opera glasses I could make out the countless, unevenly shaped stones of the mosaic, and the way this brokenness disappeared when I looked back with a naked eye was yet another riddle. Despite the riddle and the sadness of the cage, on that last day the mosaic dome spread a canopy of comfort above me, protecting me as I passed by the attractions, surrounded by people, and entered the quiet district, where it acted as a charm against the sensation of my own oddness.

When we left, the streets were wet from a thundershower, and the dark cloud mass had not fully moved on yet. We sat in the morning traffic among crooked buses, the dust washed away by the rain, and people on their way to work stared down from the bus windows into our car, causing me to look away.

Hours later, once we were already past Bologna, our car broke down and had to be brought to a repair shop. The mechanic got out chairs for us to sit on in his concrete courtyard while he fixed the car. We sat in the whitish summer air of northern Italy, so different from the air in Rome, and listened to the highway roaring in the distance and ate our travel provisions, while my father explained the great art of laying mosaics, which involves positioning thousands upon thousands of small, roughly rectangular pieces—semiprecious stones, colorful glass and white glass, and clay mixed with gold-leaf—at just the right angle, so that in the finished picture everything can be seen equally well and appears, even in the curvature of a cupola, as if spread out on a plane. Just like here, said my father, pointing with a sweeping gesture to the flat, shadowless landscape, with a poplar grove and a dilapidated farmstead lying like an island amid stubble-covered fields.

Swimming

WE SPENT TIME AT THE SEASIDE, some days vacillating indecisively between the open, free beaches and the private ones, which, subdivided into named zones, were enclosed by blue and green, colorful beach cottages. Lounge chairs stood in rows and a tanned muscleman, when presented with a receipt, would distribute them and assign visitors to a beach cabana.

The free beach lay outside of town, at the end of an avenue lined by stone pines. A path led up a narrow dune crest, no higher than an embankment. From there one looked onto the cornfields up country, pierced by rows of poplars, small farms and cars, glittering in the blazing sunlight on the coastal roads beyond. In the other direction one looked to the beach: to the stripes of garbage the surf would wash up, take away, throw back onto land. To the bathers, families with colorful sun umbrellas, large beach towels, dogs. That was the beach for people who lived at the seaside resort year-round, for the families of waiters, gelato shop employees, gas station attendants and car mechanics, of the small-shop owners and the intrepid drivers of the gray, three-wheeled delivery vehicles that overran the streets, transporting everything from fruit and vegetables to gas cylinders and balls of dirty laundry from the guesthouses. The mothers, children, feckless teenage brothers of all the businessmen, craftsmen, and employees also had to get this hot summer over with. Here the coconut and melon slice vendors, black from the sun, must have dozed away their rare breaks as well, without being afforded any shade. My father probably leaned toward the open beach—he had his notions about what constituted the real Italy—but we finally ended up in one of the monitored sections, furnished with bathing huts and lounge chairs and emblazoned with a name. My father paid the rental fee at a kiosk and the beach attendant presented us with lounge chairs and the key to a pale-blue beach hut, whose smell of mildew and salt and wood and urine left an indelible impression on me.

My father was bored at the beach. He read the newspaper, doled out the small fragments of language that we asked him for in order to communicate with other children and, once or twice a day, went for a very long swim. My father was a strong swimmer. In his youth he swam in the Rhine, from one bank to the other, where the river was wide and the current treacherous. After half an hour my mother would become nervous, and we would stand beside her at the edge of the water, shading our eyes with our hands, my nearsighted mother looking through her opera glasses out to the sea, which, in the afternoons above all, glittered insufferably, stinging the eyes. Of course we never could see my father. Near the beach there were always too many people in the surf, and farther out the tiny dots of brave swimmers were too small to recognize as individuals. But eventually we would catch sight of him, near the shore, exhausted, offering a faint, apologetic smile as he came out of the water. After these excursions he would sit motionless in his lounge chair and stare absently ahead, even mutely putting us off when we needed words.

One day a strange atmosphere prevailed. The sea was like glass, and the sky was overcast, hanging heavy in the warm, leaden air. Only a handful of people sat on the beach, and for the first time I saw washed-up jellyfish, their small, translucent bodies, round with rippled, crown-like edges and a reddish, pastel-colored stripe running through them. The sea lay too still to send any salutary waves to draw them back into the surf. Hardly anyone bathed. Swashing idly against the shore, the water was covered in a film, which no one wanted to wade through in order to reach the clearer blue-gray farther out.

But my father soon decided to go in. At the water's edge he appeared to hesitate—surely, he too was disgusted by the film. A moment later, however, he was submerged and had almost pierced the cloudy stripe. Then he was but a single small dot in the still water, navigating steadily out.

My mother looked anxiously to the sea again and again; today she had forgotten her opera glasses. But we children couldn't find him, either. The surface of the water lay like a cloth, unbroken by any swimmer. No one had noted the time when he went into the water, and my mother was panic-stricken, which had a paralyzing effect on us, and we stood stock-still next to her, helpless as ever in our lives at the sight of the sea, the heavy sky, the emptiness, the absence of a tiny point that we could have set our hopes on.

A few other bathers came over, speaking insistently to my mother, but she didn't understand Italian and ran back and forth, blurting shreds of sentences in French, beside herself with anxiety. Someone fetched the beach attendant, who scanned the water's surface through his binoculars, and we could tell from his face that he had discovered no one. Two women accompanied my mother to our lounge chairs and we children stood around cluelessly, while the beach attendant explained something to the Italians and walked away, and a small crowd formed around us, with a number of women bent down to us, saying nice things, but it was all misguided, and then my father emerged. He came through a narrow passage in the row of cabanas that formed the border to the neighboring beach. He looked blue and pale at once, like the sky and the sea on that day. He plopped down into the lounge chair, wrapped himself in a towel, and I saw how his legs trembled. We said nothing at all and I was overcome by a strange despondency, but the Italians clapped their hands in relief and patted my mother on the head while she cried quietly and a woman brought us gelato, probably because she already saw us as half-orphans—a hasty token of sympathy, which now couldn't be undone. Soon the Italians settled back into their places with a certain sense of tact and someone notified the beach warden, waving, and we remained, a foreign islet of panic beneath leaden air. It thundered lightly, but it was more a growling of the sky, too heavy and hazy-gray to put forth thunderclouds. We left for the hotel. On the next day we traveled inland, even though for a few more days the hotel was already paid for. The round-faced innkeeper gave us each a luntsch-pecket, as he called it, and released us into the hinterland. It had stormed throughout the night and the day broke clear with everything enveloped in a silent, early morning blue, but now something different was in the air. Perhaps it was already autumn.

Lapis Lazuli

MY FATHER DESCRIBED HIMSELF as an expert on the color blue. He would look to the sky and have a different name for every shade: the gray-tinged Trieste autumn blue, for instance, whitish Mantua blue, a purple-toned Naples blue and—almost unthinkable in our region and found nowhere in Italy—the dizzying, *pure* Bregaglia blue. Every place had a different blue, every blue had a different name, and he even described painters as followers of this blue or that one. His desk was always covered with unfurled maps, showing large surfaces of variously dense blues with lines and writing running through them, scarce compared to those found in the gray, brown, green and white surfaces, and for a long time I thought they were the most important part of any map.

When I turned seven my traveling grandmother gave me a necklace with a small blue stone pendant. My sister had received the same necklace for her seventh birthday, but her pendant was rose quartz, and from then on, I had envied her somewhat watery, rosy stone, which looked as if it were translucent, and I imagined that when held up to the sun it would cast a pink light. My stone was now blue. A very intense blue with tiny sprinklings of bright yellow, but matte and sturdy and with none of the rose-quartz pendant's light milkiness. Blue was my favorite color but all the same I was disappointed; I would have preferred rose quartz. By now I was accustomed to it being the object of my envy and expectations—I had never pictured any stone but this one when I thought of the necklace that lay ahead of me. Now I had this blue stone called lapis lazuli, and even if I had to admit that the name was more beautiful and suffused with mystery than rose quartz, I had trouble warming toward it and at some point, when I was supposed to wear it for some occasion, I imagined it lay on my chest like lead, preventing me from breathing. This hostility toward the lapis lazuli stone continued until one day my father, standing before of a painting of the Madonna at a museum in Italy, explained that the blue of her cloak, which was so angelically beautiful that the painter himself was eventually declared an angel, was made from lapis lazuli. He pointed to the garment's tiny sprinkling of gold and claimed that it came from small embedded particles, just like those found in the stone on my necklace, because tiny delicate veins of real gold traversed this stone, which lay hidden, deep in the mountains of distant lands. We were on a trip and I didn't have the necklace with me, but after hearing this story I began to miss it. That evening my father told us about lapis lazuli. Where the stone was found, the various tones it might possess, and how variably precious it can be. The most precious lapis lazuli was unearthed deep in Persian mines, where elect, particularly small miners would find and loosen it carefully from the rocks. The miners must not be any larger than a child of approximately my size, but required all the sagacity and prudence of the wise to avoid being sent astray by the glowing false blues of stones that, as if to mislead and deflect their gaze from the true lapis lazuli, placed themselves bluely in its proximity, and would emerge in the daylight as crumbly fragments of an especially dull gray. He who brought such a false blue out of the mountain on more than three occasions was sent to the lead mine—a severe punishment. The king of Persia had no use for men like that, said my father, and then he described the lamps that the miners wore on their heads, and the tools they used for their work—a very fine hammer and chisel—as well as the baskets, wrought from a very fine gold wire, for bringing the stones out into the light of day. The extracted stones were sorted according to blue tones and thickness of gold veins and then pounded into a powder—a task completed with the utmost caution, for anyone who breathed in lapis lazuli powder would fall into a deep sleep from which he would not awake for months, and never again for the rest of his life would he be happy, as he would think only of the incredible blues that he had seen in his dreams during the long sleep. With this powder, painters produced the color of the Madonna's cloak. This most precious pigment came from very far away and for that reason was called ultramarine: from beyond the sea.

With these stories I became ever fonder of my lapis lazuli stone, which lay far away in its box at home, and on no occasion did my father neglect to draw my attention to the blues produced from lapis lazuli in museums. In Florence, on an oppressively hot day, we walked past an art supply shop, where pigments were displayed in the window, and the three different powders from lapis lazuli overwhelmed me, each in their own way, for their sheer blueness, and I pressed my face against the hot, dirty glass pane to see if I could make out any gold dust in the small dishes of powder.

I learned that the painter who became an angel for his blues was named Fra Angelico, and with time understood that my father would stay out for hours when my mother insisted that we rest in the guesthouse beds after hours of walking around in the sun. Among other things my father looked for paintings by Fra Angelico, immersing himself in the blues of the robes and the gold of finely decorated angels' wings. After becoming acquainted with the use of lapis lazuli, I came home with a fondness for the blue stone on my necklace, and could occupy myself for long periods of time, picturing how it had been extracted from a mine deep in Persia, examining the small sprinklings for their golden luster in the sunlight.

Sparrow Hawk

THE BIRDS IN ITALY SANG differently than the birds in our garden at home; they might have been different species, though I recognized blackbirds and tits and crows and a few others that I didn't know by name. We spent several days in a village on a mountain where, again and again, I heard a call without ever having seen a bird. The village hillsides fell steeply into the valleys, which in summer were a tired green. The birdcall echoed from the valley that our windows opened to—a bright, hacking sound, at times like unfriendly laughter, at other times like an accusatory, woeful call. I brought it to my father's attention several times to no response, but once he pricked his ears and said: sparrow hawk, and this name pleased me. At the same town, which could be seen sitting atop the hill from a long way away, I learned that the cliffs there were formed from tuff, another word that I would hold onto. The village sat atop the cliff like a jagged growth; the windows were holes and the towers its gangly, rigid offshoots. Nevertheless, it looked friendly, and on our journey there my curiosity for the town grew with each curve brought behind us. The stone emanated warmth and the lanes smelled of bread, metallic like geraniums, of thyme, and sweet like anise. We obtained two rooms in a guesthouse which looked down the cliff into the distance, to the forest, traversed by paths, and more hills and mountains in the background. We were given sinewy meat, fried in thin slices, and tomatoes for dinner, and took a walk through the village. In front of a church children were still playing outside in the dark, their voices echoing off the wall, and it became imprinted in my mind that the church, with its facade of forbidding smoothness, was called San Rocco. As was so often the case when I watched children playing in a foreign place, I imagined that I was one of them; I would keep my name, but speak a different language and live day in, day out in this mountain village made of tuff where there were no gardens, but lanes and squares where children played without adults watching over them, and in front of this San Rocco church I must have also wondered, as I always did, what I would have thought—as one of these children who belonged, with a command of this language and not my own—about the family that brushed by our playing field on this hot August night, with children who stared and said nothing. Upon seeing this family, how would I have felt about myself? With this thought, which I often abandoned myself to, I always came up against a boundary, where I sooner or later would turn back. The thought touched upon a division of myself into possibilities, and that overwhelmed me. But in passing something dawned on me—even if to this day I don't know what to call it—which appeared like a foray across a boundary of reality, tempting to the point of vertigo and eerie at the same time. Or a suspension of the boundaries of reality. The thought that I could be faced with myself as a mere part of some family from who-knows-where, that I could be evaluated and judged by myself, kept me awake at night. What would be *me*, in this encounter? Here I reached the point where I always foundered. To think any further, to hazard envisioning this sight, was not possible—perhaps because my intuition told me that such a division would have allowed me to see the profound solitude of our family, of every individual member in it, from the outside. That was something I wanted to avoid.

In this mountain village I often lay awake. Almost every night I saw heat-lightning around a tall mountain in the distance. In the valley it was quiet but for the sounds of animals, nocturnal birds, perhaps foxes too—sharp, flat noises that seemed to communicate fear.

My father was always searching for traces. Usually it was the Etruscans that he was tracking. Books about Etruscan cities piled up on his desk, and *necropoli* was an everyday word during our stays in Italy. In this town of warm tuff we wandered through the lanes, climbed up and down, through archways and narrow walkways between houses. Wine stores, vegetable shops and butchers were located in vaults below street level, where the merchants were friendly and told my father about things that we didn't understand, and in the end were probably disappointed that their pleasant conversations led to no purchases.

We walked out of town along the terrace-like strips, from which the forest proved sparser up close than it had appeared from above, until finally we found what my father had been searching for: narrow corridors in the cliffs, where the air inside was damp, cooler, but nevertheless heavy, with patches of moss creeping across the walls. The corridors were variously wide, some as narrow as crevices, and we were afraid, so my father went in alone, shouting back something intermittently, and then it became quiet, flies buzzed, we heard a sparrow hawk somewhere, and my father returned and we continued. We became lost on our way back to the village and, passing through a broken gate, ended up in a small cemetery. The cemetery was on a kind of rock terrace, from which we looked past the road and valley to the town. Viewed from here, it had something watchful about it, as if it had to steel itself against a threat, which might have risen up from the valleys or spread from the surrounding mountains. The cemetery resembled the village in a way, because it also crowned an albeit smaller cliff, and below the outer cemetery wall the hillside fell steeply to a path. Compared to the village, however, the cemetery lay bare, not safeguarded by a tower, exposed to every potential attack. Nothing but a row of high, dark cypresses rising up in the background—an unnecessary rear cover that did nothing to diminish the exposed nature of the terrain.

Until then I had known only cemeteries with graves of relatives, on which we bestowed commemorative kindness once a year. To stand surrounded by foreign graves, in a foreign place, was new to me. My father brushed aside the needles, leaves and coarse-grained sand that had gathered on the grave markers, and a writing in unfamiliar letters appeared below, which he deciphered for us. We followed him, somewhat embarrassed, from foreign grave to foreign grave, while he also needlessly read the Italian first and last names aloud, which stood on the individual graves in Latin characters. It was a small cemetery which seemed neglected, with several rows of graves, weeds and tree seedlings growing in between, and high cypresses in the background. The gravestones, tombs and grave markers were gray-white, some made from marble or travertine, others weathered and taken over by lichens, smooth and cool in contrast to the tuff. The cemetery lay like a small, stern hamlet of sorrow across from the reddish-yellow mountain town, locked in an invariable gaze.

As we left the village on tuff mountain, my father made a short detour to the graveyard to photograph the view. It was a very hot day, windless and white, the air full of chirring cicadas, and the town looked grayer than it had before, more sealed, perhaps because of the heat. We sat on a small wall that looked onto a meadow or pasture, framed by high trees, listening, always mindful of potential snakes, for a rustle in the dry scraps behind us. We were allowed to look through my mother's opera glasses while my father photographed. When it was my turn I saw a large bird at the edge of the trees which hovered silently in the air and then descended suddenly; I lost sight of it but soon thereafter it was back in my field of vision, swinging and flapping. With a small bird in its talons it slipped away, up to the tall trees. I lowered the glasses and could make out only an indistinct shadow in front of the treetop green. When I lifted them back up to my eyes, the bird was gone. I recounted what I had seen afterwards, once we were back in the car with the village and cemetery far behind us. That was a sparrow hawk, my father said, as if he had seen it himself. Maybe he caught a goldfinch.

maiale

Driving the unavoidable stretches on thoroughfares and highways, my father, as if infected by the general air of reckless-
ness, lost his sense of caution, put on his sunglasses, stepped
on the gas and smoked out the window. As it was for every
driver, his highway toll was a ticket for a kind of funfair drive of
potential collisions, performances of fearlessness and narrowly
avoided tragedies. The highways through the Apennine Mountains were the worst, with short and long tunnels and galleries
which looked down into abysses. On almost every drive we
passed by accident sites bearing witness to tragedies ultimately
unwilling to be missed. On a journey home through the Apennine Mountains we were overtaken by a large truck, a livestock
carrier full of pigs, peeking with the unflinching curiosity of
their kind between the bars of the trailer's small stalls. It was an
excruciatingly long passing maneuver, as seldom occurred, an
idle game of faster-than, which, on the narrow road with tunnel stretches and no shoulder was difficult to end. Behind both
the pig trailer and our car, other drivers honked their horns
with perceptible anger, because they saw this increasingly sluggish and roaring truck robbing them of their own driving fun.
When the livestock transporter was careening at a level with

us, I observed the pig trailer, which, as if dizzy from speed, occasionally swung out, coming very near to our car. The trailer was a kind of steel frame on wheels, lined with wooden slats. Through the horizontal interstices between the slats one saw the pigs, standing on two or even three levels—an apartment building of sorts came to mind. I had never been terribly fond of pigs, never would have touched one, was disgusted by the smell of their stalls, and after hearing stories about sows biting off human fingers and eating their own piglets, I must have been afraid of them as well. In these minutes alongside the pig transporter, I felt a benign curiosity for the animals for the first time. Greedy for the view, they crowded against the observation slits in order to see outside, to a world that must have been so totally strange and unfamiliar to them. I saw only fragments of the animals—the area around their eyes, their snouts, strips of their bodies, legs, twitching ears, the pinkish beige of their bristly skin, the greed of their snuffling snouts, the nimbleness of their eyes, the droll excitement of their ears—and something about the ravenousness of the pigs' curiosity suddenly pleased me, and I preferred to imagine that they were going on an outing, rather than to the slaughterhouse.

The race came to an end at last when my father exited the highway. For him every Italian rest stop was a place of promise, a temptation to succumb to. We children roamed around magnificent chocolate sculptures and gigantic toy figures, which I can hardly imagine anyone would purchase on a trip in passing, and watched our father, how he stood with coffee and a cigarette among other transients, easy, alone, on the road.

When we got back on the highway a traffic jam had formed. Endless, the line crept ahead, eventually into a tunnel. A short pipe. Inside the air vibrated, heavy from exhaust. The right wall soon turned into a half-open gallery, fetid smoke blowing in through the arched openings, fetid smoke blew in. Passengers got out of their cars and crowded against a railing so high that no one could see much of anything, aside from those who had helped themselves up onto the ledge; there was a babble of voices, eventually drowned out by the raspy clattering of a helicopter. My father got out to smoke, ambled over to the railing, spoke with spectators of the scene. We followed him with our eyes, curious and frozen in the terrible suspense that follows a foreboding of something gruesome; he stood on his tiptoes, steadying himself somehow on the masonry, and carefully bent over the railing. A moment later I saw his hand fly in front of his eyes, and he stepped back onto the street, doubled over and vomited. It couldn't have lasted more than a few seconds—it happened too quickly for us to react—but it remained in my mind as a scene of agonizing length, and with each remembrance it has blended with horror, compassion and aversion in different measures. My father walked back to the car, keeping his head down as if to avoid all eye contact, and silently flopped into the seat. Slowly we moved out of the tunnel, my father said nothing and tried to avoid looking to the right, where the road barrier was open. The pig transporter hung from a ledge below, brownish plumes of smoke rising from it. That evening we stopped somewhere, already in the Alps, at a small town on a river which we could hear murmuring in the distance. Later a light rain set in and dripped onto the summer leaves with a comforting, faint rustle and whisper.

Disco

ON OUR TRIPS we occasionally stopped along the way in northern Italy, where my father had an acquaintance whom he sometimes referred to as a friend. The friend was a doctor and a communist and his daughter was learning Russian. When I was ten she boasted about having a pen pal in the Soviet Union, and proudly showed us the letters written in Russian that she had received from the girl, riddled with thick lines from the censor. They lived in a large house with many rooms; everywhere except the kitchen and dining room smelled of mothballs. The doctor's wife was often indisposed and he usually entertained us in the company of his daughter, his young son, and their elegant grandmother, who always carried a hand fan. We would swim in Lago Maggiore, which I dreaded—I feared the algae, where I thought I had caught sight of eels on our first swimming trip to the lake. We ate at inns with playgrounds boasting equipment shaped like enormous Disney figures. Among this loudly colored equipment, which we were much too old for, we felt out of place. The doctor, whom my father now always referred to as the *dottore*, talked incessantly and always left a deserted landscape of crumbs and stains around his plate. Sometimes we drove long stretches with him to towns where rallies or festivals were taking place, barren suburbs of Milan, separated from the city by wasteland, in the vicinity of factories. On grassy areas between residential blocks, tables were set up where books, brochures and posters were laid out for sale, but there was always also something to eat and drink and they played music between the speeches, which echoed off the concrete walls in the residential blocks. That evening, before the dancing began, we had to leave and drive back with the *dottore* to his house and his suffering wife. In poor small cities there were festivals with music and dancing, which did not wait for nightfall to get started. Musicians played on wobbly stages with microphones and spotlights, and everyone danced and sang along freely, and when a thunderstorm hit the crowd would run to a bar with a dimly lit banquet hall where chairs were piled into a corner. A pool table stood in the center of the room, and the partygoers would start a game. The women at the rallies were energetic and loud, laughing a lot and walking arm-in-arm in self-contained rows behind the men, who carried signs. It was new and exciting, and a bit unsettling, too, because I understood very little, but the effervescent energy of the movement was contagious. All over Italy people were striking, and the word *sciopero* was on everyone's lips. In the evenings when we sat in the *dottore*'s dining room, eating a late dinner, the television would be on in the background, reporting of rallies and demonstrations much larger than the ones we had seen.

The garden encompassed a small wood—a *boschetto*—which also lent the house its name; even in this diminutive form, it was a big word. The *boschetto* comprised a group of thin-trunked trees, which, contending for light, had probably grown too quickly; a small path wound through the trunks, lined by stinging nettle, and on the floor of the small wood crept thorn bushes, feigning a thicket. With the doctor's daughter we wandered about the path and tried to communicate using the few Italian words we knew. One day we found a small dead bird, with yellow-black wings held tightly against its greenish body. At first sight it appeared unscathed, like a toy, and I picked it up. It had a small wound on its neck, around which clotted tufts of feathers and down had accumulated, and it lay cold and stiff in my hand. We mourned it without needing to communicate about it and, in the end, we buried it in a hole, dug with our heels and some twigs, and covered it with soil. The doctor's daughter insisted we wash our hands thoroughly. But having been the one to pick up and hold the bird, I felt leprous for hours, perhaps because the girl stretched out her arms in order to hold a book up to my face, which I was not allowed to touch. The open pages showed several small, colorful birds, among them the kind we had found and buried. *Lucarino*, she said. That was the bird's name in Italian. The next morning I searched for the spot where we had buried the *lucarino*. It lay bare, and ants had formed a broad trail between its now half-existent bird body and the underbrush. On the second morning I found only the bones, a frail carcass which one could no longer recognize as a bird since it looked more like some mysterious item made from very thin porcelain, whose maker might have thought had turned out badly, and thus wanted to dispose of or hide here. When, not long thereafter, I learned the word *lucus* in Latin class, I couldn't not think of the bird.

We paid our last visit to the *dottore* one spring. The small wood greened reluctantly, and it was cold and the mountains across the lake still wore large spots of snow. We took a trip to a larger neighboring town, where this friend of my father was presented with a medal at a formal celebration. I can't recall if it was for his services as a doctor or an activist. In any case, afterwards, as dusk fell, we went to a large restaurant for daytrippers, located not at the lake, but in a frayed no man's land at the edge of town. In front of the restaurant men stood bunched together, many holding onto their mopeds, some waving to greet the *dottore*. Inside, set tables stood in long rows, but there were not many guests. A glass wall partially separated the dining area from an additional room, which was totally empty and lit only by large aquariums. That was the *discoteca*, the doctor explained. While we ate, more and more men entered the adjoining room. A shutter was raised on the rear wall, behind which was a softly lit bar with a long counter, and music played, Italo pop, to which glittering lights spun on the low ceiling. It was a kind of parallel world to the restaurant, where a few families had now gathered; people were laughing and eating while waiters wandered about with wine and dishes, and in the room behind the glass wall a kind of dim circus unfolded. The men stood at the bar or against the glass wall, staring into the restaurant, drinking and smoking. A man came over to our table and asked the *dottore* something with almost deferential politeness. He nodded and the man stepped back and stood in a dark corner near the glass wall, where he remained until we had finished eating. My father then told us that we—my sister, the *dottore*'s daughter, and I—were now allowed to dance in the disco. I was eleven, twelve at the most, and the prospect of dancing in a disco made me both excited and embarrassed. On the *dottore*'s signal, a few men came over right away, led by the one who had waited in the shadows, and took us onto the dance floor behind the glass wall. The men might have been in their mid-twenties. They appeared old to me, and I felt strange. A short man laid his hands on my hips and slid me about to the slow and somewhat campy ballads; he had serious eyes beneath very bushy brows, and his forehead was furrowed, as if he were exerting himself or concentrating, and sometimes he tried to smile or said something which, even without the music, I wouldn't have understood. After this dance, he bought me a cola, without asking, and I saw that his hands were scratched, the grooves in the balls of his hands black. I politely thanked him, although I didn't like cola. Men communicated suggestively, with looks and brief finger gestures, probably to decide who they would be sliding around next. The second man was serious as well and not very tall either, and he also moved me back and forth stiffly, as if I were on trial, feeling my waist and hips in the process, and when the music came to an end I declined in advance, no cola. Other girls were led out of the dining room onto the dance floor and I wasn't sure if I should flee or stay—something about being slid around to the heavy music was enjoyable, as if I weren't entirely myself anymore, or as if who I was were wholly irrelevant. Then the music became faster and louder, and the slow dancing enthusiasts stepped into the background and loitered at the bar. Finally I ended up with a boy who was maybe sixteen, who had long hair and danced like they did to pop music at school parties, without touching.

The next day we left and drove farther south and the plain beyond Milan lay in its usual soft, quiet light, which mollified every contour. My parents fought about the course of the *Linea Gotica*, a name I would never forget, even if I didn't learn what it was until much later.

A year later we received news of the *dottore's* death. My father was shaken, and spent days writing a condolence letter to send the widow. That summer his daughter came to visit us. My sister and I were nervous before she arrived. We hadn't known anyone our age whose father was dead. But the girl got off the train and appeared unaffected. She now lived in Florence with her grandmother and had a floor-length dress in her suitcase; perhaps she expected to be taken to a ball. She now spoke only of Russia and her Russian pen pal. She had a pile of censor-blackened letters in her suitcase and talked about an upcoming trip—she dreamed of seeing the steppe. I want to visitate the steppa, she said in her somewhat crumbling English, the steppa has no end.

Tarquinia

Even outside of our trips to Italy, my father devoted a great deal of time to his passion for the Etruscans. He spent hours poring over maps, marked archaeological sites, connected the archaeological sites with thin lines, transferred these networks of lines onto tracing paper and pondered the resultant patterns. At the connecting points he scribbled names, dates, made margin notes, compiled new drawings, larger ones, smaller ones, unmarked ones—a whirl of routes that was blind to impassibility, a labyrinth without beginning or end, a network of routes in blank space. He hardly ever spoke of it, but when we were in Italy, the Etruscans were always nearby. From inaccessible terrain shrouded in hearsay at the edge of the Apennines down to the sulfur-steaming mountain valleys and coastal hinterlands, traces of the Etruscans were everywhere: graves, *necropolis*es, collections of grave goods. *Necropoli* was a word that caught your eye on countless signs. At some point, in my mind it inevitably coalesced with the secret word necrosis, the incomprehensible name for what ended my other grandfather's life. Those who searched for the Etruscans couldn't avoid death, which, embedded in landscapes and vistas, nevertheless appeared almost benign, embraced, sought after, understood. The Etruscans left behind no poems, no writings or notes, just a couple of words, a few names. Only their cities of the dead remained, which once stood face-to-face with their cities of the living. Cities of the dead with pictures, reliefs, chambers and objects, which, people said, mirrored those used by the living.

On a bright day with sharp shadows we visited Tarquinia. It was cold, perhaps it was February, and a bitter wind swept across the plateau of graves, where I looked across the sparsely populated coastal strip onto the gleaming, dazzling sea on the one side, and onto the massive white rock scarring the hills on the other side. The wind ripped through the sparse gray-silver olive trees, which stood scattered and low on the winter-sallow terrain, buffeted the leafless tree crowns with balls of mistletoe and the parasol pines at the street's edge. It howled around the corners of the huts through which one entered the graves, and drove clouds of dust across the burial site.

The gravesites themselves made me feel uneasy. Not because of the dead, but because of their hollow subterranean nature and the related imponderability of what one might find alive there. When we visited Tarquinia it must have been much too cold for snakes; the wind was so icy that the small city's residents had all withdrawn behind closed doors, and any grass snake that risked coming out into the open would have been frozen into a small stick and carried away by the wind. Nevertheless, my father brought along a torn-down, winter-wizened tree branch which had lain in the way at the entrance to the site, in order to pound at the ground in warning as he climbed ahead of us. Already on the first step, the branch burst into countless pieces; my father tried to continue with the small stubs, but then gave up and merely tramped ahead with heavy steps, having drawn his flashlight, which he had brought along to illuminate the tombs.

In the chambers a kind of roaring silence prevailed, so that the wind outside was no longer audible. There, in these parlors of the dead, other rules applied; light, weather, wind and outside sounds didn't count here. Perhaps the dead had their own light, for contemplating the paintings on the walls, and this light would fade once the living entered. Our voices sounded different, flat and echoless, as our words bumped bluntly against the walls with their painted figures and patterns, falling dryly to the ground as if the chambers had rendered them unsaid. The dead had their beds and their niches, and here and there carved into the walls were their everyday things—a rigid order of stone, which must have been agreeable to them in death as softness had been in life.

Next to the first huts were vessels for the ashes of the dead, large cracked stone receptacles and smaller containers shaped like mushrooms and boxes, gnawed by the salty air and covered in lichens, which formed patterns in the raw light gray and dark gray surfaces. I reached my hand across the low barrier to touch a mushroom urn, which felt softer and less rugged than expected. I pulled back my hand and felt as if I had done something forbidden.

Outside, the vast terrain lay in pale greens and almost-yellows beneath the wind, which skimmed the grasses in ever fiercer gusts and entered low, coniferous creeping bushes. The dust clouds formed small columns here and there, which, like an advance guard to the wind, flew over, close to the ground; fleeting angels from the finest particles of matter around here. The brightness spread, gleaming, across the *necropoli*s's surfaces, uneven, pervaded by dry paths. The paths led between the huts like lines from the Etruscan network that my father drew onto tracing paper. A soundless writing of the living, over all the excavated and yet-hidden homesteads of the dead, whom no one had mourned for a long time. The massive whitish asperity, so barren on the opposite side of the thicketed valley that sunk behind the *necropoli*s, this scarred surface of the city of the living, abraded and now visible only in its absence, lay tarnished as if in the shadows—the light fell there, too, but only trickled down into the dense rock.

Ponte Cavour

YEARS LATER, we went back to Rome. It was a different city.
Windy sunny days alternated with gray sleet days, squalls blew
through loggias and rattled antennas on roofs. On the wet evenings the streets were nearly empty. Lights reflected off the sidewalks and asphalt, women dashed home with shopping bags,
and the iron roller shutters were let down earlier than usual.
Around Stazione Termini men who wore caps and had turned-
up coat collars ducked beneath the wind, which caused signs
and barriers to vibrate, filling the air with an incessant rattling.
Upon our arrival, my father took a wrong turn and couldn't
find his way out of the square around the train station. While
we circled astray, brief views of the city's layers opened up. On
lit sidewalks, above which café awnings stood crooked in the
wind, disgruntled waitstaff looked out for customers without a
hope. In the middle of an intersection without cars or pedestrians, in front of dark building blocks without a single illuminated window, stood a trio of traffic policemen, in long raincoats,
who raised and sunk their arms like machines into the empty
evening. On narrow streets full of rain puddles, women wearing
make-up, pants and high heels huddled in building entrances,
smoking, buzzing, laughing; here and there behind half-shut-

tered shops one saw only their legs and high-heeled shoes. Customers walked up carefully, looked around, bent low enough to peek beneath the shutters, negotiated with the women or ran off. They were not young, the women I saw there—most were probably around my mother's age. They had bouffants and were heavily made up. Dresses, skirts and headscarves—that's what the women were wearing back then on the streets of Italy, and so the wide-leg pants worn by these women of the night behind Stazione Termini appeared like a kind of occupational dress, which would at least keep them warm during their covert business this inhospitable spring.

In Rome, the old order had shifted. The division into residents and transients, into the momentousness of history and the inaccessible lightness of contemporary life was less noticeable. Rifts now ran through a different terrain, and belonging was rewritten. In every district an unrest had taken hold of some locals, and visitors absorbed the upheaval and took it with them when they went. There were roadblocks, groups of police officers everywhere, demonstrations rolling past; it was all new to me and pushed its way in front of everything I was supposed to be seeing. In the crowded buses we no longer stood like a foreign islet, pressed against our father, surrounded by tired and mistrustful men and a few women on their way to work or home. Every man now had a hand ready to mutely harass, to be alarmingly intrusive. Once on the bus I saw a woman slap a man in the face. She was wearing a polka-dotted dress much too thin for the weather and a headscarf, and tears ran down her cheeks as she darted for the exit. Perhaps she had been holding out and was frightened, and risked slapping him only when her stop came. When she stumbled on the step and my father bent down to help her, she rebuffed him with anger and leapt out into the cold rain. The men in the bus grumbled and laughed at once, and after seeing the woman's tears I also started to cry.

In the evening we went to a café near Ponte Cavour. We sat there for an hour or two without my father, who had little patience for sitting in cafés and was happy to wander the streets alone. The chairs and benches had green-and-white striped cushions, and from the backrests of the benches up to the ceiling, the walls were covered in mirrors. It was a large room, at this evening hour apparently never full to capacity, and guests sat at the round tables, smoking, talking, reading. Every evening a woman in a fur cap sat enthroned on the bench across from the shimmering bar, consuming, very slowly and with elegance, one cake after another. After hours of walking through this street theater, I felt well there. The café lay like a distinguished harbor in Rome's sea of motion, and although I had no predilection for the distinguished, in this harbor I could simply sit and look out the window, watch as it became dark outside, while a long line of headlights crept across the bridge, and young people with Vespas gathered along the wall to the Tiber and talked every evening for as long as we were there, and for who knows how long into the night after we left. I was watching for signs that made the city decipherable. This gathering under the sycamore trees was one such sign, as were the demonstrations where skinny girls marched with raised fists, which I liked. On a calm day bathed in white, northern Italian light, Ostia Antica became a sign, too. This slow deciphering of the characters that composed Rome took place during the short stage of my growing up, when I—like every child, at some point—almost abruptly, nudged by accident, recognized the *world without me*, which I would have preferred to spend the entire day watching through the window panes of this café. One evening my gaze wandered aimlessly from the window to the high mirror that reflected part of the café, the entrance and the bar, and I saw someone walk in and was startled several moments later when I realized I was staring at my own father.

Eventually the wind abated. The rain had failed to materialize. Beneath a white sky, which the sunshine filtered into a uniformly soft brightness, we visited the grave of John Keats. The cemetery was full of cats, which rambled about the graves, rubbed against our legs. At John Keats's grave cats had a good chance of finding affection. Near the entrance, placed beneath pruned cypress trees, were small plates, as if set out for a society of dwarves; an elderly woman came over with a pot of food scraps and distributed them onto the plates, which were already thronged with cats. Next to the cemetery a sharp pyramid protruded above the traffic, an angular sign that seemed to refer to this island of the dead, lying here surrounded by the swells of the city. A Roman general had the pyramid erected as his tomb, perhaps consumed by a yearning for the sands of Egypt where, despite his warrior trappings, he had been a different person than he was here in Rome, where his eyes were inevitably drawn, day after day, to somber clusters of dark parasol pines.

From the cemetery with the pyramid we drove toward Ostia. We wandered through the lanes overgrown with grass, between the remnant houses of seafarers and traders, small merchants, intermediaries between the sea and the city upriver from the swampland surrounding Ostia. A calm terrain around this fragmented shell of a place, beneath a seaward sky. Nothing evoked urbanity and yet one could imagine the erstwhile life of things better here, in this dilapidated state, than in any re-creation, as if the grass, weeds and small flowers in the cracks between bricks and cobblestones were a kind of protective skin that preserved as much as possible, and even that which couldn't be seen. Seagulls circled, calling in mid-air, and the half-round empty openings in the urn walls of the old *necropolis* looked like small versions of the hunched, crumbled houses along the cobbled road, which belonged to the former city of the living. City of the dead, city of the living—both were empty, flayed of all presence, and in this emptiness they stood in reference to one another just as they had in former times, filled with the living and the dead, across the road that allotted them all their places. Entirely unlike in the city, things here, in their hull-like state and in their emptiness, in their refusal to bear witness, acquired a kind of beauty.

Ostia near the sea appeared even more empty than the ruined city. Most of the shutters were pulled down, and the shops were either still barricaded against winter or in the process of being repaired for the season. The sea lay gray-blue and calm, rippling gently around the mouth of the Tiber at the end of the beach. Small and wedged between functional terrains, the river came from the swamp and marshland and emptied into the sea.

Caccia

OUR LAST FAMILY TRIP to Italy fell on a languid summer that augured ill. We stayed in the outskirts of a village surrounded by vineyards, olive groves and small clumps of trees, where brambles crept up forbidding slopes, whip snakes rustling in their shelter. At some distance was a small forest of holm oaks. We were there for the third or fourth time and had observed a bit of affluence settle in the village houses. Ragged olive groves were cleaned, pruned and cared for, the vines were blue, stiff from copper sulfate, and black and white lambs were slaughtered, the fruitless little rams of the spring litter. In a garden at the village edge was a sounder of pigs. They, too, would be slaughtered, but not until winter, when the blood wouldn't spoil so quickly, the farmer explained, before describing in detail the slaughter, how the blood and intestines were processed, how the feet, ears and snouts would be used.

Throughout the years that we were acquainted with the place, a small trash dump had accumulated in the holm oak grove. Occasionally an old man with a long cane came around the house where we stayed, and I once saw him at the trash dump, hunting rats with his cane. He would let it crash to the ground, hissing curses; I couldn't say whether he nabbed any rats. My father often walked to the village, bought wine and cheese and had long conversations about the advantages of different grapes, steel barrels, certain insecticides.

Hanging above the landscape in those weeks was a heavy heat that refused to give way, and at night we often saw heat-lightning in the west, but no storms reached us. My father always returned from his usual walks exhausted, recounted little, and then sat for a long time beneath the mulberry tree. He looked to the landscape, to the church steeples, roofs of houses and rows of cypresses in the distance, trying to find his bearings, to give them names he had found on the map.

One morning a large group of agricultural workers, men and women, showed up to harvest the grapes. They brought along two or three donkeys and would take turns leading a donkey loaded with filled baskets over to the winegrowers. In the afternoon they would sit in the shade, eat, drink and sleep. The donkeys twitched their ears, warding off flies, and were watered. It took three days to harvest the vineyards around the house and then the agricultural workers disappeared again. They had made my father uneasy: they only reluctantly agreed to a bit of small talk and moreover responded in a dialect that he had difficulty understanding. At night after the harvest they would bring out nets for catching birds. They did this in the dark, while the birds slept. Men with flashlights moved between the rows of harvested vines, and we didn't know what they were doing, until the next day someone explained the purpose of the nets. Upon seeing the men with their nets, collecting their catch, we all fell silent. The next day the hunting season began. At dawn a jeep parked next to the house, and two men with dogs got out and unloaded their weapons from the bed. All day long shots echoed from every direction, occasionally the barking of dogs, too. My father didn't risk a walk. He went into the village and returned somewhat tipsy, offering statistics about shooting casualties among the hunters. The next day we decided to take a trip to an Etruscan *necropolis* that my father wanted to learn more about, but the day broke already in such a heat that we abandoned our plan. Despite the heat, the hunting fever prevailed. The jeep was parked next to the house, shots and barking echoed in the gentle valley. Neither on the first nor the second day of the hunt did we see them return with their haul; the jeep would disappear unnoticed, and we wouldn't hear the slightest panting of dogs, or the dull thud of their bagged haul hitting the jeep bed.

In the afternoon of the second hunting day, a dark blue cloud front formed in the west and edged closer. The clouds, bulging with brown, glowed greenish yellow around their borders, but soon this halo disappeared also, and the landscape lost all color. The storm lasted an hour. The power went out, candles flickered behind us in the dark rooms, and we stood, each alone at a window, watching the thunderstorm. The next morning the bird nets hung ravaged between the trees and vines. After the rain, the soil was no longer light brown and dusty, but red. On the slopes small landslides had formed from sludge and gravel, which lay like wounds in the landscape. A large branch had broken off the mulberry tree, knocking down the chair where my father liked to sit. The birds sang as they had on no other morning during these hot weeks, and not a single shot was fired. Aside from the birds, all was dampened and ducked. The sun was stinging once it broke through the clouds, the light now dazzling and sharp. That afternoon the sky was blue again,

the red earth visibly lost its rawness and the landscape straightened up to its usual gentleness. We ate dinner by light of the gas
burners in the kitchen, because the power wasn't turned on yet,
and we had used up all the candles. There wasn't much to say,
and perhaps each one of us was filled with relief, busy thinking
that our time here was now coming to an end.

Birds

YEARS LATER, I again spent a few hours with my father at the edge of Italy, in Trieste. He had given up his profession and now worked as a tour guide. He spent little time at home. When I came from abroad to visit, my father spoke only of his travels. He had specialized in tours of Early Medieval mosaics and Etruscan *necropolis*es which he presented, explained and—surely with countless digressions and detours—elucidated in great detail to knowledge-hungry tourists. With a shrug of the shoulders, he accepted that he wasn't always able to lecture on his preferred subjects and that he also had to take groups through the Roman Forum or even into the Colosseum, which he had always hated. But usually he succeeded in finding time for a mosaic, he said. At least one.

The tour group had spent the night in Trieste, where I arrived very early in the morning. At twilight the train had emerged from the mountains, and I stood at the window and for a time couldn't say where the sea ended and the sky began. The world hung suspended until the Earth and sky came adrift and the small lights in this blue-gray materialized as ships. It was my first trip to Italy in years, I had no intention of lingering and preferred to restrict my visit to this peripheral city, which in my mind already leaned toward a different Europe, more Eastern than Southern, the air filled with the melodies of various languages—a knotted sound that muffled the Italian my father had so fully devoted himself to.

We sat in a large square which at this morning hour was still empty, in the only café already open. The sky was gray and low without being oppressive, even though the air was so humid and warm that I continually thought small raindrops were falling. I felt alien and peculiar. Something about our brief meeting in this border city on the periphery—which to my father was so Italian, as he explained without my asking, and to me, without my interjecting, so un-Italian—appeared false and artificial to me. Perhaps I missed the familiar gestures of his hands while smoking, which he had given up a few years back, or walking, which at that moment I suddenly felt was the one requirement for communication. After eight or ten days of leading tours, he was still entirely in his role of explainer and now no cigarette or, so early in the morning, glass of wine could distract him; he wanted to describe everything, to hold a short lecture about his last presentation in Ravenna, where I had never been. What had I wanted to tell him? I no longer knew. His accounts of artworks made me tired. I looked around at the large, foreign square while my father spoke, and my distracted, wandering gaze might have disappointed him. The large square abutted the port promenade at its far end. Nearby, where a water-filled gutter ran through the square, flocks of seagulls and pigeons swayed, squabbling over the crumbs and scraps in the cracks between the stone slabs. A fight broke out between a seagull and a pigeon, silencing my father, and together we mutely watched the seagull slowly gain an upper hand and hack into the pigeon with indescribable savagery. Eventually it flew away, leaving the lifeless pigeon on the square, a drop of blood pooling below its beak. Other seagulls, screeching, crashed back and forth between the square and the water, while a small flock of scout pigeons circled once or twice above their lacerated companion, before ascending and alighting on a rooftop. My father shuddered with disgust, and we left. We walked along the pier and viewed the city panorama. The sky was now white and seemed to hesitate letting the sun break through. Viewed from this distance to the sea, the city had a certain sadness—it had reasons enough—but at the same time this sadness, or the absoluteness of it, had a placative quality like the kind that often opens up in places where affiliations are unresolved and possibilities are enmeshed. Had my father asked, I now would have agreed—Trieste is very Italian—silently knowing, however, that by Italian we both meant something entirely different.

I walked him to his hotel on the hillside, where the tour group was waiting to depart. The sky had meanwhile decided against the sun, and a thin rain had set in, which appeared not so much to fall as hang in the air. Years had passed since our walks together, and I noticed for the first time that the steep street's inclination was difficult on my father. Now and then he had to pause and catch his breath. I saw the bus already waiting and said goodbye. Imagining my short-winded father on this tour bus, ever so diligent, was disconcerting. I pictured him as a small, hunched over *professore* with a weak heart, perched on his seat beside the driver, issued full freedom to stray off topic, and this image frightened me. As we parted he recommended the mosaics in Ravenna. Above all the harbor picture, he said emphatically, and without further explanation walked away. I wondered what had become of his expertise in shades of blue and his related affinity for pictures by Fra Angelico, whom he had long since ceased speaking of, and I decided to ask him about it the next time I had the chance.

My father died the following June. I saw him once more in winter, but we didn't say a word about Trieste or the blues of Fra Angelico either. In autumn he had made an Etruscan tour, as he called it. Across the upper half of Italy, from the northeast to the Tiber. Spina, he said, Spina in the Po delta, there's another great mystery. I avoided a longer conversation and the detailed explanation presaged by the maps, already deployed on the table.

The following spring, shortly after returning from a mosaic trip, my father suffered a heart attack. While he was still conscious, he blamed it on his suitcase, which he had carried such a long way. Somewhere along the Rhine he had asked the bus driver to let him out, on the bank opposite his house, and then he hauled his suitcase to the ferry pier. Perhaps he didn't want anyone to see him exit the tour bus. Perhaps he wanted to cross from the left to the right side of the river. The right, eastern bank is where he grew up—that side had a lesser reputation. He had nonetheless always considered it more beautiful, admitting, however, that its greater beauty could be recognized only from the left bank.

The day of his return was said to be very hot. In my mind I have often pictured my father with his suitcase, bent to one side by its weight, in the white, sharp light of the Rhineland on humid days; he walks north, the bend already in sight, where the river, having left all hills behind, turns west. He stands on the dock waiting for the ferry, his gaze riveted on the opposite side.

As time passed after my father's death, he became ever smaller in my mental picture of this walk along the river, and his suitcase ever larger, into which he had stuffed who knows how much of his life that he never found a name for.

Rain

ON THE DAY that we buried my father, rain fell in sheets. Overnight the weather had suddenly changed. A violent thunderstorm broke the heat that had crouched above the landscape, felling a tree on the narrow street to the cemetery. We had to park on the roadside and walk the last bit. The wind whipped the rain against our legs, and the skirt of my black summer dress, which at home I had thrown into my suitcase as if this heat could never cease, was dripping wet. A man with a large umbrella came out of the mortuary and whispered something to my mother. For a final time she asked me if I really didn't want to see my father once more, and again I said no, and the man rushed away officiously, as if he were either awkwardly touched or feared a family quarrel. At a safe distance, from the open vestibule of the mortuary he called out: Then we'll screw it shut now!

We were a tiny funeral party, following the coffin through puddles. My mother had not notified anyone aside from our immediate relatives. My father would have been ashamed at the sight of this scanty crowd—he had his own ideas about mourning and saw it as a kind of duty to participate in funeral processions. He certainly would have pictured a long cortege behind his coffin.

The cemetery was completely new to me and the grave appeared to be very far away. The trolley with the coffin rumbled over the wet, stony road, the gravel crunched underfoot, and the men pushing the trolley were probably biting back curses. We had to wait at the grave because part of the dug-out earth had slid back down due to the heavy rain. A small complication, the man from the mortuary said apologetically, with a hint of annoyance. I was struck by the vocabulary of hospitals spoken in this place. The man whispered with the pallbearers. They had to decide if the grave was still deep enough.

It was as cold as in October. A sheep's chill, they once called it. The summer had dog days and sheep's chills, as we used to say. In mid-June the sheep were shorn. I thought about the herds of sheep that we had seen on our trips. They lay at the edge of a village near the Swiss-Italian border, near Bergamo maybe. From the road one looked down onto flatland. The sheepfolds stood empty after the shearing and in the shelter behind the sheepfolds was the shorn wool, neatly separated: on the left side was the white wool, on the right side, the dark.

The pallbearers and the man from the mortuary nodded affirmingly. Yes, they assured one another in a muffled tone, the grave was deep enough. The rain drummed against the umbrella, and from the Rhine the ships and the trains on the other side sounded so loud, it was as if the tracks ran very nearby. It was always like that in the rain there on the river, which past the next bend would leave the hills behind and flow through flatland, where the sound was sure to take a different course. Here the sound was bandied about between the low hills, from the right side to the left and back again, a relentless game of echo, especially in the rain—that was a law of nature.

The coffin was lowered into the grave and shovels of wet earth clapped against the wood below in the grave. The rain held out for days.

III
COMACCHIO

Le parole. Già.
Dissolvono l'oggetto.

Come la nebbia gli alberi,
Il fiume: il traghetto.
Giorgio Caproni

Bassa

THE EARTH IN THE BASSA PADANA is bright brown in the light of these bitter-cold winter days, in which I've never before seen it, cast almost purple, a surfeit of blue in the air under the vast sky. To the northeast the Euganean hills are a wispy blue, a timid sketch in the lower cusp of the sky. The fields are neatly plowed into small, broken-up clods of soft earth, alluvial land. The farms lie like islands in an ocean of fields, surrounded by trees, their bare branches reddish and motionless in the frosty, still air; everything rooted, bound to the ground has these bright, earthy tones against the sky. In the open farmyards, between sheds and barns is agricultural equipment, and no sign of pasture as far as the eye can see—perhaps a lesson learned during flood years, when the river, risen quietly above the banks overnight, wrested cattle from the meadows and carried them downstream, belly-up, until they became tangled in unwieldy thickets or wedged between splintered beams from the wrecked roofs of barns and farms, while the water level sank and farmers began counting what they had to mourn.

The age of alluvial land is past and the Po is lined on both sides by a dam; small hamlets and villages lie in its shelter and shadow. This January very little water runs in the river and bright gravel islands have emerged; from the dam the flow toward the delta, which begins already on the eastern horizon, is barely discernible. Between the dam and river are plantations of fast-growing trees, their spindle trunks like lines drawn into the fallen leaves. At a bend the causeway retreats a distance from the river, making room for a construction site which seems to lie fallow, as if left in haste. Arranged in a circle, pipes are overlapped with pallid grass and a collection of rusty objects, pressed into the concave embankment of the dam, shows just how well this uneven brown-red suits the landscape, as if it stemmed from the river-blue and earth-brown, from the thin wood of the willow thickets and the thorn bushes, which appear either yellowish or violet depending on the fall of light and shadows. Between thickets a large crane-like machine stands against the sky like hastily scribbled punctuation devoid of meaning; all of the equipment gathered here can at most be regarded as letters, signifying nothing but colors. On the other side of the river a tall church steeple stands crooked against the coppice, where lines from the grove jut out of the ground in taut, regular rows. It is a slash on the horizon, punctuation as well, but here, clustered around it is a run-on of roofs. A flock of pigeons takes to the sky next to the village, a small script in the air, shifting from a dark speckling to a brightly shimmering flourish. There, across the river, lying below it, is a sentence addressed to the plain. This short sentence, made unforgettable by the forward slash, forms an introduction to the curve that the river is preparing for in a gesture of peaceful generosity toward the land, which in its flatness must be prepared for every interference, every invasion, yet is embraced by the river with such mercy that it succumbs with all the willow-thicketed grace it has at its disposal. This curve, too, is a sentence, a small, murmured excuse from the river on the brink of unraveling into the countless waverings concealed beneath all inconsistent names.

On top of the small river-promontory, formed at the beginning of the curve, a man in high boots fishes. The gravel islands and sand banks are a stone's throw away; the water cannot be deep here. The fish must be sparse during the low flow, and all the more so in this coldness, which drives most fish to huddle in riverbed cavities to survive. The man, the fishing rod, the line—everything is motionless, the water flows almost imperceptibly. A short verse, as well: the man by the river, the catcher in the gravel, without a hope of a catch he nevertheless clings to his fishing rod.

On the path along the dam, a woman approaches, striding decisively. The sun lies low, encircling her figure in a halo of light. Difficult to tell her age. Her gait is young, but her get-up is from another time. She wears a white coat with a wide collar and a belt, tied tightly around her waist, causing the coattails to stick out. Hanging from her forearm is a black handbag suited for a town promenade and her hair is styled stiffly and sits around her head like a bonnet. She walks resolutely, her gaze lowered slightly, in elegant shoes with high heels. In the direction she comes from I can't make out a village. She passes by the small village behind the *rocca*, becoming smaller and smaller against the afternoon sky. An extra from one of the many films shot here in the past, perhaps she didn't want to give back the beautiful coat, and walked and walked from one scene into the next, unhired, attuned to all the transformations around her, *la donna del Po*.

The stout edifice of the *rocca*, a small fortress, which in earlier days was situated directly on the water that has since receded from it, casts a long afternoon shadow in the corset of scaffolding that it wears to keep from breaking apart. A crack, broken open by an earthquake, extends along its wall. The church steeple across the river may also have the earthquake to thank for its slant, which transformed it into an exclamation point, in order to remind the region of the shifting terrain.

A chirruping drifts from the fields at the foot of the embankment, the succinct, rattling winter syllables of sparrows, which flutter in swiftly shrinking spots of sun. A man climbs up to the path. He wears high boots, a weatherproof jacket, a leather cap and around his neck, binoculars. Like a hunter who wades in reeds might look. Only the dog is missing. The woman in the white coat is a tiny figure, far away. Should I follow her or continue walking in the other direction? Helpless, I turn toward the hunter. Which direction is more beautiful? I ask. It's beautiful everywhere, he says, raising his hand to gesture to the path, the small municipality, the fields and farms, the tree plantation and the construction site, the river and the distance. Just as beautiful everywhere, he repeats.

Later, at dusk, small rural roads lead me back to the city. It is a holiday, the last detour of the Christmas season. Around lunchtime there was hardly any traffic in the streets; parked cars are now crammed in the villages. A family day. On the sunlit, uneven village streets, children, shivering in their holiday clothes, clumsily tested their new roller skates, scooters and remote-control cars until they were called in for dinner. Now it's quiet between the houses, here and there lights are already on, dusk is falling and the last flocks of crows assemble and take to the sky—clouds of birds flying toward the trees where they roost, bare elms, alders, willows, poplars, standing like drawings against the thin evening-blue. Running outside of the small villages are long avenues, moats, plowland. Here and there an abandoned farmstead in the middle of plowed, tended fields, slumped and buckled under the load of its broken rooftops. A very thin ground fog rises from the fields and ditches, imperceptible from the perspective of the town.

Corso

I RETURNED TO FERRARA to walk up and down Corso Ercole I d'Este and look at the gardens—read-about, imagined and real— on both sides of the street, and to peer over walls and through gates in the walls, and into the small side lanes that forked off from the unswerving street. It was January once again, and I wanted to walk until I reached the Porta degli Angeli, and continue from there onto the city wall. With this in mind I arrived at the small station and stepped out onto the courtyard where African refugees, who whiled away the lonely, cold, and hungry days in the vicinity of the station, were waiting for buses to return in the night to idly quiet and half-abandoned industrial towns, whose factories had either been shut down or were now operated merely for the sake of appearances. There, in the outskirts of the city, they had accommodations in sparsely furnished erstwhile public buildings which were still able, just barely, to pass as basic shelter. They frequented the small urban area around the station on the fringes of Ferrara, loitering, perhaps meeting other refugees, and on market days they would wander to Piazza Travaglio, hoping to find odd jobs, to trade, to help out the Chinese merchants spreading out their textiles, to be given a sac filled with pairs of socks which they would be allowed to peddle in the streets.

I arrived on the commuter train from Bologna. It was already dark and the fog that had formed began to freeze. I welcomed the fog, I had hoped it would cast its veil over objects and dissolve distance, familiar as I was with other lowland landscapes teeming with rivers. But it was deceiving to be received by the evening fog. Over the next few days the sun shone in a cold sky, hoarfrost covered the grassy areas, and a thin sheet of ice formed on the body of water that surrounded the castle in the city. I rented a bare bones apartment in a sloppily renovated building. It was in the attic and every morning the reddish landscape of bricks, gables and chimneys in front of the kitchen window materialized in the bluish light. Once daylight broke, pigeons would appear on the roof ridges, silent for frost, and in the grooves and cracks of the old tiles, moss and short-stemmed weeds, which even bore tiny white blossoms. A construction site projected into my field of vision where a modern house, rising above the other rooftops, was either being repaired or given an additional story. A building crane was in motion there daily, and on the scaffolding men began work at dawn in the freezing cold; now and again snatches of their exchanges in Romanian reached me.

On the night of January 5, it was loud in the lanes and after midnight raucous groups rambled about, awakening memories of the street festival honoring the epiphanic witch in Olevano, of that intensifying echo which moved so erratically between the hillsides and houses, causing the monotonous music and shrill voices to hover in the air for so long.

My first walk down Corso Ercole blurred the lines on the maps that I carried around in my head. The uneven cobblestones seemed eager to imprint on the soles of my feet like a tactile writing, directing my footsteps over to the severe, sleek house facades with closed windows, which seemed so unblinking and stiff, as if the whole facade were merely a mock-up. Behind there anything was possible: no man's land, overgrowth, the disturbed territory of old stories. Then someone stepped out of a house, a lady in mink, closing the door so rapidly behind her that I couldn't catch a glimpse inside. Towering above the walls that occasionally interrupted the facades were the rigid branches of bare treetops, cypress crowns, listless winter palm fronds. Nothing moved in the frost. Bassani's winters, too, are icy, not as bright as this Sunday, but rather misty, rimy, gray or full of snow. Hardly anyone was out on Corso, the long street lay hushed in the sun, and I found no hint of the vague traces that I was looking for. Before long I abandoned my search for his mythical garden; I had trouble locating it on the city map and found nothing to help orient my mental picture. The garden of the Finzi-Contini remained a space that was shaped and reshaped by memory and interpretation, an area of loss that refused to be found. The meaning of my search in these foreign streets with familiar names lay in sensing the narrow tracts of intuited borders which hemmed -in that area of forlornness. The names alone had to make do for a stop, together with my memory of actual walkways between the green burial mounds of Cerveteri.

At the end of the Corso I came across the Porta degli Angeli, the gate of angels, on the path up to the rampart encircling the city; there one looked down to the city's outer border path, the still waters of a canal, which must smell foul in summer, and a heavily trafficked arterial road, leading to the—at times rural, at times eagerly suburban—fraying urban fabric of Ferrara, flat and traversed by rows of poplars; here and there was a sparse grove, situated on a piece of land evading all utility, or a thicket, left to its devices to conceal some decay. Everything had been repeatedly disturbed, was forever suspended between traces and effacement.

Joggers in loud tracksuits passed me by in droves on the path to the Montagnola, a kind of gallery in the city wall, where it veers to the southeast. The gallery looked out onto the random, overdeveloped sprawl at the outskirts of the city, nothing rural about it left. I pictured young men on bicycles, who emerge from the foggy plain, tools or food in their packs, and climb the fortress wall day after day, attempting conquest, and upon reaching the top simply cycle on, scatter in different directions to find their market stands or workshops, and in the evening hit the pavement again through one of the city's eastern-bound gates. Without being recognized as conquerors, they cycle off into the dusk, which slides across the plain. Now there were no longer farmer boys climbing the grassy wall, shouldering bicycles, in order to avoid the brief detour to the open city gates. There wasn't even a market anymore in Ferrara, aside from the stands run by Chinese vendors selling textiles and household goods made from brittle plastic at Piazza Travaglio, at the mouth of the city.

The bell tolled noon as colorful joggers trickled off into the distance, and before long the path, lined by rows of sycamore trees, was empty. Stretching below, along the foot of the wall with the sycamore path, were gardens and meadows with fruit trees—small countryside idylls within the city, lying inside the city wall, invulnerable to the openness outside. A trail led down into this quiet landscape, bound by thorn bushes and hedges, where in the dense shrubbery the jangling chirrup of hedge sparrows spread out like a thin cloth beneath the silence. A man sat on a bench wearing an old tweed coat, bright white sneakers, and sunglasses with wire frames, which had something American about them, a touch of the 70s, recalling photographs of New York with laidback men on the Atlantic shore, skyscrapers reflecting in their lenses. Between his coat lapels a matte-brown, tiny dog peeked out, with a pointy muzzle. Its hair was so short it looked practically naked. The skin on the dog's neck formed thick wrinkles. The man stood up when I approached, as if he had just been waiting to join a solitary passerby. *Ha freddo*, he said, jerking his chin toward the dog, and for the first time in years I thought of how my grandfather's sister would mutter *I've got so cold* under her breath, as if nothing in the entire world could remedy it. The man was very small and had trouble keeping up with me, but he didn't let off. I bet you want to go to the Jewish cemetery, he said, as we reached a long, bright wall. Just watch—, he advised, without my having answered. Watch your step. The dog let out a quiet, plaintive cry, as if he too wanted to comment on the matter.

You have to ring the bell there. The man pointed to the gate. He wore a perforated glove made from crochet and brown leather. The old word *motoring gloves* occurred to me, nearly forgotten; it had been so long since I had seen a pair. The cemetery caretaker opened the gate and allowed me to enter, wordlessly. He held a napkin in his hand, and from rooms behind a door inside which was ajar , I could hear a clattering of plates; he was in a hurry to get back to his meal. Without turning around to the man in the tweed coat, I stepped into the graveyard.

The layout of the cemetery followed an opaque plan. Perhaps it reflected the complex system of the Ferrara Synagogue on Via Mazzini, where the Italian, German and Sephardic synagogues all lay side by side and nested into one another behind a single entrance to the street. Guarded from the outside only by this large, yet rather unremarkable portal, it formed an interior world that you could lose yourself in, partitioned into various levels of meaning and importance. Spread out over a large area and despite the wide, open lawns, the cemetery—sectioned off by the hedges, narrow avenues, and groves—also had something disorienting and nested about it. Situated below the city wall, it had a view uphill to the promenade lined by sycamores, where at midday there were no more colorful joggers out and about. The sycamores, clinging to what rigid leaves they had left, their color faded almost entirely, stood motionless against the cold blue sky. In the distance I heard the brief call of a pied flycatcher, no trill, only a succession of diphthongs, which always sounded to me as if the bird's throat were trying to reverse and swallow the uttered call with its second syllable. A tone for empty, bright February mornings, which was befitting to the smell of the city; it smelled like February in the lanes, a not-quite-winter-anymore scent from my childhood with thin, fragrant veins of deep-fried dough—an air that reveals more frost lying ahead. I couldn't spot the bird anywhere. He must have been sitting, guarded in a strip of sunlight between the last leaves, which waited in January's drought to be unsettled by a storm. In the shady areas of the cemetery, hoarfrost covered the soil, the grass and the withered leaves. In places the ground was littered with gingko fruit, which emanated a nauseating odor. Perhaps that's what the man with the dog referred to with his word of warning. The frost had caused the fallen fruits to burst and the stench cloud crept in every direction; it seemed to stick on my shoes for days, hanging in the air.

A few visitors walked among the graves, searching, deciphering epitaphs. An older woman had taken a seat, exhausted, on a sarcophagus-like grave, and a young man with a shadow of a mustache stood next to her, letting his shoulders hang, looking utterly clueless. Where's Bassani's grave? The woman called to me in a shrill voice, tampering with her ankle boots. She sent the young man to ask the cemetery caretaker. Two men, both in elegant winter coats with distinguished hats on their heads, walked purposefully. I saw them stand in front of a family grave, where they lingered, perhaps praying, before sauntering about the other graves, inspecting names. I found Bassani's grave by chance, situated at the edge of an expansive lawn, a dog rose bush with large rose hips casting its shadow onto the memorial stone. Later, as I contemplated the inscriptions on the headstones at the other end of the lawn, examining them for traces of stories I'd read, I saw the two elegant men also stop at his grave.

Herons

ONE MORNING A WOMAN ARRIVED to clean the apartment, a haggard woman with a broad dialect unintelligible to me, who tried in vain to explain something. Again and again she made a wave-like gesture with her hands. While pondering it later, I had a peculiar hunch she might have been talking about eels. Perhaps she wanted to communicate that she came from an eel-fishing region, or a family of eel fishermen, or maybe she had even brought along an eel concoction for sale in her large, woven plastic bag, from which she also pulled out her work clothes. Once she realized that I simply didn't understand her, she took a small radio out of her bag, set it in the kitchen window, and tuned into a station playing Italo pop.

It was the kind of misty morning I had imagined I would find in this region. I walked through the streets of Ferrara, arrived at the station, and took a train to Codigoro. While looking at names on the departures board, I had an image of fragments before me. Details arose from Bassani's story of Edgardo Limentani and the heron; blending with memories of entirely different, distant places, they formed a picture, frayed at its edges, and a web of vast veins of emptiness spread out between these unrelated snippets of memory. In a rundown hotel on the main square in Codigoro, Edgardo Limentani wiled away the hours before and after hunting game birds in the Volano lagoon. It was a winter day, two years after the war. My father had most certainly never held a gun in his hand for the purpose of shooting birds, and I could recognize no parallel between his life and, unfolding in that slim volume, the chagrin of Edgardo Limentani, who lived in a house on Via Montebello, the road leading to the powerful portal of the Jewish cemetery in Ferrara, but while reading it I pictured my father all the same.

It was a small regional train. Sitting across from me was a woman in a worn-out quilted coat who led an elderly man with a hanging lower lip, step by tiny shuffling step to his seat. The man wheezed. As soon as they had taken their place, she occupied herself with a bundle of official-seeming letters which she carried around in her large handbag. The envelopes were cleanly ripped, and my father's letter opener came to my mind: an ugly item with an ebony bird's-head handle, which my grandmother had brought back from her late travels. I never knew whether it was due to the sharpness of the letter opener or my father's skill, but when the envelopes lay flat I could never tell if they were opened or closed.

A number of passengers were visibly infirm; a few stations later it became clear why, as the train nearly emptied at the regional hospital of Ferrara. The procession of invalids, with their tentatively tapping canes and exhausted companions, remained in my sight for some time, as it inched its way across the platform and onto the path between sloppily greened embankments toward the bulk of a hospital, while other infirm individuals, their doctor's visits already behind them, embarked.

Past Cona the view opened out to the countryside. I had hoped for landscapes hung with fog, for that silent intermediate world of forms and colors, which carries every river along with it, occasionally casting one away, in order to transfix those living in its proximity. But on this January day the haze soon thinned between the acres; it wasn't a fog of rivers and canals, but a sheer veil hung from the heavens, which became ever thinner and eventually dissipated beneath a pale winter sun. The sky still held onto the distant dove blue of indecisive sunny days, but every outline was clear, and the landscape lay unfurled, its flatness broken by individual groves, avenues, canal dikes, which altered the view to the whitely flickering horizon in the east, where I presumed was the delta, with its branched water veins, and the sea. Flocks of birds rose from the edges of fields, and pigeons, drawing their oblique half-circles, rose darkly and lay into flight so that their undersides, too, appeared bright in the hesitant light; a game of steering toward and avoiding the light, which I knew so well from flat river landscapes and estuary regions, and which I never could stop seeing as a sign, without ever having learned to decipher it. Fruit plantations ran along the railroad embankment, nothing but bones, the trees forced flat as if stretched onto the trellises, bare and crowded into this restricted growth, but even so, winter-green weeds spread between the rows. White foil from cheap greenhouses hung in shreds and waved, flapping when the airstream seized a strip. The high greenhouse tunnels vaulted, hollow, above herbaceous undergrowth, and seasonal neglect was visible all around except in the neatly plowed acres, with their precise furrows. Above a field with a touch of green from germinating winter seed, two gray herons flew low. The train stopped in small villages, where, beside overgrown remains of abandoned huts and farm estates, small settlements of uniform houses had emerged, their front yards leafless, with decorative shrubbery splayed next to pruned evergreens. No one crossed the streets, no one climbed aboard on this mid-morning, to commence the brief trip to Codigoro. The invalids left the train little by little, standing, squinting on the unpaved narrow platforms, as if they had to recall the way home. The region appeared to have been settled by trial and error, and, despite the overgrown ruins, only recently; even the church steeples looked experimental, crowned by strange small cupolas, which faintly recalled Orthodox churches, but without their radiant polish, somewhat shabby overall. As if deliberately, the railroad cleaved into the intimacy of the villages and their separate cemeteries; each city of the dead, girded by a brick wall, was found across the tracks from the village it belonged to, always in an open field, surrounded by acres or meadows; like friendly fortresses, the rearward walls of grandiose tombs on the fringe, facing the viewer on the train. The winter sun shone on the tops of the white angels and stone crosses. Here and there a sparse avenue—with lindens, sycamores, chestnut trees—edged between the train and the cemetery, simulating the cut made definitive by the railroad tracks. Funeral processions would always have to be planned to prevent the interruption of a train on this admittedly seldom-traveled road. Or funeral guests, the *Onoranze funebri* hearse with a decorated coffin, and the priest were all prepared to be detained by the level crossing, where the gates sunk with a tinny ring. Funeral processions might even occasionally become divided, with the coffin already beyond the gates and the bereaved left to persevere on the other side. At an old train station we came to a halt. Two passengers exited the rear car, and I watched them walk across the gravel-strewn platform. The main building of the train station, with its suggested portal and beautiful arched windows, was closed, but an open door in a wing offered a glimpse into a bleak waiting room with graffitied walls. Only two benches stood inside, but they were as wide as beds and placed so near to each other that it might have functioned as a consoling encampment for the stranded who had missed the last train, or, upon arriving at this small station had begun doubting their ultimate goal. The carriage doors closed at last, but the train didn't budge. The conductor stood on the gravel, talking on the phone. He ultimately knocked on the windowpanes, urging the slim handful of passengers to step out. I joined the three women with shopping bags who stood around the conductor. The train couldn't continue. A bus would come, though it was not clear when. The small group moved out into the courtyard, to a narrow waiting strip on a tree-lined street, scattered with whitish pebbles. Through the trees I saw roofs, the ochre and pink plastered walls of village houses. *Lidi* was written on the bus that finally came, the bus to the seaside. A vague location, perhaps because of winter, when no one headed to the seaside resorts, anyway. The three women got on the bus, but at the last minute I decided against it. While the blue bus drove eastward on the avenue, I suddenly felt relieved that I was denied Codigoro. What should the sites of Edgardo Limentani's doubt mean to me, anyway? Or the imagined shadows of my father in bars, small inns at the ends of narrow streets, where winter-pale reed fronds waved on the banks of canals?

I wandered through the small town, which despite the sun lay in a silent winter stiffness. Sparse clientele gathered in a grocery shop, where a black woman stood behind a counter with cheese, sausage and pieces of dried cod in a small pile.

While customers were busy deciding what to buy, the woman stood with her hands folded on her stomach, as if after a bit of practice she had memorized the old Italian *alimentari* shop assistant's pose of twenty, maybe thirty years ago. Today shop assistants no longer stand like that, but this black woman, who might have been cast away here, had the idea of exercising this shop-assistants' language, and who knows why. Perhaps she had watched old Italian films at home, their sounds mixing with the street noise from the town where she lived—beeping and calling and omnibuses rattling and the clattering whir of a fan—so that this gesture from the films gave her a feeling of familiarity.

In front of an inn with a covered veranda, the proprietor stood without a hope of customers. A small hotel was attached to the restaurant, dedicated to the heron, as the wall above the awning announced in old-fashioned writing. Perhaps the writing even glowed on summer nights, imprinting itself in the minds of people passing through. The narrow streets through town were empty but for cats, all of them brownish tabby. In a garden an elderly man bent over a pile of firewood, slowly filling a basket. He took each piece of wood from a neat stack beside the barn, tested its weight in his hand, and turned it over before laying it in the basket. The garden was narrow and deep. In the crowns of plumpish trees, pruned by a green thumb, blackbirds ruffled their feathers while chickens stalked, stiff-legged from the cold, through the grass. The town, in addition to the Heron Hotel, also had a Piazza Giorgio Bassani, where on warmer days and bright evenings people would presumably come together, for a chat or a drink, and lay eyes on a shop whose display window had written above it in large letters: *Game Over*. Past the town, two canals or river offshoots nearly met, but then decided better of flowing on together, after all, and a dam ran between them. Over on the other side of the water sprawled vast, sunken farmland, traversed by ditches—the drained delta terrain where the *necropoli*s of Spina once lay buried. The photographs in the archaeological museum of Ferrara, enlarged to the point of distortion, show peasants at work beneath wide-brimmed hats, standing barefoot in rolled-up pants, leaning on spades and shovels, looking into the camera, toothless and shy, the Etruscan grave-goods before their feet and the enormous nascent arable land, previously under water, behind them and at their sides. The photographs were meant to illustrate this accidental discovery, made while digging ditches for the land-reclamation project, but they appear clumsily staged. The ostensible finders grin stiffly, strained—woe to the grubber with silt-crusted calves, who might have thought to bend down for a vase.

The town was not large, and the friendly, old-fashioned nature of the gardens, bars and small shops petered out at its fringes, where a pair of new functional buildings towered angular above pruned bushes. Behind them a beltway ascended. *Lidi* was written on a large street sign, which pointed east. After the bus to the seaside, here was the street to the seaside. Hardly a car on the road. The word *lido* had the connotation of elegance for me as a child, until we once made a brief stop at the Adriatic Sea on a spring trip. We wanted to see the water, and my father had to lift us up so we could catch a glimpse of its blinding emptiness through a hole in a wooden fence. A flat beach and restless seagulls without prey above distant, shallow-breaking waves. In the town we also found a café, whose owner was nearly alarmed by our arrival. *Tutto chiuso*, she said, as if she wanted to get rid of us. Men in overalls stood around the bar, drinking to the inevitable tune of Italo pop. They certainly wanted to remain among themselves, undisturbed by foreigners, whose time had not yet arrived. She finally served us sweet-bitter lemonade in small bottles, and we sat on the café terrace in the cold wind beneath a flag that flapped, looking through the path between beach cabins, onto a narrow strip of bright blue sea.

On the road to the *lidi* I came across a cemetery, which appeared new. In the middle of fields, a bare concrete park where crows pecked. Yellow-blooming weeds and grasses stood offering solace around the wall, which, with its stony angularity, gave the eye little to hold onto or otherwise take comfort in. Through the iron gate I saw a wall with columbaria, rows with grave markers, artificial flowers in plastic containers, all things garish and unbreakable, put to use here in place of the vases, plates, and pieces of jewelry from Spina. The light of the small grave lamps, those eternal lights I knew from Olevano, couldn't be made out in the bright day, but I imagined how on misty nights the cemetery, seated here between the fields, so solitary and separate from the village, might appear an assembly of will-o'-the-wisps: hovering, flickering, erratic. Before I had a chance to eye the names and dates, a vehicle appeared from the local *Onoranze funebri*, a dark-gray hearse with a casket covered in colorful floral arrangements and ribbons. A lank cortege of a dozen mourners in practical winter clothing, quilted coats and anoraks with artificial-fur trim. They glanced, distrustful, in my direction.

I left quickly, ashamed by my ill-timed curiosity in this utterly foreign place, where I had happened by chance. Hesitant, I stood at some distance from the small cemetery and again saw two herons sitting on a cable stretched between two poles. Were they a sign? Were they themselves waiting for a sign? They had turned up at the right place, anyway, these guardians of the dead who kept watch at a proper distance, unobserved attendants to the gathered mourners.

A bus stopped on the side of the road, seeming to appear out of nowhere. Ferrara was written on a small sign stuck in the window. An elderly couple dressed in black stepped out, the woman wearing a bright synthetic rose, offering an arm to her hunchbacked husband. I stepped onto the empty bus and looked out at the slowly shuffling couple. A mourner rushed through the cemetery gate, waving both arms after the bus, his red tie fluttering from his shirt front, the laps of his unbuttoned coat seeming to brush against reeds in the roadside ditch. The bus driver actually braked and went into reverse to pick up the funeral escapee. The man collapsed into a seat, and I heard him wheezing a while. He dabbed his forehead with a large handkerchief, pulled from his pants pocket, and exhaled, as if he had escaped a certain danger. The bus drove through a landscape that lay quiet and flat, without stopping for some distance. Gray-white reed fronds lined the road, willow bushes stood between fields, lindens and acacias encircled farmsteads, and in the distance were rows of poplars. Flocks of crows stalked slowly around the light brown soil of plowed fields. Here and there industrial patches emerged, small factories; along a body of water a worker snipped reddish reeds. When the bus arrived in Ferrara, the mourner had long stepped off, without my having noticed.

Amber

THE NIGHT AFTER MY ABANDONED TRIP to Codigoro, I had a dream. I walked into a ditch with high walls, wet on both sides; the ground was covered in puddles, which mirrored the sky. The dirt in the walls was riddled with blunt pebbles. Despite the sky reflected in the water, it was dim in the ditch, and smelled damp and earthy, even a bit salty, like veins of clay. On my walk, and even before it, I was afraid of stepping with my bare feet onto something alive, which would slither out from under my toes, and that the walls might cave in. As I was dreaming, the gravel quarry from my childhood came to mind. Against all rules, children hollowed out caves in the walls there; some collapsed and buried children under sand and gravel, and there were fatalities. I spent time at the small, eye-shaped lake at the quarry's floor, surrounded by the funneled, ascendant walls, from which a trickling of sand always came loose, somewhere. Shortly before reaching the wooden stairs in my dream, I pulled a pebble from the wall and, feeling as if I were doing something forbidden, closed my hand around it. The stairs swayed beneath my feet like a rowboat. Above, at the ditch's edge, I stood on a stretch of land overgrown with thin, pallid grass. The sharp blades lay flat on the ground below a wind that I nevertheless didn't feel. Although the puddles on the ground in the ditch had reflected a blue sky with puffy clouds, here above it was a whitish-gray. It was hot as summer. Far in the distance I heard bird calls, curlew-like and mournful, but saw no birds. It was an utterly empty landscape, with nothing looming on its horizon. I opened my hand and saw that the pebble was a piece of amber shaped like a head. The face's profile, with its very straight nose, was recognizable, but this amber pebble was particular for the marked rearward curve, which in my dream immediately summoned to my hands how it felt to hold M.'s head near the end of his illness, the frightening palpability of his skull's every detail under his skin. I had one last thought in my dream, while waking: it was the memory stored in my hands that had turned the pebble into head-shaped amber.

Later I thought about my amber necklace from childhood, which for a long time was the most beautiful thing in the world to me. These edgeless, irregularly formed drops of amber—with their inclusions, recognizable as small written messages or shadows of messages in the yellow glow of the stones' seeming transparency—supplanted marbles and their undeciphered mysteries. I had received the necklace from a distant, vaguely related aunt, who had spent her youth in Königsberg. Every story she told about this place revolved around the extreme coldness that prevailed there in winter, which caused the waves to freeze in the middle of the surf and stand motionless at the water's edge, with delicate spired ends of frozen spray arching over the snowy beach, until weeks or even months later a thaw would set in. The image of spray, frozen into a lace-like web, was forever accompanied by a quiet, high-pitched humming and tinkling, and I couldn't bear to imagine what a sad sight it might have been, when a thaw set in and this beauty—with the wind's quiet, incessant whirring and singing hovering around it—collapsed inward with the sound of shattering glass. Snow always fell in these Königsberg stories, the world lay quiet and still in a winter fairy tale—I couldn't have imagined it any other way. And yet, there must have been other seasons as well, because along with the necklace came a tale: during autumn and spring storms above all, the Baltic Sea cast amber, as if with colossal hands, onto the white sand near Königsberg. Once, not long after I was given the necklace, we made a midday stop in a small town on the Po on a trip to Italy. We had watched the river from a bridge and afterwards sat in a tavern garden at the foot of the embankment. My father told a story about amber, which led far away from Königsberg and the Baltic Sea. It was the story of Phaeton, who, in an impetuous attempt to drive the sun chariot, gave his horses the reins and set fire to half the world, stopped only by Zeus, who killed him with a lightning bolt. Phaeton plunged into a river—the Po River, according to my father, even if it bears a different name in the legend. Phaeton's sisters stood crying by the riverbank. Their grief transformed them into poplars, and their tears became drops of amber. I saw the poplars of the Bassa Padana and the river, but nothing about this environment could be reconciled with the fairy tale of snow and ice called Königsberg, and that unsettled me temporarily.

The legend of fallen Phaeton's sisters' tears is anchored in the Po delta, in this vast terrain on swaying ground, traversed by river courses that lead to the sea and saline waters, which grasp inland like fingers reaching from the sea. In a Ferrara museum I had seen the artefacts of Spina and a bit of time passed before

I realized what the name reminded me of. I hadn't expected to find the Etruscans here; they had hitherto belonged in my memory-landscapes of central Italy, far from Ferrara and its environs. The Bassa Padana was a land of passage—an overnight stay or two came to my mind. There were no excavation sites to visit. Perhaps that was the reason behind my clueless fondness for the region, which I had so often watched pass me by, untrodden and inaccessible, like a film about uneventfulness. But in the Ferrara museum *palazzo*, on a bitter cold Sunday I learned that the eastern plain lying before the city had once been settled by Etruscans—a trade city and its *necropolis*, buried beneath sand and marsh and gravel, in the struggle between land and sea. I read that the Etruscans came to this plain east of the mountains after the Picentes, a tribe I had never heard of, which had followed the call of the woodpecker, hence the name, southeast, where they settled. In my mind it could only be the green woodpecker. I well understood the Picentes who let themselves be led to a different region, ensnared by this distraught tone, whose author took pains to remain hidden. And then, while looking at the coarse-grained photos of the excavation, it also occurred to me that my father had spoken of this place with a kind of promise, twenty-five years earlier in Trieste. I wandered along the glass cases and beheld the beautiful objects meant to keep the dead company: toys made of animal bones for children, tiny turned stone spindles for women, dishes of all sizes depicting festivities and battles, decorative bangles and rings. Colored glass came along later—forerunners to mosaics, with their watery greens and blues, their soft, pastel colors, translucent not transparent, committed to the light in silent colors, without radiance. You can see the delight that those preparing the dead for their journey took in these objects—the delight that they were meant to elicit in the dead themselves, when they opened their eyes in the underworld, or rose from the ashes. Pure testimonies of love for the dead, the departed, for those who had traveled on ahead. Even later than glass, amber was added to the treasures—a commodity, small tears fished from the Po delta. When the Etruscans first turned it in their hands, held it against the light, felt it on their skin, this mysterious resin stone that came from a sea they certainly couldn't have dreamed of might have eclipsed all other valuable and precious things, so for a time it became an object of great promise, which they gave their dead to take with them.

I looked out of the window of the last hall onto the garden behind the *palazzo*. Pruned beech trees, cypresses, and bare pergolas—everything was dark blue for the freezing cold, while in the west the sun set a misty red. I headed back to the apartment and walked through the street where Bassani grew up. The house had a memorial plaque, and although it must have been inhabited, not a single window glowed with light. Against a pale blue-turquoise evening sky, the jutting branches of a tree were stiff, sharp and black. It towered above the wall. Hanging from a branch was a single frozen pomegranate, and I could picture how shriveled it must have been, after the cold nights that followed these raw days. And there was a bird's nest between its branches; like a darkening rank growth, it hung in the lower crown, somewhat crooked, as if already wrenched by the wind; half-hovering, it lingered in the evening, which was motionless for the cold. *Il nido è in tavola!* I heard the mother in Passolini's *The Hawks and the Sparrows* shouting. Her children have nothing to eat and she has boiled a bird's nest. The man at the frugally appointed table eats the nest and, in my memory, he always wears a cloth spread over his head, like the diners of small ortolans, caught by bird hunters in summer. Why do they eat beneath the cloth?—a perfectly reasonable question. The answer: so that God cannot see them.

Marshaling Yard

FERRARA IS DIFFICULT TO GRASP. The narrow lanes in winter light often led to unexpected locations, and on the shifting red and brown tones of facades, what the light revealed about the time of day was unreliable; the blend of quiet northernness and a presage of sharp, deep shadows in the glaring heat of other seasons was dizzying. A sobriety lay over everything, a reticence, almost reminiscent of Ottoman cities: gardens were to be surmised, the depths of houses divined, all their magnificence held behind closed gates and modest facades. On my last morning in Ferrara, I visited the Po di Volano, the river offshoot that grazes the city's southern side, surrounded by walls and through-streets—a border to everything suburban, to the outskirts, a dividing line between the shielded city and the few industrial areas found there between fraying settlements. It was a bitter cold early morning. On the bank with its back to the sun, small ice crusts had formed on the drooping branches of waterside bushes. The river had been straightened up to the city's height and thus appeared more like a canal, a functional body of water, which was perhaps still navigable and used for a stretch, until it finally lost itself in the delta behind Codigoro and flowed into the lagoon where Edgardo Limentani had watched the heron die. The street across Via Pomposa up to the sea would still be the same today—foggy on winter evenings, when dampness rose from the *Bonifiche*, from the sections of drained land pervaded by ditches and canals, infiltrated by the Po's thousands of small, desolate arms.

Away from the river, I ended up on Via Piangipane, the street of bread and tears, as I read it; what a name for a street that previously housed a prison. Although it lay within the city's walls, it was visibly pushed to its outermost edge and there was something inherently out of bounds about it, something shunned—a quarter one wanted nothing to do with. Here and there brownfields abutted the road behind rusty fences, and the houses were a half or a quarter new construction, perhaps with old huts tucked away at their cores. Now they seemed to do their utmost to be respectable; dogs barked behind gates, a Chinese family stepped out of a car. Between the houses were small shops—a nail salon, a takeaway pizzeria with standing counters, without customers at this early hour. The prison was a long brick building, its lowermost windows still barred. Women would have lined up here at the portal, begging for news, bringing food, bribing prison guards with cheese, eel and wine—to pass on letters, perhaps even a book or cigarettes. The sidewalk in front of the portal was practically made for protestors, for the helpless; barren and empty, in summer it was probably insufferably hot. The prison of Ferrara no longer harbored prisoners; flanked by strips of wild fallow land—perhaps former vegetable gardens, where the inmates had to work—the building was now adorned with a menorah, hung askew, which declared it a Jewish museum. It brought the cleanness of the facade, the intactness of the windows, the new respectability of the street, entirely adapted to the disused jail, into a framework in place for emptiness. It was a sad sight in its maladroit solicitude, which might have sent some viewers fleeing back to the pretty lanes farther uptown. Behind the prison, beyond the city wall, was the small port of Ferrara: a narrow basin, once used for fishing boats and barges, today used for pleasure boats, now in hibernation. The small square next to the harbor basin had surely been a place to trade, to haggle, a breach in the permeability, where the wall might have been climbed and vanquished with a secrecy greater than that of the country boys at Punta della Montagnola. The bus station now occupied the gap between harbor and rampart, an indecisive area that was animated in the morning by arrivals, mostly women with large bags who stepped off the regional buses in a rush, their heads sunken against the cold, and walked to work. In the blue information-and-tickets window a tiny Christmas tree, spray-painted silver, still blinked, and the employee stood at the rear door, smoking with the bus drivers on cigarette break. Behind the next bend of the city wall was the train station, forming an acute triangle with the prison and the harbor, which despite the city wall stood out from serious and austere Ferrara, wanted to be something different—a piece of city with traces of the interwar period in its apartment blocks, in its cracked sidewalks, where passersby, wrapped in scarves against the cold, clasped their briefcases, struggling to make it to the train station on time. At the edge of the triangle, ascending like a throne was the sports stadium, perhaps still a central place for workers and lower-ranking employees who lived in the apartment blocks. Tired and shying from the cold, residents walking their dogs shuffled past the stadium's numbered entrance doors, greeting one another with brief nods, breathing fragments of words into their scarves, while their old asthmatic dogs, hoping for a hasty return home from the frost, relieved themselves between pieces of trash blown by the wind into corners under the stands. At the Porta Po I returned to the rampart. The street crossings with grassy areas, streaked by paths; the gas stations, businesses, and apartment buildings on the network of arterial roads; the brick building visible in the distance at the edge of the train station grounds, which must have been a former freight rail station—all the casual activity, laundry flapping on balconies, young men lingering on street corners, the two idle police-men, who stared into the distance, suddenly reminded me of the Italy of my childhood, of my childhood in general, of an approximate hope connected to the light, to the vastness, to not knowing where unfamiliar arterial roads would lead into the countryside, a hope that was bound to the Bassa Padana's clipped horizon and opened up in small, narrow interstices out-side the city. Central Europe is full of similar freight and goods stations, of crumbling times in the wide strips of several un-used tracks—goldenrod, corn poppies, and chicory blooming between them. Full of brick sheds with signs corroded by rust. *Freight office* was written on one such damaged sign at the train station near where I grew up—a flat, windowless building that was always wrapped in a burnt smell, made of dark clinker-bricks with a high platform, behind which the iron *slidi*ng gates occasionally stood open, offering a view into a gruesomely dark depth. The marshaling yard from the story of the Finzi-Conti-nis and Micòl's recollection of the sound of trains, *slidi*ng back and forth, which she could hear from her window as a child, had blended over the years with my own memories of listening,

half-anxious, half-curious, for trains in the dark—this mixture
of horror and hope that was connected to the echo of trains,
roaring through the night along the Rhine. For days in Ferrara
I had followed the map of fiction, attempting to spin threads
between place names, cardinal directions, quotes, and only now,
upon realizing that my own memories had blended with what
I'd read about listening out for shunting trains, only now, after
walking along the city wall and through the streets that swerved
from the Corso Ercole I d'Este, after pacing Via Arianuova and
attempting in my head to locate the garden, only now did I understand that the place in the story is a commemorative place,
whose paths and perspectives followed rules that I as a foreigner,
decades later, couldn't understand. It was a place that could be
found only by sensing its absence, by recalling what was lost;
therein lay its reality, sovereign to every walkable and touchable
place in Ferrara.

That afternoon I took a bus to the *lidi*. I arrived too early at
the stop across from the train station and stood in a bar with a
view of the street, clinging to a cup of coffee. Guests came and
went, the television was on, boxes of chocolates in Christmas
packaging and leftover Panettoni glittered in the light of the
low sun. Students gathered outside, along with tired women
in thick quilted coats, who, having finished their shifts, now
wanted to go home, and three African women who had sealed
themselves off from the world with headphones. The bus was
full of schoolchildren, who got off past Ostellato at requested
stops in open land, next to strips of reeds, poplar groves, willow
copses, where someone in a car waited to drive them home to
one of the widely scattered farmsteads or bleak duplex houses.
The bus emptied slowly, canvassing the deserted seaside resorts

on a sluggish drive through long roads outside Comacchio, past rows of shuttered houses, their rooms turning dark forlornly behind shopfronts. Where did the schoolchildren live? What was keeping them in these empty places? What did their parents do for work? Only in Porto Garibaldi, Ferrara's old seaside port, was a little bit of life visible between boat workshops, a filter bed, and a long, boat-lined canal leading to the sea. I exited at Lido degli Estensi. Here began the pine forests outside Ravenna, clipped down to artificial small groves between the summer housing estates, yet tall, severe, and nearly black now in winter. Behind a parking lot I saw the sea, light blue beneath the sky, which was already preparing for twilight.

Salt Pans

BEHIND THE SEASIDE RESORTS lay the Valli di Comacchio, more water than land—canals, ditches, and basins with narrow paths running alongside them, southern offshoots of the delta between Po di Volano and the Reno river. In former times they extracted salt here, just as they had across the Adriatic curve, in Strunjan, between Piran and Koper, where years ago on a hot April day I wandered around with M., and among the fissured, dried-out planes and basins, divided by low grass walls, I experienced an emptiness and a stillness unlike in any other place I'd been. Everything appeared as if it had moved unattainably far away—the cliffs that concealed Piran, the houses above the escarpment in Strunjan, the vineyards, even the sea at our backs. Nothing counted anymore except the rugged ground, the still water surfaces in ditches, the windowless small huts. The word *zone* popped into my head then—a salt zone—where time passes differently, where altogether different va*lidi*ties prevail. Far and wide, we saw no one. It was afternoon and the air shimmered over the terrain in the unusual heat beneath a whitish, clouded sky; as we headed back to Piran, along the cliffs, beneath the threat of falling rocks, we both observed having lost all sense of the time that had lapsed while we wandered around the salt fields.

I had ended up here by accident, in an accommodation with a view to a half-wilted potted palm tree, reeds, willow bushes, and ample sky. Far from the coastal road, inland of the deserted seaside resorts. The owners had given up all hope for livelihood—a slight bitterness was in the air, a melancholy astonishment that the desolation of the seaside destinations and view to the emptiness of salt pans in winter could leave the viewer overwhelmed not only by doubt. The owners' family lived in a house secured by an enormous metal gate, with small guest cabins flanking the property. The house and cabins lay like random objects at the edge of this emptiness; to the south a plowed field extended behind a water ditch, and in the distance I could make out a farmhouse, surrounded by poplars. Acacias, alders, willows, poplars: trees found in all regions that sway as a thin layer above the groundwater, which can rise at any moment in grooves, furrows, small hollows, and suddenly mirror the sky. What thrives here roots claw-like; trees grow quickly, as if fearing the water might cause them to vanish in the marshes. Poplars shoot in such a rush that they don't have time to form growth rings and become hollow with accumulating summers. Their hollows become habitats for all apparitions that emerge in the ground fog: Erl-King-like creatures and their retinue. Tempests have it easy with the gangly, hollowed trees. They topple, block paths, cause disasters; the ghosts become homeless and resettle in other woods. Poplar wood had always appeared splintered and inferior to me, until I eventually noticed how many pictures painted on poplar panel have outlived the centuries. Fra Angelico, whose blue could send my father into raptures—whose blue he could go on and on about—painted on poplar, and I wondered briefly if some quality of the poplar was behind this particular, enrapturing blue.

In front of the guesthouse was an open terrain, pervaded by silt furrows, which appeared to function as a campsite in summer. Small lopsided information boards protruded from the ground, and along a driveway, silt-splattered signs pointed to a reception area, which was impossible to locate. A dirt-crusted backhoe now stood on this stretch of land, as if a long time ago someone had abandoned a big project and forgotten the machine. Next to the backhoe was a covered terrace with tables and benches, a Christmas decoration still jammed into the edge of its roof, recognizable up close as a reindeer-drawn sled.

The owner half-heartedly extolled the red flamingos that he said lived in waters not far from the guesthouse. I headed out for a short walk. It was late afternoon, the sun was low, and it was becoming very cold. I followed a small path between rustling reeds, which rose like whitish small forests from the ditches. The path led to a large, square body of water, an artificial basin, like a small lake. A brittle jetty rose from the grass-covered edge above the water. Crammed into a bush at the edge of the path was the crooked frame of a rocking bench, and a bit farther, half-sunken into the earth, were two white garden chairs: battered remains of an attempted idyll that had no place there.

I followed the path around the water. The trail formed a kind of wide embankment, with more watercourses, ditches or canals on the other side, the water not still but flowing slowly, moved by an exchange with other ditches and basins, a branched system designed to drain the ground. Unlike Strunjan, in Comacchio's salt pans neither a developed hillside nor distant cliffs were in sight—the land spread flat in every direction. Standing on slightly raised turf, one would see to the north, west, and south nothing but the blurring pattern of water and

strips of grass, interrupted here and there by partly dilapidated buildings, as high as two-story houses, with few windows:
perhaps salt storehouses or former appliance sheds, workspaces
where the salt was sifted and filled into barrels. I forgot all I
had learned about salt production from the old black-and-white
film in the Piran museum—only the overexposure from the
glaring sun, the hunched posture of the women with baskets
and sifters, the flickering from the damaged sections of celluloid
and the impression of hard work remained with me, along with
a sensation of rawness I had while watching the bare hands and
feet of workers handling large quantities of salt. In addition to
these few buildings, the horizon at Comacchio's salt pans was
interrupted by some thick shrubs, which in the years since salt
farming was abandoned had been able to take root: stunted, low
trees, reeds, willow thickets, feathery tamarisks. The grounds
were much larger than in Strunjan but, already long-weaned
from salt production, had become a wilderness for birds not
needing the cover of trees. The sun set and the sky vaulted the
landscape in layers of orange, red, purple and lilac, reflecting in
the strips of water, framed by ever blacker lines of land. Birds
crossed the sky, arrow-like signs, black against the darkening
red. In the bushes at the edge of the ponds, marsh tits uttered
their quiet sounds of alarm. I heard teals on the other side of
the basin, peewits in the distance, and later night herons, too.

When I returned, the Christmas decoration on the covered
terrace was lit, the reindeer sled blinked white and glittering,
yet much too small and pale to be seen as an invitation by anyone passing on the street. Who would accept an invitation into
this emptiness, anyway? The owner loitered about the cabins
and asked if I'd like to ride with his family to Porto Garibaldi,

to shop. Perhaps I made them feel uneasy, or they didn't want to leave me behind all alone. I accepted the invitation. I was interested in Porto Garibaldi, which from the bus appeared to be a kind of intermediate place, separate from all intention and control, an animated junction of transient things, an agglomeration of preliminarities, of the kind that often—as if it were a law of physics—forms to guard the core of places, whose need of protection had gone unnoticed. The canal, the long rows of moored fishing boats, the shipyards and parking areas with countless strewn boats that remained here, left to winter—all that, in a comforting way, bespoke of a life beyond the bleak views of seaside resorts.

But now it was dark, and little of Porto Garibaldi could be seen. The route was short and confusing, on a road frequented mainly by trucks, past halfheartedly flickering neon signs of businesses closed for winter or altogether abandoned, on labyrinthine roundabouts onto the parking lot of a supermarket. To the west, where a reddish stripe of sky was about to be engulfed by night, a large darkness opened up above the land. I felt small and foreign, at a loss for phrases appropriate to this unexpected family outing. The young daughters who sat next to me silently played with their cell phones. I kept my dislike of supermarkets to myself and made a few purchases. Arriving back at home, the terrain where I had my shelter in the cover of the blinking Christmas illumination now appeared to be even more of a nameless island than it had in daylight that afternoon.

I slept little the first night. A wind arose, rustling the limply drooping leaves of the dried potted palm tree outside. From the salt pans I heard fretful birdcalls. Not only the night herons called, but also ducks, small-voiced songbirds, which surely sat hidden deep in their bush, and a hoarse, guttural bird whose call I couldn't identify. Perhaps there were small predators, silent slinkers. I couldn't imagine foxes here; it was a land without cover. I stood at the door and listened into the night. The blinking flicker of the reindeer sleigh only blinded, and did not diffuse enough light for recognizing anything. The darkness was too deep. Nothing unsettled me. The nameless island was a good place. The rustling of the palm, the whispering of the dry reed stalks, the birdcalls—all this was a new language, which wanted to be learned.

Kingfishers

IN THE MORNING the Christmas decoration was no longer blinking. Perhaps the children were tasked with turning the reindeer sled off before school and back on again once they arrived home, and I wondered if they had a name for this object. The father surely took care of mounting and dismounting it, and the reindeer must have spent most of the year in a dark corner of the garage, possibly in the company of other, long out of use Christmas paraphernalia. The girls had outgrown the decorations and now relied on the light cast by their cell phones. Upon my arrival I noticed, in a corner between the house and garage, two small toys: pink plastic shopping carts which appeared to be wedged, as if they'd collided into the wall, half-broken, with leaves and all kinds of trash gathered inside, as if they'd sat in this spot for some time. A pink dollhouse-version of the battered metal shopping carts in East London side streets that teenagers, full of defiance and anger, would ram together and send flying into buildings with such fury that no resident could pull them apart, much less remove them. Within a few weeks they would fill with trash, bulky memorials for bitter evenings regardless of the season, and no one gave them any further thought.

The night had been very cold, and the furrowed mire on the campground was frozen. Lined by tall, pallid canebrake, the water ditch, with the path leading to the basin above it, was covered in a thin layer of ice, not yet fully sealed. Beneath the ice I saw a white outline: a dead bird, buried under a translucent cover. Lying on its back, the bird was not large, like a pigeon or perhaps a tern, and its feathers shone a blunt gray-white, due perhaps only to the brownish murky water below the ice. I could make out its spread wings, the tips of the pinions—ragged in death—its head, turned slightly to one side, and the breast. Yesterday I had stood in the same spot, looking at the farmhouse across the field, and noticed nothing in the small stream. Could it, in the night, before frost set in, have plummeted from a height into the ditch, just like that, with outspread wings? Years ago, M. and I saw a bird beneath thick ice in a pond. M. pointed out the whitish shadows to me; he couldn't make out what it was. The bird had lain nearby at the marshy edge, between tall reeds, which receded somewhat there, as if the canebrake had parted to make room for the bird. The ice was much thicker there than here, as if a frost had prevailed for weeks, and I presumed that the bird had been shot. The hunter might not have found him, or had to take flight after shooting because he lacked a permit or feared someone. Evidently, no one hunted here.

The basin lake lay like glass. On its far end a small boat swayed, and male voices sounded across the still water surface. The boat's motor was left running, reclining at an alarmingly crooked angle, and the men laughed loudly, shouting brief sentences to one another. In the middle of the water the motor fell silent and the men inspected something marked by small buoys. The boat wobbled back and forth, the men tugged lines and navigated using sticks; they must have laid fish traps or nets.

They moved closer to the banks, heading back to the buoys in a zigzagging route incomprehensible to outsiders. When the motor kept silent, the air buzzed with birdcalls. Flocks of marsh tits busied themselves in the bushes at the water's edge, their long tailfeathers twitching between the tendrils, and on the electrical cable between two crooked masts sat six, maybe seven young herons. Black ducks paddled in small groups along the edge of the basin, expelling doleful sounds. The fence following the path was buckled and bent to the ground in a number of places. Behind it rose a somewhat higher-lying dam from which, looking inland, one saw nothing but strips of land and water up to the horizon. In the next body of water I discovered the flamingos that the guest house owner had spoken of. They had flocked together way off on the far side; perhaps that's how they behave in the cold. Flamingos were somehow exotic in my mind, incongruous with the world of birds I was familiar with. Their Italian name, which I had learned the day before, was *fenicottero*, the phoenix still resonating within it—a bird at home nowhere but in legend. Nor did they appear to be native here, even if they had learned to put up with an occasional frost. From a distance they were a swimming accumulation of pink pillows, illegally dumped trash, discarded props from long forgotten pleasures, now waiting to be carried on by the wind. Seen up close, it became apparent that the birds were not swimming but standing on their very tall, thin legs in the shallow water. Most had their heads submerged, searching for food, their necks serpentine. Although they hardly moved and only a few elongated their necks as if to catch some scent, they radiated nervousness. Their rosy color stood out against the landscape of gray, brown, and matte-green tones, and this discord of colors produced a restlessness; in spring, between the musty pink-hued tamarisks, it would be different. Beneath a higher, brighter sky, surrounded by greenery, the sight might even offer a certain grace. Suddenly, without my having made a sound, the entire flock raised their heads. I imagined they had communicated underwater somehow, perhaps with leg movements, brief wag-waves of the body, which caused the water to vibrate in a manner that gave warning to all. Three birds rose up, revealing beneath their wide, unfolded wings the red feathers and black undersides—sharp, determined colors, which stood in a strange contradiction to their grubby pink wing coverts. The three envoys flew in my direction, their necks elongated forward, their long pink legs outstretched; they uttered squeaking sounds, brief and bright, which I wouldn't have thought them capable of. I had expected something stronger, a kind of crane's cry, but a flamingo's neck lacks the muscles and agility of a crane's throat, and so they now produced these feeble, unmelodic sounds, while their companions who remained in the water watched them in silence. The birds flew toward me but then turned away, alighting in the middle of the shallow basin and sticking their heads in the water, while the rest of the flock in the distance moved to another location. The brief nervousness of the flamingos had spread to the ducks, which, close to shore, rocked in the water. A small fight broke out between them, with shrill quacking and a lapping of the waves; then it was silent.

The air smelled of salt and earth, of sea and land at the same time. The house with the small cabins lay dark-pink in this ashy, pale landscape, friendly despite its tall gates. Behind the house was an electrical substation with a long building and masts with short, diverging arms, flung upwards as if in panic-stricken and headless flight, and drum-like equipment, thick wires and cables behind a fence, secured by an alarm. Extending behind it was the street we had taken to Porto Garibaldi. Now an unbroken stream of large trucks passed down it, but no sound reached this backcountry from there, as if the road belonged to a different world. Besides the birdcalls, and the occasional roaring of the launch navigated by the three fishermen, it was completely silent and the endless train of cars ran like a film, a silent backdrop to this land in the care of the pink house—a land of water, grass, sparse bushes and birds—and then everything seemed to split into film tracks: the house, the ponds and birds lay in the middle, and the field with the farmhouse, surrounded by poplars, stretched to the right as a side track, with a car silently driving away beside it, and behind it, also obeying its own laws of time and sound, the road with the trucks. When I squinted, I thought I recognized a different light above the field and farmhouse, distinct from both the road and my island—even the graininess of the colors and surfaces was different there than where I walked, in this mellow air and this whitish, frosted light beneath an overcast sky.

Presepio

ONE AFTERNOON the owner offered to take me along to Comacchio. *Via Romea*, he explained in an apologetic tone as we sat for a while, waiting for a break in the traffic on the busy road. Via Romea sounded beautiful and ancient, like journeys and pilgrimages, like Rome. Now the route was above all subject to trucks commuting along the Adriatic coast, between Rimini and Venice, through the vast, staggering Po delta. The roadsides were littered with trash. The license plates on most trucks traveling in the opposite direction indicated Croatia, Serbia, Turkey, even though the writing on the sides of the trucks suggested different origins—German meat, Dutch plastics—which surely were unconnected to the routes and orders in the trucks, the hawked inventory from somewhere else. The carriers were probably just fine with these misleading advertisements.

It was not far to Comacchio. The street led past brownfields, factories lying idle and abandoned businesses behind seaside resorts. On one side, now and again we had a view to a body of water with fishing boats. The small city lay obsolete behind bypasses under the light-gray winter sky.

Everywhere in Italy, around Christmas one encountered manger scenes: some were like large panoramas in glass cases, with countless figures, humans, animals and landscapes, while others resembled clumsy dollhouses with children's room fittings. *Presepi* belonged to the churches, but here in Comacchio at every turn one came across life-sized dolls arranged in Christmas scenes: holy families in boats under bridges, beneath archways and on small squares. In the empty small city, where only a pair of hungry cats ranged the sidewalks along the canals, these group pictures were eerie in their lifeless sweetness, in the way their backs were turned to the shuttered facades and faded signs on walls and in windows. Like mock-inhabitants, the *presepi* figures stood in the damp shadows of bridges, on ledges where the wind sharpened, in corners where the wind dulled. Awkward distractions from the many weathered signs announcing houses for sale. There was a museum whose proud showpiece was a Roman ship, hoisted from the mire. And I was told by a fishmonger, who stood lost in thought in his empty, neon-lit shop, as I approached, that there was a tourist attraction dedicated to the art of preparing eel. He wore a washable apron over his anorak and rubber boots, and gazed out onto the empty square behind which ran the bypass road. The fishmonger, who had or was about to experience, a long series of dreary days, optimistically seized the opportunity to address me as I stood beholding his display. While my gaze wandered across the fish counter, forsaken of all goods, and over to the shelves filled with preserved food—cans and jars, their contents undefinable—he extolled, with sweeping gestures, all he had to offer. Once he sensed he wouldn't have any luck, he took out a leaflet for an exhibition of objects concerning local customs and eel handling. Enthusiastic, he pointed to the pictures of the large vats where eels were boiled in great quantities. I shuddered and left the fishmonger to his disappointment.

There was little to see in Comacchio. In summer it might have been friendlier, the streets livelier, the houses more colorful. Radio music would sound from wide-open windows, the doors would be open, dogs would lie out in the sun, and the curtains made from colorful plastic cords would move in the draft. Tourists would amble along the canals, musicians might play in the small squares and street cafes would open their doors. The wind would blow, soft and warm from the sea, and perhaps, at a foreseeable time and accompanied by a signal, audible for miles, it would mean: The eels are coming! Behind the storefronts of some houses, fishermen might now be dozing away the winter, dreaming of these times. I stood still and stared through a large window, in the manner of Jane Eyre staring into the redemptive cottage on the moor. It was a sports bar with men crowded around a pool table; a television was on and guests stood at the bar in small groups, talking, drinking coffee or beer, looking up at the screen. It looked like warmth, like life, like a scene that I could have witnessed in Italy during my childhood. In the middle of this lost, abandoned small town in the Po delta, a window opened into a world, familiar from a distance, which had never been accessible to me, frequented only by men; briefly it consoled me over what I had experienced, while I wandered through the northern Italian streets during these weeks, vaguely and unnamed, as absence and loss.

The guest house owner was in good spirits when I met him back at the car; perhaps he had received welcome news, a moratorium, or a tip on getting a small tax break. In any case, he had left his bulging briefcase behind somewhere, and this alone might have been enough to send him walking with a lighter step through the winter day. He took a long detour around the Valli. The road was separated from the water by a levee; over the back of the levee towered fishing hut roofs and obliquely positioned rods with nets stretched between them, which contrasted darkly against the whitish-gray sky. On the other side, inland, fields sprawled, interrupted by neither a village nor a hamlet—the *bonifiche* where digs had revealed the *necropolis* of Spina. Draining the land had broken the backbone of the delta people, the guesthouse owner suddenly explained. They were water people, not land people; here they were not made to farm. Since the draining, misfortune had spread across the region. He evidently believed that one's relationship to water and land was ruled by genetic disposition. Because he lost the water and also his profession, his grandfather became a fascist. But one of the good fascists, he quickly added, emphatically. I didn't know what a good fascist was, and suddenly, I felt small and uneasy next to this stranger, who, by telling me his story and taking me to Comacchio surely had wanted to do something kind. His grandfather had been mayor, a good human, he repeated emphatically, whom the communists helped flee to Sicily to escape detention. I learned several things on this ride between water, now dressed in the gradually dusking afternoon sky, and the plowed winter fields, which in summer might appear even more desolate than they did now, with slowly shadowed furrows extending through the bright-brown earth into the distance, where empty tree crowns hung as low clouds on the horizon. The *Linea Gotica* ran not far from here, behind Ravenna. Around the Valli di Comacchio, a fascist recalcitrant population had held out longer than in any other part of Italy— whole machine-gun nests were dug out after 1945, and even his, the guesthouse owner's childhood, was overshadowed by the discovery of weapons and ammunition in the country, along with planned and unplanned explosions, which cost many their limbs and some their lives. The landscape became a different color, and Edgardo Limentani's winter day between Codigoro and Volano, only a few kilometers north of here, suddenly lay in a different light, cast by history.

It was already getting dark when we crossed the Reno, which flowed into the Adriatic Sea south of the Valli di Comacchio. The delta came to an end here. The guesthouse owner's flow of words trickled out. But he wanted to show me one more thing. A town sign for "Piangipane" emerged on the side of the road, and a few minutes later we stopped in front of a cemetery. Uniform rows of identical white gravestones projected into the deep-gray twilight. Only these groups of gravestones could be made out and as we departed our headlights briefly illuminated a Star of David on the entrance post. The gravestones, having sunk into the evening behind us, looked like milestones along this border known as the *Linea Gotica*, which the landscape remained mindful of; it pervaded northern Italians' conversations and ran through their stories. In the spring before M.'s death, on the anniversary of the *liberazione*, we heard a gruff waiter singing resistance songs in Berlin. But only ones that were sung south of this line, he emphasized. He sang *O Vanna mia*, claiming it was about his grandparents, and M. was moved.

We drove home on Via Romea. Traffic was sparser than it had been during the day. To the right and left of the street, small woods grew dark, while our headlights grazed tall pines and from time to time small bodies of water, too; occasionally a wider view of the flatland opened up to the sea, which was dabbed by tiny isolated lights. On the left I could sense the

Valli, the night's large, open mouth. I was brushed by a memory of traveling with M. across Crimea by night, when all points of orientation dissolved. Meanwhile the guesthouse owner spoke of the years he had spent with his family on a catamaran off the Antilles. Here in this flat, wintery, war-damaged delta-land, his story seemed so implausible that I at first hesitated to believe him.

During that sleepless night, I contemplated the connection between the town, the cemetery and the road leading to the former prison in Ferrara. Was there really a bread-and-tears village here, in this country absorbed by evening, behind Ravenna? Or had it lent its name, only seemingly related to bread and tears, to the road?

Man Canal

I BECAME ACCUSTOMED to the wind's nightly rustling in the potted palm and the birdcalls in the dark. The disquiet of my first
night did not repeat. Occasionally I heard night herons and
peewits, at times sharper, brighter sounds, as well; I didn't know
if flamingos were night singers or how far their calls would
carry. Either way, what I heard at night was always birds, never
other animals. During the days I wandered around the salt basins and always discovered the terrain anew in the varying light
of winter days. Each morning I saw young herons sitting on the
power cables. They were bold and stayed put for a long time as
I approached. At some point they would fly off in groups of two
or three, unfolding white wings and white tailfeathers unexpectedly from under their brownish cover. Usually one would
stay behind until I was almost under the cable. A test of courage, of sorts, suited to their great serenity. I previously hadn't
seen herons in larger groups—usually they were alone, sometimes in pairs; gray herons by flowing waters, on rare occasions
little egrets in estuaries, unblinking, as if petrified. These young
birds, too, sat entirely still in a row, without visibly communi-
cating with one another. Not a single feather quivered on the
backs of their heads. Up there on the cable they all resembled—

equally in head and body—the ancient Egyptian depictions of herons that had lent the deity Bennu his form. When the day drew to an end, the Egyptian heron god would transform into a falcon, flying into the setting sun, only to be reborn a heron at dawn. A touch of the phoenix could be recognized in the herons living here in the vicinity of *fenicotteri*. But I never saw falcons in the salt pans.

The three fishermen were out in their boats daily. They were always inspecting something, never hauled a catch or fished. Past a few ditches, there was a long building which resembled a low stable. I had learned that the semi-dilapidated brick buildings in the salt pans are called *casoni* and formerly housed the salt-field workers. The stable-like building once also served as a lodging, located at the end of a tract with small basins, with wider paths between them. Every day an open delivery vehicle was parked there and someone in a glowing yellow safety vest would pace the grounds, bending down here and there over something, squatting to inspect it up close. Usually I could also make out a white bird somewhere on the grounds. Each morning I searched for it as if looking at a puzzle picture. It stood motionless and alone, white like an egret, but from this distance I couldn't determine anything else. Perhaps it was hiding from the man, playing a game.

The path abutted a narrow road, lined by an embankment; on the other side of this embankment the water basin was connected to a canal and the Valli. A small bridge led across the canal. Men lingered there, catching mussels. Their cars were parked on the wayside, they smoked, laughed, and carried on while handling their nets, their traps and devices. The dam rose behind them, leading to another network of ditches, canals, and basins. Between winter-rusted blackberry vines one looked past the water's still surface to Comacchio in the north and, in the other direction, past the guest house and substation onto the parasol pines, which stood on the other side of Via Romea, like clouds above the houses of Lido di Spina. Rising above the yellowed reeds not far from the guest house was an old watchtower, a relic from centuries when salt reigned, a lookout where the area was once scanned for salt thieves.

On the dam a path followed the canal toward the sea. The embankment was overgrown with thorn bushes, entangled with litter, and here and there trails led down to the water's edge where small sitting areas had been leveled into the land and cleared of vines. On the other side was a row of fishing huts, the poles and nets standing rigid in the air, waiting for schools of eels, setting about on their journey home. Here one could study the ancient mechanics of the nets being dipped down into the water and lifted back out with a ball of anxiously writhing eels, thus deprived of their return home. Somewhat farther, on the opposite side of the canal, I could recognize flat, shed-like houses among the trees, and a row of wire kennels with dogs clamoring inside, throwing themselves furiously against the walls of their cages. Surrounding the kennels was a kind of scrapyard with two men working inside; one shuffled over to the dogs and moved the kennel steps, which only intensified their furious cries.

I hesitated crossing Via Romea for some time. The traffic was incessant. Around the crash barriers on the bridge above the canal, bulges had formed from paper and plastic—all the packaging that truck drivers had thrown out their windows: cigarette packs and small liquor bottles, wrappers from chocolate, peanuts and condoms with Croatian, Serbian or Albanian labels.

Across the road, the canal bed widened, and at the foot of the embankment, planks led to floating fishing huts which were barely more than lean-tos on rafts, rigged together from everything imaginable. Some had small rowboats lashed to their sides, and outboard engines curved beneath thick plastic film, while fishing rods towered like the grid poles in the Valli. No one was on the dam, but bikes lay in the grass and as I took out my camera and looked through the viewfinder I noticed men on a number of rafts, standing motionless, half-hidden among their tarpaulins and devices, watching me in complete silence.

It was quiet here—even the trucks on the street were hardly audible, and the sparse gulls and terns circled, seeking without calling. Only around a boatyard and workshop on the opposite side was there a brief cacophony of metallic grating, the sputtering drone of a tool-engine starting, and an exchange of words between men, one of whom wore a suit, while the others were in workshop overalls. But ultimately this exchange of words led to laughter and slaps on the back, and the hammering, screeching and droning petered out as well. The apartment blocks and pines of Lido degli Estensi framed a large strip of fallow land, weather-torn advertisements at its edge, announcing additional new construction. The streets lay deserted; nearby, smoke rose from the chimney of a single house, with light in its windows. In winter it must be very dark in the pines. The exterior walls of the house, under the cover of trees, appeared mildewed and dirty, and the embellishments on the alpine, pseudo-carved decorative balcony and gable were torn by weather, their futility exposed.

The sun didn't shine, but the wide beach was blindingly bright. The sea lay smooth and still; swimming in the shallow waves that curled around the furrowed mouth of the canal were terns with black heads. Mourning terns? How quickly we attribute grief to the color black in nature.

Everything in this corner of the beach looked like discarded accessories from a different time, from films, from forgotten, half-remembered, lost, rejected scenes of fragmentary recollections, gathered from entire generations of travelers to Italy: the abstract concrete sculptures, the switchback slide with its sallow-red plastic embellishments leading to a tiny pool, the crooked construction site fences, the angular, awkward beach furnishings utterly absent of humans, deceptive in their functions and assaulted by time and weather, the exposed rim of the flowing canal, onto which a small cliff landscape made from excess concrete was glued. Surely, they had hoped this failed thing would remain forever underwater. But on this maltreated coast, damaged by the violent rhythm, the rushing and retreating stream of occasional residents—even here the sea remained its own master, and in the absence of cliffs to break upon, it would turn at times here, at times there, as it wished, and it now lay bare this concrete growth that had been accounted for as sunken.

Near the mouth of the canal two men were working in a boat, lifting gravel and sand from the canal and poking around in the water to measure sediments. They spoke to one another in loud, sharp words as if they were arguing and stood up, causing the boat to sway. I momentarily feared they might scuffle, but then they settled back down into their seats. A police car drove at a walking pace along the canal, turning onto the street that ran behind the beach. Both police officers stared, as if dazed, through the windshield straight ahead into the emptiness and forlornness of the bright expanse.

I again walked back on the path over the dam. I left my camera tucked away in my pocket and tried not to mind the silent figures who, half-hidden among the accumulated fixtures on their knocked together water refuges, followed me with their eyes. No one said a word, but I felt like a foreign body in that area along the canal—an unsolicited intruder who made herself witness to something between the embankment and canal, which wanted to remain hidden.

The hotel owner had gathered people around the backhoe to help, and together they evaluated the motor below the open hood. A dog jumped around them, and one of the men entertained him by throwing sticks, which the dog would retrieve. Barking, it rushed at me, an assiduous animal who wanted to impress its owner with obedient alertness; it turned back at a whistle with disappointment. Talking and wracking their brains, the men stood over the machine. They tapped, handled, flicked their cigarettes in high arcs above it, throwing the dog into a frenzy each time. The reindeer blinked in the soft-gray afternoon light—the children had forgotten their morning chore.

Spina

THE NEXT MORNING the mechanics returned to work on the backhoe. A thin crust of rime had spread across the silt and the reindeer sled was still blinking in the gray early light. This time a man sat in the backhoe cab; they exchanged words loudly and suddenly the motor sputtered on. Then it fell silent again. Wrenches shimmered matte in open toolboxes and the owner stood for a while beside the workers, watching their attempts at repair. Then he began pacing the space, as if to survey it in anticipation of resuming his project. The mechanics' dog was calmer, but began barking every time the sputtering motor petered out again. The sun rose, the fronds on the tips of the reeds turned pink, and the sky filled with a grating call, like from wild geese, without a bird in view.

I set off for the archaeological sites of Spina that I had marked on my map. Where the men had let down mussel nets, on this morning it now murmured and bubbled about the junction of the basin and the canal, as if invisible floodgates had been opened. Dogs prowled around the legs of the idle, smoking, glancing, talking men, and vigilantly kept me in their sight. A broad, flat, partly submerged marsh opened up past a bend. At its edge, in a reddish earth-colored creeping thicket,

I very clearly recognized a white bird as a little egret. Crossing a bridge, I entered a terrain that looked out onto an emptiness that presented itself as the mere beginning of an unpeopled expanse, much larger than I had expected. A landscape or the absence of a landscape opened up, which might cause one to forget that the sea, Comacchio, the Bassa Padana existed—that anything existed at all but this swaying of the water and the tiny islands of scrubby weeds, their miniscule forked stems shimmering reddish-violet in the winter sun; anything but the decaying storehouses by the salt pans, which hung like mirages in the distance, or the faint appearance of basins, dams, tiny brush groves; here we might forget that any living creatures existed at all, except birds. The flamingos stood together in large flocks. There were curlews, snipes, herons, herring gulls and great black-headed gulls, too, whose occasional mewing cut through the sky. The path became a dam between the vastness of the salt pans and the Valli and a wide canal, with treetops protruding from the lower flatland on its north side—bare willow, alder and poplar branches; behind it one could sense the flat plain of drained, unpeopled fields, where the *necropolis* of Spina had come to light.

The dam extended for kilometers—so long that I almost lost hope of ever getting anywhere. Through the sharp winter air I wandered with a dwindling awareness of the ground beneath my feet, and with every step I fell deeper into a dream, a no-man's land, a nothing land of quietly moving, coldly glittering water and billowing islands that could offer a foothold and refuge only to birds. In the bright light of that winter day, while the mountains' blue shadows moved slowly across the southwestern horizon, I felt as if I were released from the world's rules—absolved of them—and entrusted to this unknown direction that overrode my objectives. I now saw little egrets by the ditch, standing in intervals at the water's edge, white and unblinking, guardians ordered to shepherd the emptiness. Some fluttered upward when I approached, pushing forward in the air with outspread wings and retracted heads, their legs elongated stiffly backward; they vaulted forward a bit with broad wingbeats beneath dry, tuneless, rasping calls, and then alighted once again in the ditches; the thin, long crests on the backs of their heads sprung just behind them, barely perceptible, as they resumed their mute sentry, as if they always knew exactly what position to take. How do they measure the intervals, divvy up this imponderable space among themselves?

Eventually I reached a bridge over the canal, which at its far end adjoined a small country road. I must have driven there with the guest house owner along the Valli's southern edge, along the cemetery of Piangipane. There could be no other route—even if nothing to the left or right evoked our drive through that sinking twilight. Knowing that I had passed by there once before—and, at that, with someone who, like myself, came from the far side of this terrain, but, unlike myself, belonged here and was settled in this region—stabilized and comforted me in this uninhabited space and ground, which even after leaving the dam seemed to teeter beneath my feet. Lying on either side was now an agrarian landscape: massive fields, all evenly plowed, many speckled with greening winter seed. Here and there bare rows of bushes marked a boundary between fields, or a stream. Sparse groups of trees rose isolated in the landscape. Between the farmed expanses were scattered buildings, appearing in no way lived-in, but rather like sheds, barns, silos, processing sites, where the harvest from the fields might be sorted and packed. Perhaps no one wanted to live here, knowing a *necropolis* was underfoot. You might sense ghosts, calamity—stories about the uncanny events that followed attempts to settle the land might have even made rounds. Besides, everyone knew that the groundwater rose unpredictably, flooding gardens, verandas, entrances overnight, until nothing but clouds seemed to thrive in the gardens, and even the wind dared be merciless.

Tractors stood orderly and motionless, parked next to the sheds and barns. Nothing moved but a few tiny cars, which shimmied like beetles at a great distance across the dead-straight and unauthorized blocked roads between the fields. I now understood that sentence about the area's backbone breaking when the expanses of water were transformed into cultivated land, and imagined the glaring yellow of rapeseed in flower, the dirty foliage from turnip stems, the blue-green of potato plants, the dusty air of cornfields that spread out here in other seasons. The relationship between the Valli and the *bonifiche*, between the restless water world, ruled and guarded by birds, and the farmland's rigid, lifeless way of being at one's disposal, appeared hostile, the scribbling of the bare treetops like prickly fences, which drew sharper borders than those between fields, asking us to take note.

The excavation sites of the *necropoli* differed from farmland in that they were surrounded by fencing. The way in lay behind a locked gate with a sign, featuring a black halting hand—entrance prohibited. On the other side, at a distance from the narrow road was a building with closed shutters; nothing moved. On the archaeological site a path, lined by slender trees, led up to an open area, and behind bushes I spotted sheds, low buildings, tilled-brown soil. A bit farther along the fence I came to a site trailer, which had something bulky beneath foil beside it—perhaps tools, equipment that would force the handler of found objects to be cautious. Tire ruts extended across one site, just like those before the guesthouse by the salt pans, as if a large, heavy vehicle had been operated here since the last rainfall. Behind this site, traversed by tracks, a broad, empty terrain extended: bare earth, brighter than the surrounding tilled acres, perhaps because it wasn't plowed. In the distance a man suddenly appeared out of nowhere, walking along the raised earth. He wore a neon yellow safety vest and had a hat or a helmet on his head; he looked very similar to the character whom I saw daily in the salt basins and, just like him, he bent down here and there, kneeled, stood up and walked on, without turning his head. He couldn't have seen me—and even if he had seen me, he wouldn't have let me in. What business did I have there? A large flock, a billowing loose cloud of crows approached, alighting on the premises. They pecked around. A few gulls appeared, too, and circled over a neighboring field. Their gray feathers shimmered pink. The crows and gulls ascended and dipped down, never mixing, adding a glinting movement to the picture, bringing the landscape to life. They drew their crooky, grating calls across the fields; the sounds, detached from the birds' throats, hung stiffly in the air and then fell to the ground without an echo, and it might have been this absence of an echo that left me waylaid by a sadness so paralyzing it was as if I had succumbed to a state of inconsolability and never again would manage to lift a foot and leave this place. After seeing all the beautiful, precious objects in the museum vitrines in Ferrara, after recognizing the visible love for the dead in those objects, after witnessing the attentive endeavors to arrange the greatest possible well-being for the dead, this barren excavation site in the middle of an inattentive and lovelessly appointed agrarian landscape appeared coarse to me. Nothing suggested the sunken *necropolis*—one could no longer imagine paths from either funeral processions or commemorative visitors, who moved between the city of the living and the city of the dead. What could be more irreconcilable than those cities, nurtured in the faith and memory of those who had been relieved of all further service, and this terrain of the *bonifiche*—dedicated purely to utility, to exploitation, to usability. Between the *necropolis* and the plowland opened a chasm that couldn't be reconciled, similar to that between the Valli and the *bonifiche*, a tension that tipped an old equilibrium.

I felt the sharp cold that meanwhile pervaded everything despite the sun. As I set out again, the flock of crows took to the sky and the loose, buzzing, restless shadow of countless crow-bodies and wings was like a guardian cloud above me for a time whose calls even sounded gentle and encouraging. As I arrived back at the long dam along the ditch, the sunlight had already retreated from the lowest edge of the embankment and the little egrets towered above it like blueish statues. They didn't move when I approached.

At the marsh where the salt pans began, yet before the mussel nets of the men, I stopped. The flamingos had now assembled here in the large pools—an uproarious, sociable league. In the late sunlight they appeared more graceful and pleasant than they had beneath a leaden sky. A few birds came loose from the clamorous group, ascending; I saw their red and black wing speculums and the letter-like forms that the small flock in the sky yielded to. In flight they carried themselves like cranes, with their long necks extended ahead, their legs stretched back, their wings extremely wide. There was almost something comical about it, as if this flight position were designed to draw attention to the imbalance of their long-necked bodies. But then they swayed in the light and reclined obliquely until the sun sent their dorsal plumage shimmering a rosy mother-of-pearl, before they turned back to the sun and only a darkness stood in the sky, and as a result they were now nothing but signs, and their wooden wading and standing-around in brackish water sunk into oblivion. They flew above the pools in circles and large triangles, wrote squarely, then roundly in the air and erased it all at last with a bright mother-of-pearl stripe. Wings beating, they tumbled to the low sun, uttering the same calls that in the morning had reminded me of wild geese: hoarse and sharp, trumpetish noises from strained throats, a sound that I associated more with northern regions.

Under the flamingo shadow in the sky, I realized that while hiking among the Valli's reflective expanses I hadn't succumbed to any illusion: in the light of the late afternoon sun, the foothills of the Apennines stood out on the southwestern horizon, purple-blue, cleanly contoured against the light turquoise sky, and like a salve, one of the world's old orders came to my mind. Lying at the foot of these blue hill-shadows was Bologna, and in the northwest, Milan—the land had names and directions and colors, attached to memories and interlinked like the *necropolis* of Spina and the Valli's blue-gray expanse.

As I made my way around the basin, I encountered the guesthouse owner. He wore a very fashionable quilted jacket in glowing orange, which in the light of the sun preparing to set almost blinded. He led a man across the terrain, whose arm he occasionally seized with enthusiastic familiarity. He greeted me effusively but turned right back to the stranger. From a few tattered words, I gathered that he was talking up his property. Perhaps the stranger was a potential buyer, who would enable the guest house owner to bid good riddance, turn his back to the pink house, the backhoe, campsite and pavilion, to the whole bird kingdom, whispered round with reeds, and the swaying world between expanses of water and sky—and only sometimes, upon waking, would he brush from his lashes the shadows felt in his dreams, of peewit, heron, and flamingo wings.

Dogs

SOUNDING AROUND THE SALT PANS—at times farther away, at times closer—were occasionally explosions which baffled me. I couldn't make out their source. The direction would change, as would the volume, and nowhere were traces of a blast to be found, neither columns nor clouds of dust. At times full sequences of small, dull bangs seemed to be coming loose from the pylons that towered in long rows wherever there was solid ground; other times it sounded like detonations across Via Romea. Not without cause, I drew a line between the noise and the stockpile of arms and ammunition that had survived the years and decades, hidden on this side of the *Linea Gotica*, as the guesthouse owner had informed me while we drove around the lagoon. One morning the sounds filled the air, as if an exchange of fire were taking place nearby. The invisibility of its origin made it threatening, and on this day, even uncanny—in spite of the birds, which didn't seem particularly alarmed. On this morning I walked not between the salt pans, but toward the sea. Sounds jingled into the background, becoming sparser, drying up eventually, drowned out by the waves and the gulls. It was a cold day, and on the shore a bitter wind slapped my face, bowing and bending all the used-up, dreary beach accessories.

In the streets of Lido Estensi, what had rusted through autumn and winter or come loose from weak fixtures now clattered: signs from real estate agents, awnings and satellite dishes. The long promenade street between two decorative arches, thrown together from concrete elements, ran parallel to the beach, littered with dry pine needles and cones, scraps of trash and fragments of things no longer identifiable, cast here and there by the wind. The gelato shops, amusement parlors and clothing stores were locked up, sleeping behind drawn shutters. On the seaward side of the street, between small office buildings, an apartment tower rose up, its facade clad in a light-blue and green pseudo-mosaic. The mosaic cladding—a rigid stand-in for the sea, which despite its proximity couldn't be seen from here—had already come loose in places and fallen off in large, palm-tree sized patches, leaving behind dark-gray gaps. Condominio Poker d'Assi was written on a sign unhinged by the wind and weather. A young woman stepped out of the entrance, her garments—a gleaming gold caftan and wide-leg pants—fluttering under a heavy leather jacket, with a purse in her hand, also gold. Tired and haggard, she looked up at the empty street and startled when she saw me. She lowered her gaze to her black shoe tips, which peeked out from under her shimmer-pants, and let them lead her to the only shop that was open. With a burning cigarette in her hand she came out and quickly returned to the light-blue building. I avoided looking at her; I'd interrupted her thin hibernation and impeded the dream that she had wanted to hang onto during her short trip. Silently, I wished her a mild winter, which she might have watched dwindle from the window of a condominium with a sea view during her brief waking breaks, and I was happy she'd pointed me to the shop. The gaunt saleswoman appeared taken aback by my unexpected presence. She must have been familiar with the young woman and, after her visit, had prepared for an uninterrupted day beside her space heater behind the counter with the crossword-puzzle books and chocolate that, like the summer's single toiletries, now remained as ornamental articles on otherwise empty shelves. Aside from these summer leftovers, there were cigarettes, lighters and bus tickets for sale. I asked for a map of the area and postcards, and she shrugged her shoulders regretfully. It's winter, she explained, with a politeness nearly indulgent, as if she supposed it had escaped my notice. In winter nothing is available. She pointed to the near-empty shelves with a gesture expressing resignation, which at the same time seemed to imply that she wanted to be left in peace.

I crossed the canal to Lido di Spina. This coastal resort's name was designed to deceive, surely devised mere decades ago for the heretofore empty, pine-covered strips of Adriatic hinterland, with the intention of leading visitors to believe it was somehow connected to the fabled *necropoli*s and the accompanying sunken port city. Here the streets were less straight than in neighboring Lido; they looped around complexes of identical houses in pine groves, where small front yards, their summerly spruceness having slipped away, bordered on sidewalks, and occasional garden gnomes stood like miserable quotations of Etruscan grave goods. No one was out on the streets, where a small trash truck moved along, without a single trash can on the sidewalk. During its compulsory exercise in the premises' desolation, the trash truck crossed my path so often it was as if he were lost and searching for a way out of this forsaken tangle of streets.

Lido di Spina lay entirely in the shadow of parasol pines. The small groups of houses were clustered in the forest, which towered above them. Although it slid small scraps of paper and dry needles across the ground and had blown so coldly on the coast, the wind could hardly put the black treetops in motion, as if different rules applied to them. Individual hooded crows spread out on strips of lawn. The trash truck had already been absent for some time, but now I had lost my sense of orientation. The sea was no longer audible, although it couldn't have been far, and no street seemed to lead to the neighboring town or back to Via Romea. Only the false detonations were still audible, faint and faraway, from no particular direction. I no longer knew if I was walking in circles; I would take note of bushes in a front yard, the fantasy name of a vacation house, but even when everything around appeared identical and already seen, I never again found the particular features that had left their mark on me. As I went past a group of houses, which I thought I had passed by several times already, I noticed two dogs sitting by the entrance. They were both dirty white with pointy muzzles, which, as if scenting, they stretched aloft. When they saw me, they tapped their tails lightly on the tiles in front of the house and moved into a position of watchful tension, but without uttering a sound. Light was on in the house; it appeared comforting, but at the same time underscored the utter forlornness of this —contrary to all expectations—contorted and nested small settlement. As if she had picked up on the minute change to the dogs' postures from inside, a woman appeared at the door. She walked between the two dogs, laying a hand on each one's head. The woman wore a pink tracksuit with a Disney figure on the chest and silver sneakers. Behind her the view into a dimly lit corridor opened up. I explained to her, somewhat embarrassed, that I couldn't find my way out of the settlement, hoping she wouldn't take it for an excuse designed to cover up other intentions. The woman held up her hand and disappeared without closing the door—I was to wait. The dogs now wagged their tails with muted delight and alternately made moves to stand up, but then sat back down, as if urging one another to remember the virtues of dignity and obedience. The woman appeared in a fur coat, which she had thrown over her shoulders as women did decades ago. It had a dirty white color, similar to the dogs' fur. As the door shut behind her, the dogs stood up and began moving with her. Up close I saw that she was older than I had originally thought—her hair's blond luster had deceived me from a distance. I said something apologetically thankful and she merely nodded and headed off. She took shuffling steps in front of me, somewhat bent over yet quick, flanked by the dogs. When they leaned against her fur coat, together the three looked like a single strange animal from behind, a mythical creature that hadn't yet found its way into a story. She appeared to have no interest in conversation, but again and again murmured something to the dogs. Once a fragment of her murmurs went astray, reaching me, and I heard that she spoke Russian. That didn't surprise me—Italy was full of Russians, and on the sixth of January I had seen quite a number of finely and elegantly dressed Russian families, women with large flower bouquets, and had assumed that they were on their way to local Christmas celebrations. In her silver shoes the Russian woman shuffled resolutely ahead, her hands buried in the thick fur of the dogs' necks. She bent ever farther forward to keep her coat, merely thrown over her shoulders, from falling off, and her head nearly disappeared in the process. All the old-fashioned nonchalance that she might have had in mind as she threw it on was lost with this posture, and, if anything, she appeared to be walking fraily under the fur, as if under a load which weighed her to the ground. On the back of the coat I could make out small, bare spots in the fur. Perhaps moths had nested in it, or mice had picked at it. The banter of magpies, which remained out of sight, sounded from a dark, small pine forest—a bleak place for these birds.

Past a bend we abruptly hit Via Romea. Trucks droned by and on the other side of the street, between trees, expanses of water from the Valli shimmered. I rummaged for a few Russian words and thanked her, explaining that I had come from the salt pans. The woman nodded courteously, smiled even, and the dogs, having lain down next to her, appeared to smile as well with their pointy snouts, as I spoke my Russian words. Three short explosive blasts reached my ears from the far side of the street. What was that? I asked awkwardly. The noise? The woman looked at me, uncomprehending, as another truck drove past. She had readjusted her coat and once again stood straight. She had disengaged her hands from the fur of the dogs' necks and held her coat shut in front of her chest. She shivered from the cold. The explosions, I said, explaining. The woman briefly spread out her arms to signal she hadn't a clue, as she turned to leave. That's the way it is here, she said. With hunched shoulders she again turned up her palms, and I was unsure if this gesture should strike me as very Italian or very Russian. Then she set off, back to her house among all the empty houses.

I walked down the road on the outermost edge of the narrow shoulder, as far as possible from the trembling lane, until

I arrived at the hill with the entrance to the salt pans. I had to wait a long time for a break in the traffic. There, on the side of Via Romea, the detonations hardly stood out. The passing truck drivers wouldn't even have noticed them.

Negative

THE BACKHOE WAS REPAIRED and stood ready for work. Every day I expected the blinking Christmas decoration to be taken down. Perhaps the owner had left it on the terrace roof only for me, as a nightly comfort, which threw its weak, flickering light into the darkness of the salt pans behind it, without illuminating anything. I prepared to depart. On my last, slow walks I tried memorizing what I had seen here daily: the expanses of water with thin strips of land in between, the lines traced in the sky by birds, the colors of decaying brick buildings in the shifting light, the pale reeds, the calm herons, the winter-slow flamingos and the silent procession of trucks. The ditches between the reeds were no longer covered in ice and the dead bird had been gone for days; perhaps there were scavengers in the marshland, living furtively. On the day before my departure, the thin fog I had been waiting for held sway in the delta. The farmhouse at the end of the field was a soft, swaying outline between poplars, feathery and transparent, hanging like faded fingerprints in the air. Two large rabbits crossed the field beneath the fog, appearing to perform large jumps very carefully and slowly. They might have felt safe from predators, protected by the veil of fog, and I hoped that in their frenzy on the open field they wouldn't lose their fear of the busy road.

The substation was an accumulation of coarse, sleeping animals behind the pink house, enveloped in a haze that blurred the headless entreaters into tree-stump shadows, the cables and wires between their raised arms into thin gossamer. Trucks glided dimly beneath dark-gray pine-clouds and everything revealed its potential innate Other, which remained hidden in clear light.

I began packing my things, consolidating my notes, sorting what I'd found. What would I take with me, what would I return to the landscape? I decided on a mottled night heron feather, which I placed in my suitcase, along with the dried, burst seed pod of a reed-like plant, which when held against the light resembled a dog's pointy snout—half-open—and a smooth yellowish stone which had laid, foreign and lost, contrasting with the surrounding marshland on the path where I found it. The imperceptible yet incessant movements of the land might have brought it to this place, a lone stone from a gravel load delivered years ago, or made to rise from deeper layers. One way or another, it came from somewhere else. I spread my remaining finds out on the windowsill, as to not forget them after my last walk before departing. I counted the exposed rolls of film and packed them carefully. Before they are developed, exposed rolls of film remain a fragile secret, as if one could see yet unknown dreams, lined up in so many identical hulls. If unopened dream pods really existed, waiting to unfold in sleep, what would happen if a rupture of light, tones, color, was allowed to pierce the undreamed world?

I had learned a thing or two about departures. How to eliminate traces, stow what I had accumulated and collected, to moor pictures of interior spaces in my memory, which would never be printed. What will ultimately prevail in memory is never clear in advance; it defies every intention. Were I ever to come back here, everything would be different to how I had stored it in my memory, what I'd read in the developed, printed photographs. No photograph is a copy. Once chosen, the frame determines the boundaries of a world, which the eye, while contemplating the finished picture, is forever reinterpreting, forever extending beyond the limits of its frame with new imaginings.

While tucking away the film, I felt an angular contour in a seldom-used side pocket of my camera bag. I pulled out a carrier for negative strips, a small narrow case made of soft cardboard—the kind I hadn't used for ages. I held the negative strips up to the light. I recognized M. immediately. His somewhat raised shoulders, his head turned slightly to the side. He was on all four of the negatives, all of which were taken in quick succession before the same background, variations of a portrait. Squinting in the light, half-smiling. It must have been a windy day, since a small tuft of his hair stands askew, a strand lying across his forehead. His hands are stuck in his jacket pockets, and behind his neck, his hood forms a small bulge. He wears the raincoat that I lost inexplicably half a year after his death.

It was a bright day on the negative and in the bluish darkness of the open expanse, I recognized delicate webs of empty trees, white in the distant background. I could no longer remember the occasion and walked closer to the window to see better, puzzling over small details that seemed out of keeping. I ultimately read the trees as rows of poplars and was gripped by a peculiar horror: for a few seconds, I thought I recognized the local landscape. I stepped outside with the strip to assure my-self that here the arrangement of trees and objects in the back-ground was different. As soon as I held the negatives up to the field and farmhouse, surrounded by poplar-webs in thin fog, I recalled the day that I had taken these pictures. It was years ago, at the Thames estuary in February—the days were already noticeably unwintry, in terms of light. Afternoon, low tide, the sinking water was still retreating to the channel in the center; at first the boats swayed in the slight waves, and then they sat in silt while thick-beaked gulls ascended in restless flocks, land-ing on the silt, on the boats, stranded buoys, screeching and piping and heavily beating their wings. Even if they took off in flocks, the gulls always seemed solitary. Each took its course and searched for its prey with a kind of nefariousness that never failed to shock me.

At the time M. had needed a picture for a specific purpose, hence the many similar shots—but that surely wasn't the reason for our excursion. It probably first occurred to us while we were there to take a few experimental shots, thinking something might turn out useful. The proofs came back to my mind; as we went through them, M. always noticed different things than I did, like the protuberance of his collar at his neck, which with a peculiar determination he found to be disfiguring. I saw the row of poplars before me, which on this late afternoon stood black and sharp against a red-orange sky, while a deep blue, slightly violet at first, slowly expanded across it. Between the shots and the sunset we went for a long walk. The train station where we had stepped out popped into my mind—Leigh-on-Sea, a kind of long wooden shed, perhaps from the twenties and almost like an old-fashioned, country conservatory with a view to the Thames, which here was almost the North Sea, revealing massive tidal flats when the water was low. But again and again I returned in my thoughts to this row of poplars, which, as I now seemed to remember, stood delicate and gray in the bright light at first and then, after a brief, smoky blueness, took on such a deep black before dissipating into the dark ink-blue of evening.

For years these memories were stored somewhere in my head and now they surged up only because here, at this place, I came across the missing negatives, which must have been tucked away in the unused side pocket for a long time, without my ever having missed them. That afternoon on the Thames, the late winter light, the unexpected discovery of a landscape with so much emptiness so close to London—all that suddenly drew closer, and after spending days with a view to the small grove around the farmstead at the far end of the field, the sight of this poplar row, which on that sloping February afternoon, before the backdrop of the vast tidal estuary, had gone from light-gray to blue to black, suddenly seemed so significant to me that I couldn't comprehend how it ever could have slipped from my memory. Again and again I held the negative up to the light, reading the white, thin scrawl of this row of trees in England, deciphering moments of the past, till this winter script—the burgeoning tree branches, evoking feathers from a distance—stood as a symbol above this short chapter of my life with M., which opened here once more.

Harbor

ON MY LAST MORNING in the salt pans a heavy wind blew. The sky hung low, and it began to rain. The rain pattered on the small canopy above the pavilion, landing with a whisper on the dry palm leaves. The wind propelled some object to strike a surface again and again, producing a sound both tinny and wooden. My last walk through the salt pans was short; the rain let down veils across the landscape and nothing could be sensed lying behind them. Even the birds remained under cover, and no herons sat on the cable.

The guesthouse owner drove me to the bus station. The bus was late and while we sat beneath the rain he told me how tired he was of this region. He wanted to return with his family to the catamaran off the Antilles, he explained. I live in a broken land, he groaned from time to time, in his very Italian-sounding English, as if he were trying out this sentence. He might have imagined how it would sound when across a strip of deep-blue sea off the Antilles, from his catamaran he would cry to another sailor: I lived in a broken land!

Beneath the rain, which slowly turned to sleet, next to the bus station sign, protruding out of kilter from its mooring, in this abandoned seaside resort—I believed him.

I asked him about the explosion sounds that had filled the air during the frost days. At first, he looked at me cluelessly—the comparison to explosions must have startled him. But then he appeared to have second thoughts, to understand what I meant. They're from the substation, he asserted. *Sottostazione elettrica.* It's always been like that, he explained after a brief silence. You get used to it, even if it only happens in winter. Every winter it makes you jump at first, but then you remember why.

I wasn't sure if I should believe him, or if he really had understood me, but the bus to Ravenna appeared and I said goodbye.

After my days in the Valli's landscape of emptiness, between reeds and water and bird sounds, everything connected to my daily life lay just as far away as my memories, and in its reliability appeared to be just as approximate and unstable, just as dependent on the light and weather. Years after my father's death, in the salt pans of Comacchio, with a daily view to the mute droning of trucks flowing from and to Ravenna, I suddenly felt as if I had to fulfil a mission. To complete some set of instructions. To visit places, inspect terrains, to fumble my way along the thin string of clues stretching between my memories and pictures, places, names. I had searched for Spina, now I was on the way to Ravenna.

First the bus drove to Lido di Spina. Like the garbage truck some days before, it wound through the convoluted network of roads, which couldn't have been large. But as on my walk, now too I seemed to lose my sense of direction. The bus seemed to leave no street untraveled. I kept an eye out for the Russian woman's house, but so many houses resembled it that only the dogs would have been a telltale sign, and I didn't see them.

Nor did I see light burning in any house. On Via Romea we moved forward slowly and the wind drove wet snow onto the windshield, which during the brief seconds between the wipers' up and down became obscured again. The tires of oncoming trucks sprayed dirty water. On the right side of the road lay the gray Valli, coalescing with the sleet into a contourless cloud; after crossing the Reno I looked through obliquely falling, fat flakes into pine forests on either side, where treetops spread out, black above the high trunks, keeping the snow from reaching the dim space below.

Ravenna appeared brighter than Ferrara, open toward the sea, even if the port had since moved far away. The city was less solemn, despite the day's harsh winteriness. The wind ripped through the last leaves on the sycamores, and occasional passersby braced themselves against the sleet. At the train station the displaced African men crowded against the glass doors in the hall, looking out. From the window of my tiny hotel room in Ravenna, I stared through the gaps between the houses onto the other side of the street and the train station's side tracks. The colorful regional trains glided past, sailing in the middle of the wide bed of several dozen tracks; here there was no shunting. It was a provincial train station like Ferrara's, weaned of past significance and at this time of year used only by commuters, among whom we can also count the homeless, who surely arrived here every morning—just as they did in Ferrara—in order to at least be in the keeping of the train station's myriad ways out, in order to, freezing and hungry, exchange a few words with other homeless, perhaps even pick up an odd job, paid in cigarettes.

The mosaics—where should I begin? I followed signs to the largest church, my head lowered, like the locals, against the wet wind. By now it was only rain, which fell harder and denser than the heavy flakes had that morning. The leftover Christmas decorations on the kiosks flickered miserably as the wind ripped into them. I liked Ravenna's emptiness, the way it was buffeted by the weather. Was it the last Italian city that my father saw? I tried picturing the streets in light and heat. With tour groups, which moved forward in fits and stops to the sacred mosaic sites, my father among them. The guards at San Vitale were pressed against space-heaters in half-glazed cubbies, subjecting the half-dozen freezing tourists to their bad moods. The enormous church's cupola spread over me with its gold-shimmering colors, until, while beholding the pictures, I forgot that it was a cupola at all—a curious effect, which for moments dissolved my every sense of direction in the space, so that everything seemed to hover, and what was up or down, every perspective was uncertain. I remembered how my father had explained the art of laying mosaics to us. The miniscule differences of the angles at which the small stones were embedded, the meticulously considered order of the glass and semiprecious stones and ceramic and gold—I imagined the mosaic artists standing on teetering ladders beneath the vast yet empty cupola vault, clinging to a vision of the picture that led their hands from lapis lazuli to green glass, to rock crystal, to rose quartz, to malachite to carnelian, to beveled points of glazed clay. Could it have been like that? What calculation went into the shoe tips of the group that surrounds the emperor and empress, in order to bring about this impression of levelness, flatness? Who laid in the panel of Moses climbing a mountain? On the cliffs are small fires like hands, growing out of the rock. Moses ties his shoe and looks up at the white hand reaching from the clouds, held out in blessing. On the rocky mountain's peak is a bare tree, black as if charred by fire. This image stuck with me, causing all else in the room to fade away.

In the mausoleum of Galla Placidia, one was allowed to stay for three minutes only, according to the sign at the entrance. No one was there to enforce this; perhaps the guards were hiding in a chamber less cold and damp. It might have been a precautionary measure concerned less with the fabricated reason—the complicated task of regulating humidity—and more with the fear that by staying too long, viewers might melt into this blue, lose the ground beneath their feet, and wander weightlessly between the mosaic's ornaments, stars and birds until they had lost all sense of the earthly. After their shifts came to an end the guards would then have the tiresome task of picking these visitors inebriated with colour out of the air and, somewhere protected from every blue, bring them back to their senses. That was a task no guard wanted to stoop to.

I found the harbor mosaic last at the Basilica of Sant' Apollinare Nuovo, after contemplating at length the mysterious movement and centrifugal force of the elegant, sumptuously clad—yet at the same time, jester-like—three Magi, who headed with their gifts through the fairy tale grove of the apse's abundance. The harbor depiction lay at the very beginning of the row of mosaics and shows three red-brown ships on a dark blue sea—the uppermost ship's sail hoisted—beneath a sky of gold.

It was a beautiful mosaic, the waves were full of movement, as was the weak twinkle of the sky, which along with the choppy sea-blue would unfold an entirely different animation in sunlight. It was an image without reference to the holy, without a sign in the sky or from the city walls, which rose around the port exit. A glimpse, a view to the possibility of a vastness that was nevertheless still bordered and captive, hadn't yet opened up, was only implied. I wasn't sure if it was actually the mosaic my father had referred to back then. I looked up at the image for a long time, puzzled, even as the light became dimmer and weaker. It was an insignificant corner of the mosaics, in winter poorly lit. As I turned to go, I looked back at the wall across from the harbor picture, and saw something that with abrupt certainty I recognized as the picture my father had spoken of. It was an express counterpart to the harbor picture, also framed by city walls, but another framework ran above it, with three white figures too small to be made out exactly. Angels would be gold, I assumed, perhaps they were children. I couldn't make it out. Three white figures for the three white boats on the harbor picture across from it; I wished them a skilled hand at sailing. In the middle anyway, between the masonry frame, a bright, delicate, clear blue-greenish *nothing* opens up—a vastness, a sea or a sky, which would slip away from all definition as soon as the viewer turned away. In the middle of this light blue-green, an outline looms faintly—it could be anything: a boat, an island, a sunken city, the shadows of a cloud, even a figment of the viewer's, a trick of the eye. These two mosaics—the dark blue, bordered harbor with its still unsteady boats, and the light-blue expanse with no destination, nothing nameable, not even a horizon— have for centuries been in a tête-à-tête about life, light and the open air outside, a whispering of countless small, gold-dusted stones, which my father must have overheard in part, and that's what he meant by the harbor.

•

The wind subsided late that evening, and even the rain stopped. The night was silent, until long before daybreak the first announcements sounded from the train station into my room. In the morning the sun shone. It was cold and very bright. I took the train from Ravenna to Bologna, then continued to Milan and from there into the Alps, where evening fell early. I looked out the train window and saw shadows of landscapes glide past, which illustrated my childhood. The orchards around Bologna—now stiff, reddish small trees, their branches stretching upward—and villages, abandoned factories, small cities in the slanted winter light. Past Milan I kept watch in vain for the settlements of uniform apartment blocks with green spaces in between. The train had already reached the foot of the Alps when it seemed as if objects and views were *gliding* past, just as I had seen them long ago: the ruggedness of the hillsides, aisles from outflows of scree, small forests, groups of needle trees, which in the somewhat unstable light of the afternoon sun appeared almost blue. Small, seemingly out-of-order train stations passed by, their names seeming unfamiliar to me at a distance. In Chiasso, the border police came and led away a young black woman who had been sitting across the aisle from me. She had stepped onto the train just before it departed Milan and spoke with three black men in a heavy West African French, of which I understood nothing. The three men had spoken insistently to her, until finally she sat down and leaned her head against the curtain on the window. For a long time the sun shone on her face. Her eyes were closed. Like a child, I later thought, who closes her eyes in order to avoid being seen. The three men disappeared in Chiasso. Quietly and without a word, the woman allowed herself to be led away. For her there was no way out of Italy, and no way home.

Lamentatio

NEARLY SIX HUNDRED YEARS AGO, *Fra Angelico painted a picture in memoriam, depicting the lamentatio, or requiem, of Francis of Assisi. The three-part predella on poplar panel hangs below Fra Angelico's painting* The Last Judgement, *a picture replete with blues, with angels mantled in gold and purple tones. Beneath it the predella appears matte and small. In the past, it formed the base of an altarpiece; it has thus always been accustomed to contenting itself with scant space at the foot of the sublime.*

The predella, with its small blue detail and matte colors on both side panels, tells a story without visions of angels or depictions of the Madonna, without all the lapis lazuli-imbued and ultramarine otherworldliness. It is a picture with death at its center: to the left is life, to the right, bereavement.

The left panel displays a scene of an encounter. Francis and Saint Dominic greet each other in a circle of other monks. They are in a world of mute colors: behind them is a building, beside them a landscape opens up—Umbrian hills, matte green, a vast valley, scattered with church towers, cloisters, villages and, if we look closely, what appear to be walled cemeteries. Among the places of the living are the places of the dead. Above the landscape is a piece of sky in angelic blue, almost as if it had been added later. O, this blue—it might have crossed Fra

Angelico's mind as he completed the landscape. There's room for a bit of precious blue above on the left, a place for angels above all earthly things—that, too, belongs in reality. The right panel shows a chamber. Here linger the bereaved. An angular opening in the background, a window or a door, offers a glimpse of nature. In night-green hues, it's overgrown outside; it is dark and a faint light leaks through the plants, which block entrance more than they invite one in. The open landscape is barred from view. The chamber itself is painted in brownish rosy tones, tamarisk colors, flat and shadowless, and it draws the eye into the trepidation and fearfulness with which the monks—transported by their grief to a foreign place—witness the apparition of the dead. One has taken flight, only his foot and a fold of his billowing habit can be seen in the door on the left. Another hides his face, half-lying on the floor in shock. Are they dreaming? How will they awake from this dream? Each in his own way touched by this encounter with the dead. And how will they ever agree upon what has appeared to them? Not a drop of blue can be found on the painting. In the absence of the sky the bereaved remain trapped in the unpredictable space of a dream.

Death itself, the lamentatio, occupies the largest space in the center: the monks are gathered around the dead. They wear their dark monk's habits, two of them holding a red book in their hands, to either read or sing from. The red of the books contrasts with the dull color of their dress, and stands between them like a message that will be passed on—an answer to the red robe of he who kneels before the coffin. The body lies in the coffin, which is surrounded by a yellow-and-red striped cloth. At his head are two church dignitaries in colorful clothing, and, at some distance from the foot of the coffin, beggars in dark brown and black. Behind the coffin are the monks. One bends in disbelief over the dead man's face, another over his feet—just as the Virgin, the apostle John or Mary Magdalene bend over Jesus's feet in countless depictions of the Descent from the Cross. The feet of the dead are a merciless sight. They say: Death, even before the hands do, and still we want to hold them, warm them, cover them, by shrouding and touching find a way to undo or at least to hush their deadness. The helplessness of the bereaved before the dead body while fumbling around the feet of the dead is inscribed in this painting. The monks are shocked and dazed, praying or waiting by the body. A younger monk has turned away and covered his face with his hands. He stands rigid in his inconsolability. In this picture of mourning, the blue triangle above the towers and walls of the monastery courtyard catches no one's eye, means something to no one, just hangs there like a small obligatory exercise on the upper edge—the precious lapis lazuli was painstakingly extracted and pounded into a powder in vain, it bestowed no consolation in bereavement.

Appendix

Pier Paolo Pasolini, "Significato del rimpianto": Part i
I mourn a dead world.
But I who mourn it am not dead.
Pier Paolo Pasolini, 'Significato del rimpianto', La nuova gioventù, Poesie friulane 1941-1974, (Einaudi, 1975).

Eugenio Montale, "Sorapis, 40 Years Ago": Part i
I've never been very fond of mountains
and I detest the Alps.
Translated by William Arrowsmith, in E.M., *The Collected Poems of Eugenio Montale, 1925–1977*, (New York: W.W. Norton & Co., 2012), 527.

Eugenio Montale, "The Eel": Part 2
spark that says that everything begins
when everything seems charcoal,
buried stump
Translated by Jonathan Galassi, in E.M., *Collected Poems 1920–1954* (New York: Farrar, Straus & Giroux, 2012), 385.

Giorgio Caproni, "The Words": Part 3
The words. Indeed.
They dissolve their objects.
Like a mist the trees,
the river: the craft
Translated by Michael Palma, in Poetry 155, no. 1/2 (1989), 34–35.

ESTHER KINSKY grew up by the River Rhine and lived in London for twelve years. She is the author of three volumes of poetry and four novels, including *River*, and has translated many notable English (John Clare, Henry David Thoreau, Iain Sinclair) and Polish (Joanna Bator, Miron Białoszewski, Magdalena Tulli) authors into German. *Grove* won the Leipzig Book Prize and the Düsseldorf Book Prize.

CAROLINE SCHMIDT was born in Princeton. She has translated poetry by Friederike Mayröcker, and art historical essays, museum catalogues, and exhibition texts for Albertina in Vienna and Pinakothek der Moderne in Munich, among others. She lives in Berlin.